S0-AYE-788

River Forest Public Library
735 Lathrop Avenue
River Forest, IL 60305
708-366-5205
October 2023

Sweetness All Around

by
SUZANNE SUPPLEE

HOLIDAY HOUSE ● NEW YORK

Copyright © 2023 by Suzanne Supplee

All Rights Reserved

HOLIDAY HOUSE is registered in the U.S. Patent and Trademark Office.

Printed and bound in August 2023 at Maple Press, York, PA, USA

www.holidayhouse.com

First Edition

1 3 5 7 9 10 8 6 4 2

Library of Congress Cataloging-in-Publication Data is available.

ISBN: 978-0-8234-5369-6 (hardcover)

Do all the good you can, by all the means you can,
in all the ways you can, in all the places you can,
at all the times you can, to all the people you can,
as long as ever you can.
—*John Wesley*

For Nannie

Summer 1974

This

I'm leaving," Mary Josephine Willoughby said. She stood by the open door, waiting for Mama to respond.

Without even turning to look at Josephine, Mama said, "Close the door behind you. And don't go far." Then she added, "And don't talk to strangers."

A small brown moth floated into the trailer, then seemed to change its mind and floated out again.

Josephine's fingers itched on the knob. Her teeth were gritted. A hot tide of anger surged inside her.

Since yesterday's yard sale, when Mama sold nearly everything they owned—*everything!*—including the dang TV, Josephine had been feeling this way. Like she was just barely hanging on to a rope. A rusty pipe fixing to burst. A girl who at any second would begin to scream and never stop.

Mama's full attention was on the Singer sewing machine, something *not* sold at the yard sale because Mama earned her living as a seamstress.

Josephine squinted and said in the hatefulest voice she

could muster: "I'm not five years old. You can't tell me who I can talk to. You're not even sorry for ruining my life!"

The *whirr-thump* of the machine stopped, and Mama turned around. "*You,* Mary Josephine, are on my last nerve today. And if you don't want to be treated like a five-year-old, stop acting like one. After everything that's happened, surely you can manage some grace."

Josephine glanced around the terrible room. This. *This* was where she lived now! "I can't stay here," she said. "I won't, and you can't make me."

"Mary Josephine, you know our circumstances are beyond my control." There was the slightest hint of pleading in her mother's voice.

Josephine's grip on the doorknob loosened. She blinked. She waited for the pendulum of fate to swing in the other direction and put their lives back in order.

"And just to be clear," Mama went on, "*you* are the one who should be sorry. Honestly, the way you behaved in that leasing office this morning . . . well, it was rude and completely uncalled for."

Josephine let go of the rope, burst the pipe, and did the thing she'd been wanting but also trying *not* to do. She stormed out and slammed the door behind her.

It was a thunderous slam, so hard she expected the glass to shatter.

It did not shatter. Through the now-closed door Josephine heard Mama return to her sewing.

Out on the highway cars and trucks whooshed past. *Nobody cares.* It was a thought that made Josephine feel small and insignificant, like an ant crawling over the sun-parched earth. The ache of misery inside her was so strong she wondered if her knees might buckle.

Josephine stood still, waiting. Her knees did not buckle.

In any challenging situation, there was usually an obvious thing to do: read the instructions again; retrace your steps; try harder. Miss Lake, Josephine's teacher, was always asking students if they needed clarification.

Josephine very much needed clarification, but Miss Lake had left on a trip to Maine for the summer. Even worse, Miss Lake was no longer her teacher, because Josephine had been successfully promoted to fifth grade.

Josephine sat on the splintery porch stoop and tried to put her feelings into words, something else Miss Lake encouraged.

Her heart was like a wedge of corn bread somebody had crumbled into bite-sized pieces. It was like a shiny red Christmas ball. One minute it dangled and shimmered. The next it fell off the branch and shattered.

Josephine imagined writing these similes in her journal, a yellow spiral notebook with flower-power stickers on the front, but her journal was inside the trailer, and she wasn't about to go back in there and get it.

Her brain swam home to Redbud Avenue with its swaying trees and smooth sidewalks. On a hot summer day like this one, Josephine might sit in the living room where it was cool and watch game shows on TV. Or dig through her old wooden toy box and look at what-all was inside it.

Most of the toys were from when she was little, but it was fun remembering. The lid sometimes fell and smacked her on back of the head, and for some odd reason this made her miss the toy box even harder. Because it was sold now. All the toys inside it were sold, too. Things that had kept her company her whole life, yet she had betrayed them.

Technically, Mama had betrayed them. She was the one who'd sold them.

And she'd sold the TV. And their old clothes and shoes and coats, anything they didn't "absolutely need or frequently wear." All of it, gone.

Not just their stuff, but their entire life was gone. A pretty life it had been. Mama's delicate dishes and brass candlesticks, even their polished furniture, gone.

Josephine put her face in her hands. The worst thing that could happen to anybody had happened to her, and it gave her the heavy, suffocating feeling of lying beneath the thick wool blanket on back of the green sofa.

Except the wool blanket and the sofa were gone now, too. The blanket Josephine didn't much care about—it was scratchy—but the sofa was the color of emeralds, with feather cushions you could sink right into. Just yesterday, Josephine had watched two men put their emerald sofa on the bed of a truck and haul it away.

Josephine could not stand to think about her lost life another second. She would walk. She would walk until she found clarification. She would walk until she formed a plan of action. Her brain was very good at that.

The Dump

Even with all the fast walking, a plan of action wasn't coming to Josephine just now. She was too overwhelmed by the eyesore that was Happy World Trailer Park—*Dandiest Little Place on Earth!* Too overcome by the loss of her old apartment.

French provincial bedroom furniture, all of it matching: dresser and mirror and nightstand and bed. The gold and white finish and drawer pulls shaped like delicate leaves. The way the sunlight slanted through her windows. Ballerinas framed and hanging on the wall.

The pain in Josephine's chest felt like someone punching her.

Happy World Trailer Park—*Dandiest Little Place on Earth!*—was a washed-out dirt path and tall weeds and rusted metal barrels with smelly trash inside. Droopy clotheslines and junky cars and busted lawn chairs and ugly power lines.

And trailers. Sad-looking trailers. The sign out front should've said *Saddest Place on Earth!* which was exactly what Josephine had told the woman in the leasing office. She was also going to point out that false advertising was a crime, but Mama stepped hard on her toe.

Josephine's trailer was number 13 and then there was number 7. Beyond that was number 10, and on the other side and down a ways was number 17. Then 15 and 19. In between were empty spots where trailers used to be, and some broken-down trailers nobody lived in now.

The grass was tall and itched Josephine's legs, and the mosquitos must've thought she was a Twinkie because they kept biting her. She'd seen all there was to see, or so she thought, until she took a closer look at number 7.

Somebody had clearly tried to make it pretty, which might've been the saddest thing yet in Happy World.

There were lace curtains in the windows. And a heart-shaped wreath on the front door. A small clay pot of red geraniums perched on the ledge of a wooden railing. Any second, it seemed, those flowers would take a flying leap and meet a tragic end.

Josephine moved closer, and something else caught her eye—a pair of tennis shoes. Not just any shoes, but stylish ones, for kids. Tiger Paws, they were called.

Josephine had seen the clever commercial on TV. "Run faster, soar higher" was the slogan. The advertisement featured real live tigers on a playground. Ever since Josephine saw it, she'd been wanting a pair of those sneakers.

She felt the sudden urge to knock on the door and meet the girl who owned the shoes. Together they would find a way out of here.

As if by some strange, magnetic force, Josephine felt herself being tugged there. Up the porch steps and knocking timidly at the door.

There was the sound of hurried footsteps and then the door snapped open. A thin woman stared down at her.

Unlike Mama, who put her face on first thing every morning, this woman did not have her face on. No eye shadow or rouge or lipstick. Just pale white skin and brown, wavy hair and what looked to be a faded house dress. Or, possibly, a nightgown.

The woman squinted hard, like her eyes hadn't seen the sun yet today. "Yes? May I help you?"

In the distance a truck blared its horn.

"May I help you?" the woman said again, firmer this time.

It had been a mistake to knock. Josephine blinked and swallowed and tried to find a way out of this uncomfortable situation.

"If you're here to sell something, you—"

"No, ma'am." Josephine held up both hands to prove her innocence. "I just moved here, and I was wondering... well, I was hoping you might have a..." She glanced at the shoes.

The woman seemed to understand Josephine's purpose then. "There's no one here," she said. She folded her thin arms tightly across her chest. Her knuckles were bony, and the backs of her hands had faint blue veins running through them.

There was an awkward beat of silence. Josephine knew she should say something, but her mind was blank.

"She'll make a nice friend for you," the woman said with a nod of her head.

"Ma'am?"

"The girl in seventeen." In the hollow of the woman's throat, Josephine noticed a rapid pulsing of her heartbeat. "Goodbye," she said, then shut the door.

For longer than was polite, Josephine remained on the porch. From this vantage point, she could see every miserable thing there was to see in Happy World—a row of battered mailboxes down by the entrance, the leasing office with scraggly green vines crawling up its cinder blocks. A washed-out path with deep gullies.

Josephine turned her attention to the geraniums outside number 7 again. Their brilliant color made her think of February—hearts and cupids and crepe paper streamers. Miss Lake's cozy classroom with its enormous windows. Valentine's Day felt like eons ago now, but Josephine could recall the smell of paste and construction paper, the gray sky spitting sleet that pecked the glass. Her heart squeezed with missing everything and everyone.

It seemed to her that the past was behind a closed curtain, like that game show on TV, *Let's Make a Deal* with Monty Hall. The grand curtain would sweep open and reveal something far better than a console stereo or five major Westinghouse appliances.

Waiting behind the curtain would be Josephine's life *before* the warehouse fire. The geranium shimmered in the sunlight, and Josephine moved the precarious pot away from the edge, then hurried off the porch.

Mars

Whoever lived in number 17 made no effort whatsoever at pretty. No wreath on the door and no curtains, either. There were cut-up grocery sacks in the windows, and on the tiny porch was a mess of rusted coffee cans and paint buckets with falling-over plants growing inside them.

Josephine tried to decide whether to knock or go back to number 13 and mind her own beeswax. Mama had picked up some chicken salad over at the IGA grocery store, and she'd let Josephine get an Orange Crush and a bag of Fritos, too.

Just as Josephine decided she wouldn't bother with number 17, the door flung open, and a girl rumbled down the steps.

"Well, hey there!" the girl said. "Where'd you come from?"

For some bizarre reason, Josephine said, "Mars." And then she added, "A big ole spaceship dropped me off right here."

The girl threw her head back and laughed. She laughed like she'd been looking for the least little thing to make her laugh. She laughed way harder than the joke deserved. And when she was done laughing, she said, "You got a right smart mouth, you know it?"

Josephine shrugged. The girl was taller by at least six inches and much older, probably.

"I'm Lisa Marie."

Josephine studied the girl more carefully. Glossy blond hair, though it was dirty looking. Grasshopper-green eyes. Big teeth. Teeth she would grow into maybe, but with a giant gap between them. *"Presley?"* Josephine was more or less thinking this out loud.

The girl laughed again. It was a boisterous laugh, without any shame behind it.

"I mean...I know the real Lisa Marie Presley lives at Graceland. *Obviously.*"

"She'uz on the news last night," Lisa Marie not-Presley said. "Driving a golf cart all over Graceland. Ain't she so lucky? To have Elvis for her daddy and a golf cart, too?"

Josephine was surprised by the *ain't*. Between Mama and her teachers, the *ain't*s had been corrected right out of her.

"What's your name and where'd you come from, really?" Lisa Marie asked.

Josephine didn't want to say where she'd come from, really. Every time she thought about Redbud Avenue it was like she'd swallowed Mama's pincushion and needles were poking her insides.

Instead of saying where she'd come from really, she said, "I'm Josephine Willoughby. We just moved here today." She tried to find some dignity in this statement, but there was none. She pointed toward the dingy trailer that brought to mind an old scab, one tattered around the edges and ready to fall off. "Number thirteen," Josephine said.

Lisa Marie's eyes went wide. "That ain't no good."

This was obvious, but still Josephine heard herself ask, "Why not?"

Lisa Marie pointed to the leasing office. "Fat lady over in the block building. Number thirteen is where Miss Connie lived at before—" And then Lisa Marie made the motion of slitting her own throat. She lolled her head to one side and stuck out her tongue.

Something close to anger pricked at Josephine's insides then. She didn't like being mistaken for a gullible sort of person. "What're you talking about?"

"Nobody knows. He just up and died."

"*Who* just up and died?"

"Miss Connie's husband. The manager of this place. Sitting in his chair watching *Gunsmoke* one minute and dead as a doornail the next. Carried him out feetfirst. I seen the whole thing, except for the TV-watching part." Lisa Marie shuddered. "Ain't that scary? That somebody died in your trailer?"

"People have to die someplace, don't they?" Josephine said, proud of herself for thinking this up so quickly. "How do you know nobody died in *your* trailer?"

Lisa Marie frowned, but then her face smoothed out again. "There was a kidnapping one time, too," she said.

Josephine squinted one eye.

"Swear on a stack of Bibles a mile high." Lisa Marie raised her right hand. "She was called Little Bit. Molly Quiver was her real name, though."

"I don't believe you," Josephine said flatly.

Lisa Marie tugged at the hem of her cutoffs and leaned in closer. "Well, it's true as me standing here talkin' to ya."

Her green eyes popped when she said this. "Happened on my birthday, so I reckon I'd know. Number seven." Lisa Marie pointed to the trailer where Josephine had just been.

Tiger Paws Keds. Geraniums on the ledge. The hairs on Josephine's arms stood at attention.

"She wasn't but ten years old when they got her. Might be eleven by now. I don't know if she had her birthday yet or not. It was her daddy and granny that carried her off from here."

They were quiet for a second, and Josephine considered the awfulness of a birthday while kidnapped. Or a Christmas or Thanksgiving or any holiday for that matter. "Patricia Hearst was kidnapped." Josephine said this out of the blue, but Patricia Hearst was the only other kidnapped person she could think of.

Lisa Marie shook her head. "And now Patty Hearst is shooting up stores and robbing banks, which don't make no sense. Her daddy's rich. She ain't got to rob people."

"Mama says they brainwashed her." Josephine felt the urge to defend Patricia, who now, according to the news, called herself "Tania."

Lisa Marie gave her a skeptical look.

"I don't understand it, either," Josephine admitted. She pressed her lips together, then added, "It happened on your birthday?"

"September twenty-seventh. I'll be eleven in sixteen weeks. Counted it up this morning. Ain't that somethin'?"

Josephine was surprised to learn the girl was younger by two whole days. "I'll be eleven the same month as you. September twenty-fifth," Josephine said.

Lisa Marie barked out another laugh. "*You?* Why, you ain't big as nothin'."

Josephine was on a seesaw of liking-not-liking this girl—up and down and up and down. "Well, I *am* practically eleven," she said.

Lisa Marie nodded and poked her tongue into the space between her front teeth. "Welp, I reckon whenever we run around and get into stuff, you can crawl in the tight spaces, and I'll reach for things way up high. We go together like butter and biscuits!"

The tightness in Josephine's chest released slightly. She opened her mouth to ask the first of so many questions, but Lisa Marie took off. In a flash of long, skinny legs and dirty bare feet, she ran toward a clump of pine trees in back of Happy World.

"Where you going?" Josephine shouted after her.

Lisa Marie turned and cupped her hands around her mouth. "I got 'maters to stake and them sticks ain't gonna pick up theirselves!" she said, then disappeared into the thick curtain of green.

Bonafide Heebie-Jeebies

Josephine slipped inside number 13 and shut the door gently behind her.

She stood watching her mother work. Mama's shiny hair was elegantly twisted up in the back, and pearl earrings dangled off her earlobes. Fabric spilled over the sides of the sewing table and pooled on the floor, taking up the whole living room practically.

This was nothing like the sewing situation on Redbud Avenue. In their apartment on Redbud Avenue, Mama had a special room for sewing with two long work tables and a squishy chintz chair where Josephine could sit and do homework.

It really did seem like they'd been dropped off in Happy World by a spaceship.

Mama eased up on the foot pedal, but didn't bother to glance at Josephine. "I fixed you a sandwich. The drinks ought to be cold by now." Mama's voice was heavy with the weight of Josephine's door slam.

An apology. Two simple words: *I'm sorry.* Yet Josephine couldn't bring her mouth to say them.

Instead, she grabbed her plate, drink, and the bag of Fritos off the kitchen counter, then plopped onto a chair in the living room. It occurred to her that Mr. Connie (that's all she could think to call the man) might've died in this very spot, a thought that gave her the bonafide heebie-jeebies.

She was about to switch to the other chair, but Mr. Connie could've just as easily died in that one, so Josephine stayed put. "You think it's bad luck to live in a place where somebody died?" Josephine asked over the noise of the sewing machine.

"People have to die someplace, don't they?" Mama replied.

Josephine took a deep pull from the bottle of Orange Crush. The sugary coldness felt good on her tongue. She swallowed and said, "Exactly. That's exactly what I told her."

Mama did not take the bait. She just kept moving the fabric along. *Whirr-thump-whirr-thump.*

"Yep, that's exactly what I said to her," Josephine repeated louder.

Still nothing.

"I said to her, I said—"

"Jo, you are beating around the *sorry* bush. You slammed the door. You were rude to that poor woman in the leasing office this morning."

"Well, that sign out front is a lie. Dandiest little place? I don't think so," Josephine said.

This time Mama did turn around, though the machine kept *whirr*ing and *thump*ing. Mama was that talented as a seamstress. She could turn to give Josephine a look and keep right on sewing. "Mary Josephine, the grace to apologize when you're wrong is an essential life skill."

Josephine buttoned her lips, and Mama went back to looking at the fabric, a polyester poplin with something called a lock-and-key design. Staring at it for more than a few seconds made Josephine dizzy.

In silence she finished her lunch, though the inside of her head was noisy. A kidnapped girl. *Molly Quiver.* Such a strange name.

Josephine pictured Molly's mother, standing at the door. How pale she was, even in summer. *She'll make a nice friend for you.* Josephine heard these words again, but now she wondered if the woman meant Lisa Marie or her own daughter.

"I'm sorry!" Josephine said out loud. The words felt disconnected. Not at all attached to her actions. More or less, she was thinking of Molly Quiver when she said them.

The sewing machine stopped, and ever so slowly, Mama turned around.

"And thanks for letting me get junky food," Josephine added.

"Did that *sorry* visit your heart before it passed through your lips?" Mama asked.

Josephine nodded, though this was a lie.

"I'm sure it's too much to ask for you to apologize to Miss Connie, too."

"Definitely," Josephine replied. She stood and went into the tiny, brown kitchen, and Mama started up her sewing again.

Everything in the trailer was brown. Brown paneled walls. Brown peely linoleum. Brown kitchen cabinets, most of the knobs missing. Drawers that wouldn't close all the way.

The faucet dripped. The refrigerator made noises that reminded Josephine of the coffee grinder over at IGA. "It's just so awful," she whispered.

The trailer was awful, yes. Happy World was awful. And

the warehouse fire, of course, that was awful. For the past week, everything had been awful!

Still, Josephine couldn't help but consider the Patricia Hearst kind of awful. The Molly Quiver type of awful. *She wasn't but ten years old when they got her.*

Got. Her. A girl her own age was got.

Are You Lonesome Tonight?

That very same evening, Josephine took a cool shower. She washed her hair in Gee, Your Hair Smells Terrific shampoo. She tugged on her yellow pajamas with the blue flowers printed on them.

Clean and with her wet hair smelling terrific, Josephine went into her teeny-tiny matchbox bedroom, which was more like a closet. Josephine was to sleep in there, and Mama would take the fold-out couch in the back, which wasn't a bedroom or any kind of room, really. It was just a place with a water heater and an old-timey washing machine.

Josephine unzipped her suitcase and took out her spiral notebook. In school Josephine wrote journal entries for Miss Lake to read. All the students did this as part of language arts. Each Monday when Miss Lake returned them, Josephine was thrilled to see smiley faces and little + + + signs. Once Miss Lake had written in perfect penmanship *You are a natural storyteller, Josephine!!!*

It was those three exclamation marks that'd prompted Josephine to start writing fictional stories. Mostly, she had beginnings without endings.

She stared at the blue lines on the blank page, then put the pencil tip to the paper and waited, but her brain zipped off toward the warehouse fire again. It had *ruined* Mama's sewing business, which she had worked so hard to build.

First, Miss Augustine, their dearest friend in the world, sold Mama the fabric. Then Mama made draperies or pillows or slipcovers or bedspreads or tablecloths or oodles of other things and kept them in the warehouse until Lucas of Lucas B. Installations could deliver and install whatever it was.

Except the warehouse burned down. Most everything inside it was ruined, either by fire or smoke or soot or water.

Josephine couldn't think of any stories, real or made-up, so she quit writing and dragged out her portable record player (something *not* sold at the yard sale) and a box of old magazines. She put her favorite Donny Osmond record on repeat.

Over and over, he sang "Are You Lonesome Tonight?" The music sounded crinkly and crackly, like somebody unwrapping a piece of hard candy, but still she listened. As it played, Josephine clipped pictures from *Tiger Beat* magazine. If she stuck Donny's grinning face to the ugly brown walls, it might cheer the room up.

"Jo!" Mama called.

"Yeah?" Josephine hollered back.

Mama stood in the doorway, but Josephine didn't bother looking up. She was busy cutting out a picture of Donny riding a motorcycle and waving to the camera. She didn't want to accidentally snip off one of his fingers.

"It's *yes*, Jo, not *yeah*," Mama said. "And where did these come from?"

"Where did what come from?" Josephine said, still focused on Donny.

"*These.*"

Josephine stopped cutting and looked at her mother. Her mouth fell open. She frowned. Finally she said, "Where'd you get those?"

"That's what I'm asking *you*, Jo. They were on our porch just now."

Josephine put down her scissors and leaned in for a closer look. She was staring at a pair of Tiger Paws, the shoes of a kidnapped girl. A girl who somebody *got*.

The shoes were not straight-out-of-the-box-brand-spanking-never-worn-new, Josephine could see this now. Still, they were close enough to new. They were very nice shoes. They were the exact kind of shoes Josephine had been wanting.

"Jo, answer me. *Where* did these come from?"

"I don't know," Josephine replied. She tried to decide if this was the truth. On purpose she hadn't told Mama about the kidnapped girl. If Mama thought kidnappers were on the loose, she wouldn't let Josephine run around outside. And Josephine was not about to be trapped in this hot tin can all summer.

"I can tell by the look on your face you have some vague idea." Mama squinted one eye.

Josephine blinked and swallowed. "They belonged to a kidnapped girl," she said.

"A straightforward answer, Jo, not one of your stories."

"That *is* my straightforward answer. I met a girl today."

"A kidnapped girl?" Mama switched off the record player.

"No. The girl I met is Lisa Marie. Not *the* Lisa Marie, you know, Presley. Just a regular ole Lisa Marie. I don't know her last name."

The tiny wrinkles between Mama's eyebrows creased into actual lines.

"Lisa Marie is the one who told me about the kidnapping. Her name was Little Bit. That's what they called her anyway. It wasn't her actual name. Her actual name was Molly Quiver."

Mama's eyes looked interested now.

"That's her name unless she changed it. You know, like Patricia Hearst who calls herself Tania. I met her mother today. Molly's, not Tania's. She lives in number seven. The shoes were on her porch."

"Goodness gracious," Mama said. She nudged away the box of clippings and sat down beside Josephine. The springs in the mattress made a *bo-ING!* sound. This was not really Josephine's mattress. Josephine's mattress, which was soft and firm at the same time, had also disappeared on the bed of that truck.

Outside, a car engine roared to life, then shut off again. The faint smell of exhaust wafted through the window screen.

Mama stared at the shoes and smoothed out the laces. "I remember the day she disappeared. I remember exactly because it was...the same day I made things official."

Josephine's mind skipped back to that warm day last September, the leaves just barely beginning to turn colors. As they left the lady lawyer's office downtown, Mama reached for Josephine's hand and squeezed it hard.

"He has such a radiant smile, doesn't he?" Mama said now.

"Who?" Josephine replied.

"Donny. All the Osmonds." Mama gazed harder at the picture. "They shine from the inside out."

Josephine recalled other details about that late September day. She'd worn a new white blouse and plaid kilt skirt to school so she could look "presentable" that afternoon at the lawyer's office. Mama was picking her up early from school. Josephine had felt better than presentable. In fact, she'd felt like a million bucks in such a cute outfit, that is until Delia Collingsworth gave her a look in the lunch line.

The look said (without actually saying it out loud), *You're a baby, Josephine. I wouldn't be caught dead in a dumb baby outfit.*

Delia wasn't her friend anymore, a fact that still made Josephine's insides twist like a pretzel. They hadn't been friends since Kitty Hawkins waltzed into Brandywine Elementary just before Christmas, fresh off a plane from California and looking every bit the movie star.

And while Josephine's dad was still her dad, he wasn't Mama's husband any longer. The truth was he might as well not have been Josephine's dad, either, since she never saw him.

A few days ago, Josephine had wadded up that skirt and shoved it to the bottom of the "didn't absolutely need or frequently wear" pile.

Mama turned the shoes over and examined the soles, which weren't worn out, not even a little. "When I turned on the news and heard the awful story of that little girl, I said to myself, 'People have bigger problems than you, Penny Willoughby.' And that was the end of my pity party."

Outside, the noisy car started up again. Mama stood and tucked the shoes into Josephine's tiny closet, which was more like a cabinet, then shut the window.

"Was it really a kidnapping?" Josephine asked.

"What do you mean?"

"If it's by somebody you know. Lisa Marie said it was Molly's father who got her. And the grandmother. She helped or something."

"What if your dad showed up tomorrow and drove you off to Las Vegas to live with him and didn't tell me?"

The hairs on Josephine's arms rose again.

"He's not going to do that, Jo, but yes. That's still a kidnapping. I can't imagine her poor mother's misery." She sighed and shook her head. "Giving you those shoes was a thoughtful gesture. She must be a very kind woman."

⊏⟹

After Mama was gone, Josephine slipped into the *bo-ING!*-y bed and switched off the lamp. Her brain skipped back to a time long ago when her dad lived with them. The memory was hazy now, almost like a dream. Josephine didn't so much remember her dad living with them as she remembered the bread crumbs he'd left.

Mostly, he was out late into the night. Gone for days and days sometimes, but there was the smell of Old Spice and cigarettes, whisker stubble in the bathroom sink, empty packets of Alka-Seltzer, and a clunky gold ring with the dollar bill symbol. Josephine could still recall the clatter of it being dropped in a dish on the bureau.

In the other room, Mama's sewing machine *whirr*ed and *thump*ed, and Josephine lay awake imagining herself getting kidnapped. She would wear Molly's Tiger Paws so she could run faster and soar higher.

The Man with Half a Face

The next afternoon Josephine and Lisa Marie were sitting on 13's front stoop, eating ice cream sandwiches. Lisa Marie had dug them out of her freezer after Josephine mentioned how much she liked them. The air was hot as a volcano, and Josephine was trying to finish the middle part of the sandwich before it melted.

"Why'd you move here anyway?" Lisa Marie asked.

Josephine shrugged. She didn't feel like talking about the warehouse fire. The ice cream was delicious and sweet, and she didn't want it mixed in with any sad junk.

"Your mama sure is fancy. She looks too fancy for a trailer park," Lisa Marie said.

Josephine ignored this and kept licking until there wasn't any ice cream left, just two soggy rectangles of cookie. She ate both halves, then sucked her fingers till the chocolate was gone.

"You sure do like them shoes, huh?"

"Yep," Josephine replied. The Tiger Paws fit her just right, and they were way more stylish than her plain white sandals.

Lisa Marie smiled, and Josephine couldn't help but stare at that big space between her teeth. Even with the gap, the girl was pretty. Not the normal kind of pretty Josephine was used to—not like Kitty Hawkins with her long, silky hair or Delia Collingsworth with eyes that shone like moonlight on lake water.

Lisa Marie was not those girls' kind of pretty.

Delia and Kitty shopped at Cooper's downtown, pretty store-bought clothes, not homemade like most of Josephine's outfits. Plus, they had pierced ears now. Got them done together, held each other's hands through the whole proce-dure, then came to school that Monday bragging to Josephine about how bad it hurt.

"You probably wouldn't be able to stand it," Delia had said. Even now, months later, Josephine felt a sharp jab when she thought of those girls' matching earlobes with glittering gold studs, a sure sign of best-friendship if ever there was one.

"Take a picture, it'll last longer," Lisa Marie said. "What're you looking at me like that for?"

"No reason," Josephine lied. But the truth was Lisa Marie's clothes were dirty. Her hair was dirty. Her face was dirty. Her feet probably hadn't been washed all summer. *This is not what I had in mind*, Josephine thought. Clients sometimes said this to Mama when she showed them fabric swatches.

"Look yonder," Lisa Marie said.

Josephine dragged her eyes off Lisa Marie just in time to see Molly's mother heading down the washed-out path. She was wearing a light blue smock and navy pants. "Where's she going?" Josephine wondered out loud.

"Work."

"But it's Saturday," Josephine pointed out.

"You get time-and-a-half pay on Saturdays and nights," Lisa Marie said, and then she sighed. It was a pitiful sort of sigh. In fact, the sigh was so pitiful it made Josephine feel guilty about what she'd just then been thinking, about Lisa Marie not being what she had in mind.

"What's the matter?" Josephine asked.

Lisa Marie stared at Josephine with her big green eyes. They were no longer grasshopper green. They'd gone a shade darker somehow. "Buster Lee used to get good overtime, too. That'uz a long time ago now."

"Buster Lee?"

"My great-uncle. He took care of me. Now I take care of him. One of these days he'll keel right over, is what Granddaddy says. Buster Lee's got part of his face cut off. Wanna get a look at him? Bet that ain't something you seen every day."

Josephine's eyes widened.

"Granddaddy's at work now, so we won't get in trouble for it. And don't be rude or nothin'. Just get a look at him. You won't b'lieve it." Lisa Marie scrambled to her feet. "Come on," she said.

⊏⟹

At number 17 Lisa Marie turned on the garden hose, and they washed their sticky hands. She spit water through the gap in her teeth and caught Josephine right in the eye. For several minutes they took turns squirting each other and squealing their heads off.

The door to number 17 popped open, and Josephine dropped the hose.

"Hey there, Buster Lee," Lisa Marie said. "We having us a water fight."

"Wisa Mawie, y'all stop that scweamin'," he said. He glanced at Josephine, then wiped his mouth with a handkerchief. "Be-ave," he added, then went back inside.

Lisa Marie shut off the hose. "Told you," she whispered. "Ain't it so awful? He won't even leave the house. Don't want folks seein' him like that."

Josephine nodded. Sure enough, half the man's face was missing, except you couldn't see his skull or brain or anything, on account of a plastic mask that covered those parts. It was like looking at something smooshed on the highway; part of you wanted to see it and the other part was scared of such a sight. "Why does he wipe his mouth like that?"

"Can't even swaller good," Lisa Marie said. "They cut the inside of his mouth out, too. That's why you can't hardly understand what he says, 'cept I understand him really good. He tells me his hopes and dreams. When he feels up to it," she added. "He has to drink this nasty stuff through his nose, else he'll starve to death."

"Through his *nose*?" Josephine was horrified.

"Yep. It goes through a tube in his nose and down his throat and into his stomach. Granddaddy says Buster Lee is going to the sweet by and by before long, and then the world as we know it will come to an end."

Josephine didn't need to ask about the sweet by and by. They sang that hymn in church sometimes.

"Got any creek shoes?" Lisa Marie asked. "There's a creek back yonder." She pointed toward the pine trees.

"Just those." Josephine had taken off the Tiger Paws so they wouldn't get wet.

"I got some old ones that don't fit no more," Lisa Marie offered.

Back when she was nine, Josephine had something called a plantar wart. It was on the heel of her right foot, and a doctor sliced it out with a knife. Josephine had kicked and cried and pitched a big fit.

Judging by the looks of Lisa Marie's feet, she had plantar warts galore. And they were contagious. The wart doctor had told her so. "I'll just go barefoot," Josephine said.

"One of them crawdaddies pinches you, it won't let go till it thunders," Lisa Marie warned.

"That's not true," Josephine said, but she betrayed herself by glancing upward. There wasn't a cloud in sight.

Lisa Marie laughed. "Be right back," she said, and pounded up the steps and into her trailer.

While Josephine waited, she wondered about Buster Lee's hopes and dreams. *He tells me his hopes and dreams.* This time last week, she'd never heard of Happy World. This time last week, Mama was planning a day trip to Opryland so Josephine could drive a Tin Lizzie car and get sopping wet on the Flume Zoom.

The world as she knew it had ended.

Rainy Sunday

On the way to church, Mama drove through their old neighborhood—not past the apartment, but close enough to make Josephine's heart grow tight. All through Sunday school and now grown-up church, Josephine felt the urge to kick something.

Of course, she knew better than to kick anything, especially in church.

So, she ripped the offering envelope into tiny scraps of paper. The tearing sound was loud enough to make Mama glare at her. It was loud enough for the old man sitting in front of them to turn around and give Josephine a hateful stare.

When she grew tired of studying the shiny crosses and flickering candles and stained-glass windows, she drew pictures of their old apartment on the back of the church bulletin.

As she drew, Josephine imagined herself walking through the rooms. She listened to the sounds of doors closing and heard water rushing through the pipes from the apartment above them.

Sometimes birds would land on the window ledge and

peer through the glass at her. Josephine drew a bird with a speech bubble coming out of its beak. "Where'd you go, Josephine?" he said in a tragic bird voice. And then she added tears pouring from the bird's eyes.

Mama leaned in close and whispered, "Pay attention to the sermon."

Almost as if he were in agreement with Mama, Brother Davis smacked the pulpit with the flat of his palm and shouted, "Hear me when I say it, brothers and sisters!"

Josephine was so startled she accidentally kicked the back of the pew, and this time the old man turned and sniffed at her.

Brother Davis pounded the pulpit again and hollered, "Blessed are the poor, for *theirs* is the kingdom!"

$\Longrightarrow$

By the time they reached Happy World again, it was raining cats and dogs. Once inside, Mama and Josephine went their separate ways, as separate as they could be in a tuna can, that is.

Josephine took off her wet church dress and tugged on a terry-cloth bathrobe. She sat at the end of her bed and thought about what she would be doing right about now—*if* they still lived on Redbud Avenue. Making toast in the Dualit, then turning on the television for *Three Stooges* reruns, but that wasn't happening here. The previous tenants had taken the TV, and there was no Dualit toaster, either.

Josephine pulled a library book from the small shelf next to her bed. Before the warehouse fire, she'd started reading *By the Shores of Silver Lake* by Laura Ingalls Wilder.

In the front room, Mama's sewing machine started up. Josephine could tell where Mama was in her project by the sound of the machine. If the machine was *whirr*ing and *thump*ing, Mama was in the middle of a project. Today, however, the machine *purr*ed, which meant she was putting finishing touches on something.

With the rain hitting the metal roof of the trailer and the terry-cloth robe nubby in the right places and Mama's sewing machine *purr*ing and the book's words so pretty on the page, Josephine's heart grew peaceful.

The urge to kick something vanished. Until Josephine came to the worst part in any book she'd ever read.

Over and over, because she couldn't believe it, Josephine studied the terrible line where Mary goes blind.

Josephine slapped the book shut and dropped it onto the floor with a loud *smack*. "The poor do not inherit anything!" she shouted.

Mama's machine stopped. There were footsteps, and then Josephine's door snapped open. "What's wrong?"

Josephine blinked. *The world as I know it has ended. A plan of action. Clarification.* Josephine did not say these things out loud.

Mama glanced at the book and then at Josephine.

"The prettiest sister went blind," Josephine explained.

"Goodness, Jo, you scared me. Don't go throwing books, especially ones that don't belong to you."

"I'm writing my own stories where nothing bad happens ever."

"Then it'll be a mighty boring book. Terrible things happen, Jo. That's part of life. It's also what makes stories exciting to read."

"You're a seamstress," Josephine pointed out. "You don't know anything about book writing."

"I'm a reader," Mama said, "and I know what makes a book interesting."

"Brother Davis is a liar." Josephine narrowed her eyes at Mama. "He stands in the pulpit and tells big, fat lies." These words were so reckless Josephine could hardly believe she'd said them.

Mama's feathers were not ruffled, however. Her face remained calm. She was doing that thing she sometimes did, which was not to play along when Josephine was trying to get a reaction.

"You're trying to pick a fight, Jo, and I have no intention of playing along," Mama said.

She made a move to shut Josephine's bedroom door, so Josephine added, "He told a big, fat lie this morning. You thought I wasn't listening, but I can listen and draw at the same time."

"What on earth are you talking about, Jo?"

"He said poor people inherit the Earth." The word *poor* blistered Josephine's tongue. It made her feel like kicking something again. The word also made her think of Delia and Kitty.

Delia's and Kitty's houses were in the nicest part of Arbor Heights. There were no apartments in their section, only houses that people owned.

"The meek inherit the land," Mama said.

"Huh?"

"The Beatitudes. Brother Davis was preaching on the Beatitudes. It says the poor in spirit inherit the kingdom of heaven."

Josephine glanced around her awful room. "You mean

after they *die*? So poor people have to wait till they're *dead* to get anything?"

"I don't have an answer for you," Mama said.

At that, Josephine's fury changed directions. It aimed straight for her mother now.

If Mama hadn't put her precious things in that awful warehouse building, none of this would've happened. Josephine opened her mouth to speak this truth, but at that precise moment came the sound of someone singing. It floated through the slightly cracked window as if on wings.

"Blessed assurance, Jesus is mine. O what a foretaste of glory divine..." The rain crescendoed, but still the music broke through. *"Heir of salvation, purchase of God..."*

Mama put a hand to her throat. Her nails were always painted. Today they were a pale pink to match the dress she'd worn to church.

Josephine scrambled across the bed to peer out the window. Like it was any ole sunny day, Lisa Marie was strolling along. Her clothes, a Dr Pepper T-shirt with orange Popsicle stains down the front and a pair of ragged cutoffs, were soaked clean through. Her hair was sopping wet, and she was barefoot and muddy and walking *through* the puddles and washed-out gullies instead of around them.

A sad feeling came over Josephine then. Lisa Marie's singing was the saddest sound she had ever heard maybe, but something else was worrying her, too. Something she couldn't quite name.

Those birds on Redbud Avenue had no idea where Josephine went, and this felt as tragic as Buster Lee's half-a-face. Josephine wanted to go home—back to the park and the courthouse clock and the smooth sidewalks with their cracks spaced exactly right for skipping over them.

They could drive there right now in Mama's ole blue car! The big historic apartment building, really just an old house divided into apartments, was still there, waiting for Josephine.

But Josephine was here in Happy World and Redbud Avenue was there in Arbor Heights. And in this instant, like something to be caught before it got away, Josephine could feel how badly Molly Quiver must be yearning to come home.

When the singing stopped and Lisa Marie had disappeared inside 17, Josephine said, "We should do something."

Mama closed the window and stooped to sop up the rainwater with a bath towel Josephine had left lying on the floor. "Do something about what?"

"If there's a needle in a haystack, it might be hard to find, but it's somewhere in there. Molly Quiver didn't just disappear. We have to find her!"

Mama dropped the towel into a plastic bin for dirty clothes. "We have to use our towels several times," she said. "The washing situation here isn't like Redbud Avenue."

"You're ignoring me."

"I'm not ignoring you, Jo. I just don't have any idea what we might do to help. And, it isn't our business."

"It *is* our business. She lives right there." Josephine pointed in the direction of number 7.

"Would it satisfy your curiosity if you knew what happened? You could read some of the newspaper articles about the abduction."

Abduction was another word for *kidnapping*, which was another word for *got her*. Synonyms, these were called.

34

"But you don't like bad things in stories, remember? Maybe it's not a good idea," Mama said thoughtfully.

"I know the story of Patricia Hearst. And I've seen those starving kids in Ethiopia. I don't know why somebody doesn't just find Patty Hearst and give those kids some food." The pictures on the news were awful.

Mama stooped to pick up the library book and placed it gently on Josephine's bed. "Lucas and I are installing some draperies tomorrow. They're for that new doctor in town. For his wife, actually. If we have time after, we can stop by the library. They keep old newspapers. And, if you really can't bear to finish that book, you can exchange it for something happier."

Josephine nodded.

"Did you ever thank that nice lady for the shoes?" Mama glanced at Josephine's closet where the backs of the Tiger Paws were poking out.

Josephine shook her head.

"I told you to write a note and leave it on her door."

Josephine shrugged. The truth was she felt afraid to go over there now that she knew about the kidnapping. Mama seemed to sense this without Josephine having to say it.

"We'll go tonight after supper. I'm going to fry some chicken directly, and I put a lemon freeze in the icebox this morning. We'll take her some lemon freeze and you can say thank you in person."

Josephine nodded. She wished she could take some lemon freeze to those poor, starving children. She'd seen the news program on Delia's big TV. Delia's mother, Mrs. Collingsworth, had said, "I don't know how you girls can stand to look at that!" and then she switched the channel. That night Delia's mother served them pot roast with boiled potatoes.

"And you will *not* mention her kidnapped daughter," Mama said.

"Huh?" Josephine replied.

"You will not bring up the subject of her daughter. Promise me?"

Josephine nodded, but inside the too-long sleeves of her bathrobe, she crossed her fingers.

Lemon Freeze

The woman in number 7 was hesitant when she answered the door, but Josephine spoke right up. "We're not selling anything. I came to thank you for the shoes." And then she extended her right foot, pointed to the Tiger Paws, and said, "It was nice of you."

The rain had stopped, and the late afternoon sun was beginning to poke through what remained of the clouds.

"We brought you a cool treat. Our way of saying thank you. It's a lemon freeze, and I made it just this morning," Mama said, and extended the Tupperware container.

For a second, Josephine felt sure the woman would refuse the offer, but then she said, "Why, thank you." She smiled, though it was not the sort of smile that showed her teeth or reached her eyes. She glanced at Josephine's feet again. "They look good on you," she said, and then she accepted the lemon freeze from Mama.

For what felt like a long time, but was probably only seconds, everyone stared at Josephine's Tiger Paws.

"My toes don't even touch the ends yet," Josephine said,

eager to break the feet-staring silence. "I'd been wanting a pair of Tiger Paws for the longest time."

"It's true," Mama agreed. "For a while it was all she talked about. I think the advertising campaign paid off—tigers on the playground."

A shadow flitted across the woman's face.

Josephine wanted to ask if Molly had seen the commercial, too, if that was why she'd picked out that type of sneaker. Instead, she bit her tongue.

Overhead a crow cawed. A bee on the geranium hummed. The woman fumbled with the collar of her smock. Her fingers were long and thin, and the blue veins seemed especially blue today.

"Well, we won't keep you," Mama said. "We just wanted to say thank you."

The door to number 7 was open wide enough that Josephine could peer inside. On the wall were pictures, dozens of them. "That's pretty," she said.

"Pretty?" the woman asked.

"Your wall." Josephine pointed, and she turned to look. "Those paintings there."

"Oh." She fumbled with the collar again—her factory uniform, the light blue smock and navy slacks and a pair of sturdy brown shoes. "Those aren't paintings. It's my needlework."

"Needlework?" Mama asked. Anything to do with sewing and Mama was all ears.

"Needlepoint, crewelwork, some macramé here and there. Embroidery. Keeps my hands busy." She looked down at her smock, and Josephine noticed a small white bird stitched on the front. "Y'all excuse my appearance. I just got home from a double shift."

"Please excuse us for showing up on your doorstep."
Mama was still gazing inside the trailer. "You did all that needlework yourself?"

"I did," she said.

"I'm a seamstress," Mama explained, "so any kind of needlework fascinates me."

"A *seamstress*?" She said the word as if Mama had just announced she was famous.

"Interiors. Draperies, duvets, pillows—"

"Tablecloths!" Josephine added.

"I always admired that kind of talent," the woman said. "Mine's just a hobby. Something to..."

"Take your mind off your troubles?" Josephine said. Judging by Mama's expression, this was not appropriate.

"Something like that. I'm Helen-Dove. Helen-Dove is hyphenated. My mother's doing." She hesitated, then added, "Quiver is the last name."

Quiver carried with it a jolt of electricity.

"I'm Penny Willoughby," Mama said, unfazed. "This is my daughter, Josephine." She put both hands on Josephine's shoulders as if locking her in place.

"Mary Josephine," Josephine added. "Not hyphenated. Can we see them up close?"

Mama gave Josephine's shoulders a firm squeeze. "Sorry, we don't mean to intrude."

"It's fine if she wants to take a look," Helen-Dove said, and stepped aside.

Josephine squeezed past her to the inside of number 7. She tried not to think about the fact that she was entering the home of a kidnapped girl.

The walls were covered with needlework, ceiling to floor,

every square inch. Pictures of baskets filled with flowers and trellises with flowers growing up them. Vases with flowers and fields of flowers. The stitching looked complicated.

Something about so many flowers this close together made Josephine think of a funeral parlor. "Mama, you have to see this," Josephine called.

"Jo, come on now. This poor woman just got home from work."

"It's fine," Helen-Dove said. "You can look if you want."

Mama stepped inside. Helen-Dove set the Tupperware container on the coffee table and switched on a lamp, which was when Josephine spotted it: Molly Quiver's school picture. The lamp had an orange shade, and it cast an eerie reddish glow over the girl's photograph.

It was in a plain black frame on top of the television. Molly's hair was in long braids, and she was wearing a top with intricate stitching—green vines and tiny red strawberries. Tied to the ends of her braids were hair ribbons, one red and the other green.

Mama gave Josephine a stern look, which Josephine ignored.

"Did you stitch that top, too?" Josephine asked, pointing to Molly's picture.

Mama's eyes went slightly wider.

"I did," Helen-Dove replied. "That's my daughter. I embellish a lot of Molly's clothes."

The room took on a funeral-parlor feeling for real then, like they were gathered around Molly's coffin instead of her picture. Josephine's heart fluttered as if it had wings.

"Molly turned ten last August," Helen-Dove went on. "This picture was taken the day she went missing. I'm guessing you heard. It's the name. *Quiver* gets people's attention. I've stopped writing checks at the grocery store just to avoid the nosy questions."

"I'm so sorry," Mama said, and gave Josephine a hard look.

"Good days and bad days."

Mama bit her lip and nodded.

Helen-Dove pointed to the Tupperware container. "Does that need to be refrigerated?"

"Oh, it's fine," Mama replied. "In fact, I think it tastes better at room temperature." Mama studied the walls again. She leaned in close to examine the stitching. "For all my years of sewing, I have never mastered this kind of thing. Your stitches are so intricate."

Josephine glanced toward the dim hallway. Molly's room was down that hallway, and judging by the layout, it was on the back side of number 7, the room that faced Josephine's window. The room that was always dark at night.

She was wearing Molly's shoes, standing inside her trailer, talking to her mother, and looking at her school picture. Molly's arms were folded, proper and stiff on the podium, and her head was tilted in that funny way school photographers always insist on.

Later that same day she would be abducted. Josephine knew now what Molly did not known then. And there it was, the feeling that their fates were somehow linked. A pinkie swear between them.

Get me home, and I'll get you home, Molly seemed to be saying.

Swimming Pools and Rich People

The next morning as Mama drove them to the installation appointment, Josephine stared out the window. She had Molly on the brain.

In some weird way, the girl was familiar, like maybe Josephine had seen her before. Not in the newspaper, but someplace else. The movies maybe? Shopping downtown? The candy aisle at IGA?

Josephine closed her eyes and saw Molly's picture again. Dark braids. Hair ribbons. The intricate stitches on her top.

Nope, she decided. *A girl like Molly I'd remember.*

"Here we are," Mama said, rattling Josephine out of her daydream.

They were turning into a mile-long paved driveway. "Is that *theirs*?" Josephine pointed to a tennis court.

"Yes, and around back is a swimming pool."

"A swimming pool?"

"No," Mama said firmly before Josephine could even ask.

"But I haven't been swimming once this summer! It would

make up for not getting to drive Tin Lizzies and ride the Flume Zoom."

"This is not a social visit, Jo. Did you bring something to keep yourself entertained while Lucas and I work?"

Josephine glanced at the library book on the seat beside her. "Nope. I'm not about to read that mess again."

"Impeccable manners. No *yeah*s or *huh*s. It's *yes, ma'am* and *please* and *thank you*. Got it?"

"Huh?" Josephine said, just to be smart.

Mama shook her head and parked next to Lucas' van, a navy-blue contraption with bright yellow letters on the side— LUCAS B. INSTALLATIONS—except the *B* was an actual bee with a trail of buzzy marks.

"Let's go," Mama said, and hurried out of the car.

Josephine stood in the driveway, taking it all in—the giant brick house, perfectly shaped boxwoods, trimmed grass. Apparently, the Morrisons were the ones who'd inherited a kingdom.

"Quit gawking, Jo," Mama said, and motioned her up the sidewalk.

⊐⟹

The Morrisons had three teenaged girls, but they weren't home because, according to their mother, Mrs. Morrison, the youngest was at sleepaway camp; the middle girl was babysitting; and the oldest was taking driver's ed.

Mrs. Morrison was pretty for a mom—poufy hair with lots of hair spray and a blue pantsuit with bright gold buttons. Also, she smelled good, though Josephine tried not to be too obvious about sniffing her.

In the basement rec room, where Mrs. Morrison sent Josephine while Mama and Lucas worked, she'd left a plate of cookies and a glass of lemonade.

The cookies tasted like cardboard and the lemonade didn't have enough sugar, but the enormous room had a Ping-Pong table and a stereo and a wall of books and records and the fattest beanbag chairs Josephine had ever seen. There were piles of teen magazines, and posters on the walls, too—bands and singers mostly.

Josephine recognized that weird Alice Cooper guy with his creepy eye makeup smeared down his face and a snake wrapped around his neck. "*Yuck*," she said, and grabbed the remote, kicking off her Tiger Paws and flopping onto a beanbag. She flipped through channels—soap opera *click* game show *click* soap opera. She was about to click the button again when a news flash caught her attention.

"We interrupt our regular programming to bring you this update," the newscaster said. "Another communiqué was delivered to the Los Angeles radio station KPFK. Kidnap victim Patricia Campbell Hearst is heard on these tapes eulogizing six members of the Symbionese Liberation Army, all of whom were killed in a standoff last month."

Josephine raised the volume and leaned in close. There was a picture of a tape recorder and then various photos of Patty—Patty as a cheerleader, Patty as a high school graduate, and Patty robbing a bank.

"She's not even the same person," Josephine said, to no one.

And there it was, Patricia Hearst's voice. She sounded more like a robot, and her words made no sense. Something about pigs and insects and sisters and brothers, not her *real* sisters and brothers, but the folks who'd kidnapped her, apparently.

"She exploded with the desire to kill the pig," Patty said about one "sister" named Gelina. Another "sister" she called a *gorilla*. And then, to Josephine's horror, the recording ended with Patricia saying, "I would never choose to spend the rest of my life with pigs like the Hearsts."

Josephine smacked a hand over her mouth. Behind her palm she whispered, "They're never gonna pay your ransom now!"

The TV screen returned to the newscaster. "We'll have further updates at six o'clock this evening," and then *Search for Tomorrow*, the program Miss Augustine watched, was back on. Josephine pressed the Off button and stared at Alice Cooper.

Patricia Hearst, the bank robber version, probably listened to Alice Cooper's music all the time. *I would never choose to spend the rest of my life with pigs like the Hearsts.* Could brainwashing do that to a person? Make her call her parents *pigs*? Or was that just being a teenager in general?

Delia wasn't an actual teenager, but once she'd called her mother a *monster*. This was after Mrs. Collingsworth refused to buy her a set of hot rollers. Delia's hair was stick-straight, and Mrs. Collingsworth said the curl wouldn't hold.

It was in that moment, with Delia and Patricia and Alice taking up space in Josephine's brain, that she glanced at Molly's shoes. *Tiger Paws* was printed on the insoles, yet the *Tiger Paws* in the left shoe didn't match the *Tiger Paws* in the right one.

Josephine grabbed the shoe and examined it. Upstairs there was the clatter of something hitting the floor. Probably one of Lucas' tools. Ever so slowly, as if it were a candy bar from Willy Wonka himself, Josephine peeled back the insole and stared at what was hidden there: a key.

The key was encrusted with dirt and badly tarnished. She ran her fingertips over the ridges and tugged at the frayed piece of yarn threaded through the hole. There were footsteps on the floor above her, and then the snap of the basement door opening.

"Yoo-hoo," Mrs. Morrison called down the stairs. "Your mother and Lucas are nearly finished."

"Be right there," Josephine replied. Quickly, she tucked the key into place again and shoved her feet into the Tiger Paws.

⊏⟹

When the installation was finished, Josephine followed old Lucas out to his van while Mama settled up with Mrs. Morrison.

Josephine hadn't detected the key in her shoe before, but now it dug into her heel like barbed wire.

"You see them draperies?" Lucas asked.

"What?" Josephine replied. She was trying to walk like a normal person.

"Your mother did some mighty fine handiwork." Lucas was the installer for Mama's bigger projects and the fella Miss Augustine was sweet on. He had a large bald head and a long nose and a pair of shoulders Miss Augustine swore wouldn't fit through her front door unless he turned sideways.

Josephine hadn't noticed the draperies. She was too busy thinking about what Mama would do with that key if she found it.

"You got something wrong with your foot?" Lucas frowned at Josephine's feet.

"I was just thinking about Patty Hearst is all," Josephine said.

Lucas hoisted his toolbox into the back of the van and slammed its double doors. "What's that girl done now?"

"The news guy broke in on *Search for Tomorrow* and played a tape. She called her parents *pigs*."

"Lordy mercy." Lucas shook his head. "I never did understand rich folks too good." He stuck his hand in his pocket and made a surprised face. "Look what I done found in here," he said, then handed over a fresh pack of Fruit Stripe chewing gum.

Josephine grinned.

"You know what to do with it, right?" Lucas teased.

"Smack it loud as I please," Josephine replied. This was their joke. Lucas had been giving her Fruit Stripe chewing gum and telling her to smack it loud as she pleased for as long as she could remember.

"I expect you'll be getting too old for Fruit Stripe one of these days."

"Not in a million years," Josephine protested, though the tiniest worm of worry bored its way into her brain.

Maybe one day soon she'd stop liking Fruit Stripe gum the same way she'd stopped liking Baby Tender Love and those Fisher-Price Little People. Last Easter instead of hunting for eggs herself, she'd helped the Sunday-school teacher hide them.

"You sure there ain't nothin' the matter with you today?" Lucas rubbed his chin and twisted his mouth sideways.

Josephine nodded and smacked the gum and thought about the key in her left shoe. "I'm sure."

Stupid Summer

Mama and Josephine said goodbye to Mrs. Morrison and Lucas, then climbed into the hot car. Josephine barely noticed the fancy houses in Country Club Estates now. Her brain had shifted from keys to kids with keys.

Latchkey kids, they were called. Their parents worked, so they let themselves inside after school. Made their own snacks. Did homework. Started dinner, even. Mama had declared Josephine too young to be a latchkey kid, which wasn't true. Josephine was plenty old enough to stay by herself.

When they reached the library, Josephine wouldn't bother to exchange *By the Shores of Silver Lake*. Instead, she would spend her precious time reading every newspaper article about Molly.

There was so much Josephine didn't know. What was Molly's favorite color and subject in school? Did she have a favorite teacher, the way Miss Lake was Josephine's favorite, or were the teachers at Molly's school dull and mean?

Newspapers didn't usually print those kinds of facts, but

maybe in this case they'd made an exception, being as Molly was a kid and all.

Mama headed east on Campbell Boulevard, and as the scenery whizzed by, a story formed in Josephine's head—if she rescued Molly, the two of them could become best friends, way better friends than Josephine and Delia had been. Way better friends than Delia and Kitty were now.

Best-friendship was something Josephine had been chewing on for months. It seemed nearly everybody had one best friend in particular. They bought bracelets with a heart split in two and alternated hosting Friday-night sleepovers and called each other on the phone. On twin day at school, there was somebody to be twins with.

Josephine hadn't had that sort of best-friendship with Delia. It pained her heart to think it, but she hadn't had that kind of best-friendship with anybody.

She realized then why Molly looked familiar. Molly Quiver was the *future* kind of familiar. Plain as day Josephine pictured them walking around Arbor Heights and Josephine showing Molly the sights—the park and the schoolhouse and the garden their landlady, Miss Nancy, kept in back of the apartment building.

Josephine spit her wad of Fruit Stripe gum into its wrapper and stuffed it in the ashtray. "What was in those news stories?" she asked, then braced herself for an answer that was likely to give her the bonafide heebie-jeebies.

Mama was gripping the steering wheel like they were about to drive over a cliff. She didn't respond.

"What's the matter with you?" Josephine asked.

The light ahead turned yellow, then red, and Mama

slammed the brakes. "I'm just making a mental list. Business is picking up again. I have to get orders turned around quickly. Not having my work tables is a nightmare. I have to measure everything a million times."

"You're in the wrong lane," Josephine pointed out. "The library's that way."

"What?"

"The *li*-brary is that way," Josephine said.

"Oh, Jo, we don't have time for that today."

"But you *promised*!"

"The installation took longer than expected, and Mrs. Morrison wants sofa cushions for her sunroom now. Oodles of them by the Fourth of July. If I don't start today, I'll never get them finished in time."

Josephine glowered at her mother. "You said if—"

"That's right. I said *if* we had time. I did not promise." The light changed to green, and Mama took off in the direction of Happy World.

"I hate this," Josephine mumbled. "I hate *everything* about this stupid summer."

"This isn't the summer you were hoping for, but sometimes work must come first. I have to work even harder than before."

Josephine pressed herself into the car door, as far away from her mother as possible.

"We can make chocolate milk shakes tonight. How about that?" Mama tried.

Josephine didn't answer. She stared out the window, and in a flash of memory she recalled Miss Lake turning a cartwheel on the playground. The kids had dared her, so at recess she removed the silver whistle from around her neck, and then, much to everyone's surprise, especially the other teachers, she turned the most divine cartwheel Josephine had ever seen.

I wish Miss Lake was my mother.

Wishing someone else was your mother was as bad as calling your mother a *monster*. It was very nearly as bad as calling your mother a *pig*. Josephine stuffed another stick of gum in her mouth and smacked it hard.

She was so busy smacking and *un*-wishing that she almost didn't notice the shiny police car parked in front of number 7.

Keys

Once inside number 13, Josephine made a beeline for her room and shut the door. She stacked her bed pillows, one on top of the other, and perched on her knees to stare out the window.

After what seemed a very long time, a policeman emerged from number 7. He was a tall, slim Black man. His hat was in his hands and his head was down. He got into his squad car and drove away.

Josephine kept watch until it was time for supper. When the meal was finished, she went back to staring out the window again. For hours Josephine wished and hoped. She imagined Molly, with her dark braids and embroidered top and red and green hair ribbons, stepping out of the photo and into real life.

Delia was a friend from Josephine's past, but Molly Quiver was a friend from Josephine's future.

"Jo!" Mama called from the other room. "Time for bed."

Josephine tugged off her left shoe and peeled back the insole. Keys were for opening things—warehouses and apartments. And trailers.

An idea bumped around in Josephine's head and made her heart speed up.

The *whirr-thump* stopped abruptly. "Jo! Did you hear what I said?" There were footsteps, and then Mama opened the door just as Josephine shoved the shoe into the closet.

Mama frowned down at her. "Why are you wearing one shoe?"

Josephine shrugged.

"This silent treatment is unbecoming. Brush your teeth. And no more spying on neighbors."

"I wasn't—"

"Lying isn't becoming, either," Mama said.

After her teeth were brushed and her face was washed and both Tiger Paws were tucked inside her closet, Josephine lay wide-eyed in her bed. Stinky cigarette smoke wafted through her screen, but it was only Miss Connie. Late at night, the woman wandered the trailer park in her pink nightgown, with her cat, Bob Barker, yowling along behind her.

Josephine thought of Miss Nancy, already asleep by this time. Oscar and Mayer, her two wienie dogs, were probably curled at the end of her bed. "Heartbeats at my feet," she called them.

Redbud Avenue was pretty at night with the hazy glow of streetlights and whisper of tires on pavement.

There it was again—the achy longing for home.

Seesaw

The next morning Josephine flung off the covers and looked out the window; except for Helen-Dove's lonely blue smock hanging on the clothesline, everything was exactly the same. Same rusty siding. Same peeling metal. Same tall weeds. Same broken lawn chair.

Mama's Singer was *whirr*ing and *thump*ing and *whirr*ing and *thump*ing. Josephine wondered if Mama had sewn straight through the night.

Hard-shelled guilt crawled into her throat then. Insect-like, it twitched. Quietly, she slid off her bed and crept into the room where Mama was bent over the sewing machine. Her hair was shiny and her cheeks were smooth, probably from all the Pond's cold cream. When Josephine was younger, she loved to run the backs of her hands down Mama's soft cheeks.

Josephine imagined living in the same town as her dad, Las Vegas with its casinos and hotels and swimming pools. "Mama?"

Mama stopped her sewing and turned to look at Josephine. "Did I wake you with this racket?"

Josephine moved closer. "I never want to live in Las Vegas." A pit opened inside her chest and gave her the feeling of falling some great distance with no one to catch her.

"And I never want you to live in Las Vegas," Mama replied. "That's not going to happen, Jo. I was just using it as an example." Mama swung her legs around and patted her lap. "Sit," she said.

Josephine sat and leaned her head so that Mama's cheek was against her forehead. Their arms were wrapped tight around each other.

"She wants to come home," Josephine said. "Even if it's terrible here, she wants to come back to her mother."

As if on cue, there was a knock at the door, and Josephine sprang off Mama's lap. "It's *her*!"

"It's Lisa Marie, Jo. I can see her through the glass."

⊏⟹

While Mama made them breakfast, Josephine dragged Lisa Marie into her bedroom and shut the door.

"What was that policeman doing here yesterday?" Josephine asked.

"What policeman? Move so I can see your pictures." Lisa Marie nudged Josephine away from the door. "You sure do like that Donny Osmond. You gonna cover the whole door?"

Josephine grabbed Lisa Marie by the shoulders and spun her around. "You didn't see the squad car parked outside Helen-Dove's trailer yesterday?"

"We was at the doctor's yesterday."

Josephine sank onto her *bo-ING!*-y bed and let out a deep sigh.

"It'uz probably Officer Frye."

"Officer Frye?" Josephine blinked.

"Did he walk like this?" Lisa Marie indicated his long stride as best she could in such a tiny room.

Josephine nodded.

"Tall and brown and on the slim side?"

"Yes."

"It was him," Lisa Marie said firmly. "He gives her updates about Molly." Lisa Marie flopped onto the bed next to Josephine.

"What do you mean *updates*?"

"The kidnappers move around. Sometimes they get in scrapes with the law."

"Like shoot-outs and car chases?"

"Naw. Money stuff. Not paying bills and tickets. By the time Officer Frye gets some news, then tells it to Miss Helen, they've up and gone someplace else. It's been cat and mouse since she went missing. Back around Christmas they was a little box of hair ribbons."

"Hair ribbons?"

"Miss Helen had stitched things on them. She's right handy with a needle. I reckon the box of ribbons was in Molly's book satchel the day they got her. Some lady found 'em in the place where they was staying at. The Happy World address was inside the box of ribbons, which was how come the lady knew to mail it back here. She sent a bill for their rent in the package, too, but I don't reckon that ever got paid. Lotsee, Oklahoma, the return address said."

"Then what happened?"

"Miss Helen 'bout went crazy that time. Said they were trying to erase her daughter, turn her into somebody else. She said them people probably wouldn't let her wear ribbons."

Josephine stared at Lisa Marie in horror. "That sounds like Patricia Hearst. The turning-her-into-someone-else part, I mean."

"I ain't never really thought of it that way before."

"Where else have they been?"

"California a few months ago. Texas. Molly's probably been dragged to the ends of the earth and back by now."

A moving target was harder to hit. Josephine had learned this the hard way in dodgeball. "Maybe Officer Frye was here because he's closing in on them." Josephine had heard this terminology on a detective show. *Kojak* or *Hawaii Five-O*, she couldn't remember which.

"I doubt it." Lisa Marie sniffed the air and sighed happily. "It sure does smell good in here. I sure am hungry."

The girl's face was grimy and sweat-streaked, and her hair, an even brighter shade of blond this morning, was a nest of snarls. There were gray circles beneath her eyes and the skin on the end of her nose was peeling from a sunburn. "What're you lookin' at me like that for?"

"No reason. How do you know so much about Molly?"

"Miss Helen told Buster Lee everything. Before he got so bad off, him and Helen-Dove was real good friends. Then he stopped being friends with anybody, 'cept me and Granddaddy."

The smell of pancakes and bacon permeated the trailer now. Mama had switched on the radio and raised the volume. Elton John was singing "B-B-B-Benny and the Jets."

It was hot and hopeless, and not even Elton John could cheer things up. "Mama promised she'd take me to the library yesterday so I could see some old newspaper stories about Molly. But she had too much work. She *always* has too much work."

"Better than not enough work. Ever since Buster Lee's cancer, we're just barely scrapin' by."

"I'm supposed to find her." Josephine did not look at Lisa Marie when she said this.

"Girls!" Mama called from the kitchen. "Pancakes are on the table!"

Lisa Marie bolted from the bed, but Josephine sprang for the door and blocked it. "I'm supposed to find her," she said again.

She was waiting for Lisa Marie to tell her she was crazy. If she'd said something this outrageous to Delia, Delia would've rolled her eyes and called her cuckoo for Cocoa Puffs.

Lisa Marie tapped the back of her wrist as if indicating the time, though she wasn't wearing a watch. "See this right here?"

"Your wrist?"

"This freckle on my wrist."

Josephine leaned in close. "What's your freckle got to do with anything?"

"It's how much faith you need. Faith the size of a little bitty freckle and you can move a mountain. It's what I tell Buster Lee, and it's what I tell you."

The seesaw bounced upward again.

"You don't need no library to see them old newspapers. Buster Lee saved everything."

"What?"

"He kept a scrapbook of the news stories. I'll show you after we eat. Now get out of my way before there's a stampede!"

58

13

The Smile of Mona Lisa

"Where did you live at before you come here?" Lisa Marie asked as they made their way down the porch steps.

"Arbor Heights," Josephine said. Her stomach was full now, and the sweet sticky of syrup and butter and bacon mixed in with orange juice was pleasant on her tongue.

"Never heard of it," Lisa Marie replied.

Suddenly, there was the sound of a trailer door slamming. Helen-Dove, dressed in her work clothes, was heading down the washed-out path.

"Miss Helen!" Lisa Marie shouted, then took off running.

Helen-Dove turned, stretched out her skinny arms, and Lisa Marie flung herself into them.

Slowly, Josephine made her way toward them. She tried to walk like a girl who did not have a key hidden inside her shoe.

Helen-Dove let go of Lisa Marie, but Lisa Marie kept her arm around the woman's slim waist. "Hi, Josephine," Helen-Dove said.

It was awkward to spend the night spying on someone and

then meet them face-to-face in the morning. "Hi," Josephine replied.

Helen-Dove's heart was not pulsing in her throat today. And she didn't look any more tragic than she had the last time Josephine saw her. Unfortunately, she didn't look any less tragic, either.

"What are you girls up to?"

Lisa Marie glanced at Josephine, then said in a joking way, "Aw, we ain't up to no good, Miss Helen. You gettin' in a double shift?"

Helen-Dove nodded.

No purse, Josephine noticed. No brown bag for a lunch, either. Just the light blue smock with its deep pockets and the white bird stitched on her shoulder, like any second it might take flight.

Helen-Dove glanced at Lisa Marie again and frowned. "When's the last time you had your hair washed? Not under the hose, but with shampoo?"

Josephine expected Lisa Marie to be insulted, but she laughed her big barky laugh and said, "It's summer. Who really cares?"

"I care is who," Helen-Dove said, then she smiled without showing any teeth. It was a sad smile, like that painting they called the *Mona Lisa*. Josephine had learned about it in art class at Brandywine.

"Why was Officer Frye here yesterday?" Lisa Marie said. "Josephine seen his car and was wantin' to know."

Josephine cringed. If she'd been standing any closer, she would've stepped on Lisa Marie's toe.

"Nothing for you to worry about," Helen-Dove replied sharply.

"Reckon when they might find Molly?" Lisa Marie pressed. "It's gettin' to be almost a year now, Miss Helen."

"I have not lost track of the months of the year, Lisa Marie. Now y'all stop being a pair of busybodies and let me get on to work." With that she strode off down the path, but turned and said, "Tell Buster Lee I'm coming to visit whether he likes it or not. And wash that hair properly when y'all are done playing."

"Why did you tell her *I* saw his car and wanted to know?" Josephine scolded once Helen-Dove was out of earshot. Josephine gave Lisa Marie an elbow jab.

"Because you *are* the one that saw his car and wanted to know." Lisa Marie jabbed her back.

"What if she thinks I'm nosy, like those people at the grocery store?"

"What people at the grocery store?"

"She said she didn't write checks anymore on account of her name and people being nosy."

"Hold up, I got a splinter." Lisa Marie dropped to the ground.

"She works at Cameron Mills, you said?" Josephine asked.

"Yeah." Lisa Marie was studying the bottom of her dirty foot.

"Why doesn't she drive there?"

"You are kinda nosy."

"I'm trying to get some clarification is all. Clarification means to make things less confusing, which is not at all the same thing as nosy."

"No car," Lisa Marie said. She was sticking out her tongue in concentration, her foot so close to her face she was slightly cross-eyed. "Sold it after they got Molly. Used the money to pay so he'd keep looking."

"Officer Frye, you mean?"

"It was some other cop at first, but he gave up. Took her money, then quit."

"Without actually looking?"

"Pretty much, yeah."

"So now she pays Officer Frye to look?"

"He ain't never charged Miss Helen a dime is what Buster Lee says."

"I thought the police were supposed to look for free."

"What they're s'posed to do and what they do, them's two different things."

Josephine thought of the Patricia Hearst search parties she'd seen on the news, back when they still had a television. Scads of officers in uniform, rummaging through garages and around people's backyards. Carrying guns and looking determined. "How far is it to Cameron Mills?"

"Three miles or so."

Helen-Dove was a tiny blue speck in the far distance now. She turned right onto the main highway, where cars and trucks would roar past her at high rates of speed.

Josephine didn't know anybody who walked such a long and dangerous way to work. On Redbud Avenue kids walked to school, Josephine included, when it wasn't raining, but Brandywine Elementary was only a hop, skip, and jump away from their old apartment.

Suddenly, Josephine remembered that walk with tender clarity—golden leaves on sidewalks in fall, sapphire skies in winter. And redbud trees. Redbud Avenue was in all its pink glory come springtime. Oceans away, her old life seemed on this muggy morning.

Josephine glanced at number 7, empty and quiet now

with Helen-Dove gone off to work. An alarming idea began to take shape in her head. Usually, her ideas had something to do with writing stories, but this idea blared and clanged, and it gave Josephine the terrible feeling she'd committed a crime.

"Got it!" Lisa Marie said, and held up a long sliver of splinter.

Smiling with Half a Face

Lisa Marie and Josephine picked their way up the porch steps of number 17, past the old paint buckets and coffee cans filled with growing things—tomatoes and hot peppers and squash and cucumbers.

Josephine tried to brace herself for the sight of Buster Lee.

"We got to be quiet. Buster Lee might be resting his eyes." Lisa Marie put her hand on the doorknob.

"Wait!" Josephine said. Maybe he would drool or cry out in pain or die while Josephine was in there. She did not want to see anybody die. "Maybe we should look at the clippings out here, so we don't disturb him."

Lisa Marie scowled. "You big chicken, cancer of the face ain't catchin'. Don't act scared or nothin'. And *don't* stare at his face. He can tell when people do that. Just act regular." At this Lisa Marie pushed open the door and dragged Josephine inside.

The room was dim, but the TV was on. "Buster Lee? You watching *Name That Tune*?"

"Hush, Wisa Mawie," Buster Lee scolded. "The Gowen Medwey is on." Buster Lee was swiping at his mouth with a handkerchief and bobbing his head along with the song that was playing. "Awawon! Awawon!" he said to the TV.

"Avalon!" the contestant hollered.

"That's right! You're absolutely right!" the game-show guy hollered back.

Bells started dinging and a lady who looked an awful lot like that mother on *The Brady Bunch* was jumping around and screaming her head off.

Weakly, Buster Lee thrust his victorious fist in the air.

"He gets the songs in the Golden Medley right every time," Lisa Marie said proudly. "Look, Buster Lee, you woulda won a car!"

Buster Lee put his fist in the air again.

"This is Josephine."

Buster Lee turned off the TV with the remote. It was so dark Josephine could hardly see his face, which was probably what he wanted.

"Josephine just moved into Miss Connie's old trailer. We're fixin' to look at that album you got with all them stories about Little Bit. Where's it at?"

Buster Lee pointed toward a narrow hallway, then gestured to the spot under his chair.

"It's in yonder under his bed. Come on," Lisa Marie said, and Josephine followed her.

Lisa Marie switched on the lamp, then flopped onto the floor. While Lisa Marie was feeling around under the bed, Josephine took in the details of Buster Lee's room: oodles of medicine bottles crowded together on the built-in desk; a pile of what looked to be clean clothes stacked on the bureau. On the wall by the door was a *Farmer's Almanac* calendar, but it was stopped on last November.

"Here you go," Lisa Marie said, and held up the album. She brushed off the dust bunnies.

Josephine scootched closer and the girls stared at the cover. In big crisp letters were the words *Molly June "Little Bit" Quiver.*

"Buster Lee wrote that?" Josephine asked, and ran her fingers over the letters.

"Yeah," Lisa Marie said.

"He's got nice handwriting," Josephine pointed out.

"He used to draw real good, too," Lisa Marie said.

Slowly, Josephine opened the book. There was the same picture of Molly that Helen-Dove had sitting on top of her TV. Josephine studied Molly's shirt, with the embroidered vines and strawberries. Molly Quiver would be exactly right for a best friend. Josephine could tell by looking.

"Turn the page," Lisa Marie said as if she could read Josephine's mind and didn't like what she was thinking.

The rest were pictures from *after* the kidnapping— clippings of police officers standing around number 7 and Helen-Dove looking stricken.

The first article was a fairly long report about the day Molly went missing and who-all had seen her—teachers at school, a person named "Mr. Sammy." He was the bus driver who'd driven Molly home that afternoon. "Let her out by the mailboxes, like I always do," he'd said.

The stories got shorter and shorter, and then the album pages were blank. "It's not very much," Josephine pointed out. "Are you sure Buster Lee saved everything?"

"That's everything they wrote," Lisa Marie replied.

Josephine backtracked through the pages again. She read

carefully, running her finger along the lines of copy so as not to miss a word.

"Is that the same Miss Connie from the leasing office?" Josephine pointed to a quote from a Mrs. Connie Godwin: "A dark green car pulled in the trailer park. It wasn't there long. I didn't see nobody get in it, though."

"That's her," Lisa Marie said. "The one day she ought to be in everybody's business, she ain't."

"Why'd Buster Lee keep this stuff?" Josephine asked.

"Miss Helen wasn't in no kinda shape to do it herself." Lisa Marie flipped to the front of the book again. Inside the cover was an inscription:

Welcome home, Molly!
From your friend Buster Lee Green
1973

Josephine skimmed the stories one last time, looking for the part about the father and grandmother. "It just says 'family dispute.' It doesn't mention her daddy or the grandmother."

Lisa Marie closed the album and slid it under the bed again. "Come on. Let's ask."

⊐⟹

Buster Lee was at the kitchen table now. The overhead light was turned on, and plain as day, Josephine could see the tube in the man's nose and milky-looking stuff dribbling into him.

Josephine shuddered, and Lisa Marie nudged her hard with a bony elbow.

"Hey, Buster Lee?" Lisa Marie said.

Buster Lee looked at her with his one good eye. He blinked. Josephine felt her heart squeeze tight with sad, but she didn't turn away. She tried to act regular.

"It was the grandmother and daddy that took her? Ain't that what they said?"

Buster Lee pinched off the tube. He made a few strangled gurgling noises, then nodded. "Mean peopuh." He squinted his one good eye. "Mean," he said again, then un-pinched the tube.

Lisa Marie went around to the good side of Buster Lee, and gave him a kiss on the cheek. It was hard to tell for sure, but Josephine was pretty sure he smiled with half his face. "Back in a little while," Lisa Marie said.

Then she grabbed Josephine's hand and pulled her into the sunshine again.

Spiders (and Snakes)

The girls squished themselves between a tall tomato plant and a rusted coffee can filled with growing peppers. They listened to the cars out on the highway and the sound of music coming from farther down the washed-out path. It was either the hippie couple or the motorcycle couple. Hard to tell which, since their trailers were so close together.

After a while Josephine said, "It's like nobody cares. It's like everybody gave up. You saw the officers in those pictures. They were just standing around, not looking!"

Sad was crawling over Josephine now, and it wasn't her own sad, but somebody else's. It was a strange feeling to have somebody else's sad crawling on you.

"I don't know what me and you can do about it." Lisa Marie put a blade of grass between her thumbs and blew out an ear-piercing whistle.

"Quit it," Josephine scolded. "I'm just saying we ought to be looking." The key to number 7 was in her left shoe. Helen-Dove was not home.

"Looking *where*?" Lisa Marie pressed.

Josephine glanced at number 7.

Lisa Marie made a horrified face. "In Miss Helen's trailer?"

It was a crazy idea. It was definitely the craziest idea Josephine had ever had, but her whole world was crazy now. A warehouse fire and a yard sale. Moving to a place called Happy World where only bad stuff happened.

Lisa Marie was boring a hole in Josephine with her green eyes. "You think. Miss Helen. Kidnapped her own *daughter*?"

Lisa Marie had blabbed about Josephine and the police car. If they slipped into number 7 to look for clues, she'd surely blab about that, too. "No," Josephine said finally. "That's not what I meant."

"Well, what did you mean then?"

"I just meant..." Josephine glanced around, trying to figure out something else to mean. "We should look in those trailers nobody lives in now."

"Aw, Josephine, that's dumb. What kinda kidnapper is gonna take their victim to a trailer right close by?"

"It isn't dumb, and that's *not* what I said."

"You kinda did."

"Maybe Molly left a clue is all I'm saying. If I was being kidnapped, I'd leave a note or a sign." Josephine hopped off the step and put her hands on her hips. "What if you were the one missing? Wouldn't you want people looking, even if they were looking in the wrong places?"

Lisa Marie scratched her head. "There's spiders in them old trailers."

"I'm not afraid of spiders."

There were three abandoned trailers in Happy World. Josephine and Lisa Marie couldn't push the door to the first trailer open because it was warped, so they moved on to the next one.

"What a mess," Josephine whispered as they crossed the threshold. The floors were rotten and the girls had to step carefully to avoid falling through them. There were weeds poking through the rotted-out places, and a thick vine twisted straight up the wall. It was bright inside, and Josephine glanced up and saw a giant hole in the roof—blue sky and a few wispy clouds. "Why doesn't somebody take this thing to the junkyard?"

"Miss Connie ain't gonna do nothin' 'cept smoke her cigs and watch her stories and pet that hissing cat," Lisa Marie answered.

There was a scratching sound in what had once been a kitchen. "What's that?" Josephine whispered.

Lisa Marie grinned. "Might be a big ole rat." Ever so deftly, she picked her way across what was left of the floor. There was more scratching and then Lisa Marie flung open the cabinet.

Out scurried a squirrel!

Josephine screamed as it streaked across her shoe, bounced over the rotting floor, scrambled up the twisting vine, and escaped through the hole in the roof.

Lisa Marie busted out laughing. "Gah-lee, it ain't nothin' but a little bitty squirrel."

"I'm leaving," Josephine said, and was out the door.

"Wanna go to the next one?" Lisa Marie asked when they were outside again. "This don't make no sense, but it sure is fun."

Josephine's heart was pounding in her ears.

"What's the matter? Squirrel got your tongue?"

A cloud passed over Josephine's mood then. It was a dark and stormy Delia and Kitty cloud.

"Let's go. This is *fun!*" Lisa Marie said, and off she ran on her long legs toward the last empty trailer.

Josephine tried to imagine what Delia and Kitty might be doing today. Buying earrings or going to that art camp downtown they both liked so much. Maybe they were up in Kitty's tree house or watching Delia's TV. Not her parents' TV, either. Delia had her very own TV, in her bedroom. She had a phone in there, too, pink to match her bedspread, and curtains and a pair of fuzzy beanbag chairs. Plus, Delia had a canopy bed, and it was so pretty it just about broke Josephine's heart.

"I have the worst life now," Josephine said as she crossed the washed-out path, but she knew this wasn't true. Molly Quiver had the worst life. And just before you got to Molly Quiver's worst life, there was Lisa Marie's almost-just-as-bad life.

"Come on!" Lisa Marie was hollering for Josephine to hurry, waving her arms and hopping around on one foot. From a distance she reminded Josephine of a strange bird.

It struck Josephine then, and filled her with what their friend Miss Augustine called awe and wonder: Lisa Marie didn't seem to think her life was bad. In fact, Lisa Marie looked like she was having a pretty good time.

$\Longrightarrow$

Josephine was sitting in a patch of clover, searching for a four-leafed one when Lisa Marie came out of the third vacant trailer and plopped down beside her.

"Now what do you want to do?" Lisa Marie asked.

The third trailer had spiders dangling from the ceiling and a long green snake with three small white eggs, which was all Josephine saw because she ran out quick.

"Did it bite you?" Josephine asked.

"Naw. Me and snakes are friendly. I know how to handle 'em good. Me and Granddaddy see snakes over at Swan's farm sometimes."

Josephine willed herself not to look at number 7; instead, she stared at the ground.

"Listen, Josephine, I ain't trying to be mean or nothin', but maybe you're not the one that's s'posed to find her."

"I'm wearing her shoes," Josephine pointed out.

Lisa Marie blinked in a way that meant she still didn't understand.

And the truth was, Josephine didn't understand, either, not really. Except that life in Happy World should have a purpose. She couldn't stand to be there if it didn't.

Lisa Marie smacked a mosquito on her arm and pointed to the mangled mess. "Ever wonder whose blood it is when you smack a skeeter?"

Josephine's heart sank lower.

"We could catch crawdaddies or turn over rocks in the creek and look at bugs under 'em. Sometimes I sit down by the road and wave at cars."

Josephine plucked a fistful of clover and said, "We could make *Missing* signs." She had seen such signs in the post office, except the people they were looking for were criminals.

"Naw, I don't want to do that. Listen, Josephine, we ain't got to do the same thing every second. You do what you want to, and I'll do what I want to." With this revelation, she was on her feet.

"Where're you going?" Josephine asked.

"I'm fixing to wave at some cars," Lisa Marie said, and then she was off and running, a flying streak of long legs and skinny arms and tangled hair.

Flying Pigs

With Lisa Marie gone, trailer number 7 practically begged Josephine to come inside. She kicked off her left shoe and peeled back the insole. The key was a comforting secret, a connection to a girl she didn't know.

Mama was sewing on a deadline. Buster Lee couldn't see anything because of the paper bags taped to his windows. The hippie couple had just left in their beat-up van, and not long after, the motorcycle couple had rumbled off, too.

The only threat was Miss Connie, but *Search for Tomorrow* was coming on. Josephine could hear the theme song from clear across the trailer park.

She glanced at the right shoe then. In the excitement of finding a key in the left one, she hadn't given much thought to its mate, but now she tugged it off and yanked back the insole.

"Tickle your tongue with Fruit Stripe gum," she whispered, and held a yellow wrapper up to the sunlight. Lemon. Every cell in Josephine's body hummed. This was what Brother Davis would've called a *divine sign*!

Josephine's favorite gum.

Josephine's favorite flavor.

Josephine's favorite shoes.

The divine signs wouldn't have been more obvious if God had pulled back the cloudy stage curtains and thumped Josephine on the head.

⊃⟶

Key held tight in her fist, she walked toward number 7. The porch railing wobbled slightly as Josephine climbed the steps, and the clay pot of geraniums made a soft clattering sound. The backs of her knees were sweating.

Time is of the essence, and a girl on a mission must not be deterred. Miss Lake said this whenever she sent Josephine to the main office with the attendance list. "Time is of the essence," she whispered, and put the key to the lock.

A distant car horn honked, probably provoked by Lisa Marie's enthusiastic waving.

Josephine tried to slip the key into the lock, but it wouldn't go. She tried again, pushing harder this time. "Dang it," she whispered, and glanced around. Molly must've stood right here on this welcome mat a thousand times. Josephine studied her Tiger Paws.

"She stood right here," Josephine whispered. "She put her hand on the knob." Josephine's palm was damp against the metal. "She squeezed and turned and—"

With ease the door squeaked open. Dust motes danced on a shaft of light.

As if stepping into a pool of quicksand, Josephine crossed the threshold, then shut the door behind her. The room was dim with the door closed, and she waited for her eyes to adjust.

Molly sat on top of the TV, her smile an invitation of sorts. Slowly, Josephine walked over to her.

The glass had a thin coating of dust, which Josephine wiped off with the hem of her shirt. "I wish you could talk to me," she said, and leaned in for a closer look. Strong white teeth with zigzags along the edges. Olive skin. Dark eyes, but not the plain brown kind. Molly's eyes had a glamorous gold tint to them. *Amber*, it was called.

The picture must have been taken in the morning. Josephine knew this from her own experience because braids never stayed neat for long. "I'm going in your room now," Josephine whispered. "I won't mess anything up, I promise. I want to look for clues."

Josephine took a deep breath, then headed down the narrow hallway. For obvious reasons, the door to Molly's room was closed. A grieving mother probably couldn't stand to look at an empty room. Josephine braced herself for what she might see, then opened the door.

The walls were paneled, same as Josephine's. And just like in the rest of the trailer, there were stitched pictures, not of flowers, but of pigs. The most charming, cheerful pink pigs Josephine had ever seen, with wings even. On Molly's bed were three stuffed ones dressed in doll clothes, a sight that made her smile.

The built-in dresser-desk was the exact same as the one in number 13. On it was an assortment of jelly jars, each filled with a different type of key. Old rusted keys and newer keys, though Josephine could see no purpose for them. "A girl who collects pigs and keys."

There was the same sort of cabinet-closet, too. Inside were a few blouses, some slacks, and three pairs of jeans. The denim things had been embellished with intricate stitches, flowers and vines that twisted up the legs. No skirts, Josephine noticed. No dresses, either. On a hook hung a small suede purse with fringe along the edges.

Molly was a stylish sort of person. Her room was a trailer-park room, but it was neat, and her walls were decorated, which made Josephine's heart flutter.

Next to the bed was a shoebox decorated with flower-power stickers. Josephine scooped it up and ever so gently sat down on Molly's bed. Inside the box were more gum wrappers, hundreds of them. Unfolded wrappers were loose on the bottom; folded ones were in plastic bags, sorted by color and secured with twist ties.

"Exactly what I had in mind," Josephine said, and held up one of the bags to study its contents. There were links of shiny foil that resembled real silver. A friendship bracelet, one skillfully woven. Josephine slipped it onto her wrist.

Molly wasn't just a flat person in a photograph. She was a girl who collected things. A girl who made things. Somewhere right now her heart was beating, her lungs were taking in oxygen, and she was thinking thoughts.

On the underside of the box's lid were faint pencil marks— *e-m* and *e-v-o-l*. *Love me*, except backwards. Josephine knew this because she sometimes wrote secret things backwards herself.

She turned the lid this way and that—*y-l-l-a-e-r* became *really*, and *y-e-h-t* was *they*. She was stuck on what look liked *mot* when the sound of Lisa Marie's hollering pierced the thin trailer walls.

"Josephine! *Josephine!* Where you at, Josephine?"

Missing Girl

It was a dreadful thing to hear your name called when you didn't want to be found. Josephine put the bracelet back in the bag, returned the lid to its rightful place, then shoved the box under the bed. As if to take a snapshot, she glanced around the room.

"Answer me, *Josephine!*" Lisa Marie's voice was insistent now. And pestering.

From behind Molly's curtains, Josephine saw Lisa Marie making a beeline for number 13. Swift as a bird, Josephine flew through the trailer and out the front door. She ran up the washed-out path just as Lisa Marie was about to knock at number 13. "Mama's on a deadline! You'll bother her!"

"I *always* knock on your door. It don't seem to bother your mama none." Lisa Marie's eyes narrowed slightly. "Where were you?" she asked as if she already knew the answer.

Guilt made Josephine's cheeks burn. "Nowhere."

"Nowhere ain't a place."

Lisa Marie was sweaty and dirty. She'd wiped mosquito guts on her shirt, not that you could see them, but Josephine knew they were there. "I'm going inside, and you can't come with me because—"

"Your mama's on a deadline," Lisa Marie said matter-of-factly. "I ain't gonna bother y'all none. Got plenty to do at my own place." And with that, Lisa Marie rumbled down the steps and brushed right past Josephine with the dignity of a queen.

Josephine felt a stab of regret watching Lisa Marie go, and judging by the grown-up way Lisa Marie squared her shoulders, she was bracing herself for some unpleasant but necessary task.

For the rest of the afternoon, Josephine drew in her spiral notebook—pictures of Molly's bedroom—and stared at the place on her wrist where the foil bracelet had been.

A token of our undying friendship, she imagined Molly saying. Then she would smile at Josephine with her zigzagged teeth.

After the rescue, when the excitement had died down a little, they would move to Arbor Heights, the section with *owned* houses instead of rented ones. They would live in separate houses, of course, but Molly's and Josephine's bedroom windows would face each other. They'd make one of those pulley systems for sending messages back and forth.

Theirs was a kind of sisterhood Delia and Kitty could not touch, Josephine thought. And because this line was so clever, she wrote it down.

⇒

With the missing-girl signs finished and ready for delivery, Josephine raced through a supper of fish sticks, carrot sticks, and celery sticks. Mama's sewing machine continued its *whirr-thump*, and the refrigerator made its usual coffee-grinder racket.

When she was finished, Josephine got up from the table and sank her plate into a sink filled with soapy water. "I'm going outside," she said.

"Where exactly?" Mama replied without turning around.

"With Lisa Marie," Josephine said, though she did not know this for sure.

"Stick close by. And come when I call, hear?" Still, Mama didn't turn around.

Josephine nodded and stood there, waiting.

"Did you hear what I said?"

The machine stopped. Mama swiveled around in her chair and frowned at Josephine.

Josephine smiled and nodded again.

"Well, if my back is turned, I don't know you're nodding," Mama pointed out.

"If you had eyes in back of your head like you always say, you would've seen me nodding."

"Come here," Mama said, and opened her arms.

Josephine slipped into the familiar hug. "I love you, Jo," Mama whispered into her hair.

"I love you," Josephine replied. And she did love her mother, so much so that sometimes it gave her a painful ache in her heart. Not just her heart, but a deeper place that had no name.

$\Longrightarrow$

With a batch of signs tucked under her arm, Josephine went out into the warm evening. The air was smoky with charcoal, and it was coming from the trailers farther down. Josephine hadn't met the hippies or the motorcycle couple yet.

Even before she knocked at number 17, she knew Lisa Marie wasn't home. Granddaddy's truck wasn't parked in its usual spot, and there wasn't the sound of Lisa Marie's singing or the smell of Granddaddy frying up a slab of bologna. Probably just Buster Lee in there resting his good eye and wishing she'd quit knocking, so she did.

Josephine wandered toward the other trailers. At number 15 there was brightly colored washing hanging on the line. Quickly, she chose her best sign and clipped it to a long, flowy dress, then hid behind the prickle bushes to watch and wait.

The weeds made her legs itch, and a mosquito kept whining in her ear. No hippies came out to collect the washing, and no motorcycle people came out to put meat on that smoking hot grill, either.

Josephine was about to head home when the door to 19 swung open so hard it banged the side of the trailer. The motorcycle man was bear-sized and dressed in leather— leather pants, leather vest, leather cap. His arms were big as tree trunks, and knotted around his neck was a red bandana.

"Make sure it's cooked through!" the woman shouted from inside. "I don't want it mooing at me."

"Yeah, yeah," the motorcycle man replied. He walked with a limp, like his right hip was missing a screw. In one hand was a platter of meat and a pair of tongs. In the other was a bottle of Budweiser. Josephine recognized the beer bottle because Lucas drank Budweiser whenever they ate supper at Miss Augustine's.

The motorcycle man set the bottle of Bud next to the lawn chair, then tossed the meat on the grill. It let out a long, slow sizzle, and soon the air was filled with cooking smells.

Through the prickle bush, Josephine watched him swig

his beer and turn the meat and scratch his beard and stare at the sky, which was turning all sorts of pretty colors now.

He might be nice, Josephine thought, but still, she couldn't find enough brave to walk over and hand him a sign. She was trying to figure out how to sneak back to number 13 when the door opened and the motorcycle woman poked her blond head out.

"Hog!" she said.

"Yeah?" he answered, still staring at the sky.

"You won't b'lieve what's on the TV. Come here a minute!"

Once they were both inside again, Josephine took off. The beer bottle, empty now, was tipped over in the grass. Josephine rolled up a sign and stuffed it into the mouth of the bottle, then waited behind the prickle bush again to see what might happen.

Sure enough, Hog came out, clicking the tongs like they were castanets. "Some good eatin' tonight," he said, and snatched the meat off the grill.

Josephine stared at the beer bottle. "Pick it up," she whispered, but Hog limped right past it. He went inside number 19 and shut the door.

"Dang it!" Josephine said when he was gone. She was trying to decide what to do when, like a miracle, the door opened again.

This time it was the motorcycle woman who appeared. She was dressed in leather, too—leather pants, leather halter top, and leather boots. The garments were edged with long strands of fringe.

"I've told that man a hundred times not to leave beer bottles in the yard!" She hurried down the steps and marched across the patchy grass.

Josephine held her breath as the woman snatched up the bottle and plucked out the sign. Slowly, as if it were a treasure map, she unfurled the note.

A tragedy has happened in Happy World!
If you know anything reguarding the wherebouts of
Molly June Quiver.
You are urged to call the police <u>immediatly</u>.
We won't rest until this girl, age 10 (almost 11)
Is found.
Signed,
Concerned Citizens

"Hog," the woman hollered. "Hey, Hog, look at this!" she said, then turned to go inside. Stitched on back of her fringy vest was the name *Joella*. And beneath her name was a red, red rose.

⇒

Josephine would not give Miss Connie a sign. For one thing, Miss Connie was the type to holler, especially at kids, and Josephine didn't care for folks who hollered, especially at kids. And for another thing, she was scared of Bob Barker.

For obvious reasons, she wouldn't give Helen-Dove a sign, either, though she did tuck one in the door of number 10, the trailer with broken mop handles and old plastic buckets littered around it.

When she was finished, Josephine stood between her trailer and Molly's. She stared at the dark window. A breeze rustled the pine trees in a peaceful way, but Josephine felt anything but peaceful.

It's strange to look at a place that has known great tragedy, she thought. The breeze kicked up again, harder this time. There was an unfamiliar clinking sound, one so faint Josephine decided she'd imagined it and went inside to get ready for bed.

Trouble on Two Feet

The following morning, a Wednesday, they were sitting on Lisa Marie's plant-filled stoop. Overhead, a tiny white plane droned, and Josephine imagined it carrying a neon banner: MARY JOSEPHINE WILLOUGHBY IS A TRESPASSER!

But there was no banner, of course, and the plane disappeared behind the clouds. Josephine braced herself for Lisa Marie's nosy questions about where she'd been hiding yesterday, but on this muggy morning Lisa Marie wasn't talking. Instead, she clutched a now-empty Coca-Cola bottle and stared into space like a hypnotized girl.

Josephine was grateful for the silence. The inside of her head was a kaleidoscope of pigs and gum wrappers and keys, all of them twisting and turning and folding into one another. She hadn't given much thought to the fringed purse, other than the fact that it was stylish, but now she wished she'd looked inside it.

Last night while Mama's machine *whirr*ed and *thump*ed, Josephine locked herself in the brown bedroom. On scraps of paper, she wrote down each unscrambled word, and like puzzle pieces, she moved them around. *They really love me* was easy to decode, but there were two other words: *m-o-t* or *t-o-m* and another one with a *t* that was too faint to read.

Lisa Marie let out an achy sigh, and Josephine glanced at her. "That Coca-Cola gave you a stomachache, didn't it?"

"I ain't got no stomachache."

"I have grape juice or orange juice for breakfast." This was meant to be a helpful suggestion, though the truth was Josephine would've traded a pinkie toe to drink Coca-Colas for breakfast. "What's the matter?" Josephine elbowed her gently.

Lisa Marie glanced back at the trailer and then at Josephine. Her eyes weren't just big today; they were huge. And frightened. "Buster Lee coughed all night long. It was the bad kind of coughing, the kind where he can't hardly catch his breath."

Josephine frowned. "Oh," she said, and then because she didn't know what else to say, she stuck her nose into a scratchy tomato plant and inhaled deeply. "Tomatoes smell kinda funny, don't they?"

Lisa Marie pointed. "And yonder comes trouble on two feet."

Josephine turned to see Miss Connie making her way across the trailer park. She was a sight this morning, in her filmy pink nightgown, with her hair in pink curlers, and smoking a long, brown cigarette. Behind her Bob Barker did little hops over the damp-with-dew grass.

Lisa Marie sighed again. "That hateful woman smokes like a chimney. Buster Lee ain't smoked a day in his whole life. It ain't fair, Josephine."

Josephine watched Miss Connie. Something about the determined way she walked gave her a bad feeling.

"Looks like she's heading for your place. Ain't never good when she comes knocking."

Now Josephine was the one looking like she had a stomachache. If Miss Connie was going to see Mama, there was only one reason. Out in front of Happy World was a black and red sign that said No Trespassing.

They watched as Miss Connie pounded hard on the door.

Wearing a trim yellow sundress, Mama answered and smiled a good-morning.

"You ain't late on rent, I hope?" Lisa Marie said.

"Definitely not. Mama paid the whole month up front." Josephine knew this because Miss Connie had tried to talk Mama into a payment plan, which Mama said made the rent cost twice as much in the long run.

Lisa Marie sighed again. "Your mama sure is pretty. I hate to see Miss Connie fussing on her. She's mighty rough when she fusses on people."

Miss Connie was talking and Mama was listening and Josephine's guilty stomach was clenching into a tight fist. Buster Lee began to cough. Even with the door closed, they could hear him plain as day.

Lisa Marie winged the Coke bottle onto the grass and clamped her hands over her ears. Back and forth she rocked. "There ain't nothin' I can do for him. Nothin', nothin', nothin'," she moaned.

Sweat was beginning to glisten on Josephine's upper lip, and the backs of her knees itched like crazy. Even from a distance, Josephine could see Mama's expression had gone from cheerful to serious. Trouble on two feet was right.

Finished, Miss Connie made her way back to the leasing office, a march of sorts, as if she'd waged a battle and won.

Josephine glanced at the sky and wished the spaceship that'd dropped her off in this terrible place would swoop down and scoop her up again.

It was in this moment, with Josephine wishing herself away, that Lisa Marie grabbed her hand and squeezed it, trying hard, it seemed, to keep her earthbound.

Carol Burnett

For the rest of the day and into the afternoon, Josephine avoided Mama. When Mama called her inside for lunch, she hollered that she was eating with Lisa Marie.

The girls had a picnic on the porch—a can of Pringles and some saltines and bologna. They drank Kool-Aid from Dixie cups and listened to Buster Lee's transistor radio.

Finally, there was no avoiding the trespassing situation any longer. "Josephine! We're going to the fabric store. Time to come home!" Mama hollered.

And with that Lisa Marie sprang to her feet.

"You could come with us," Josephine said, desperate for a buffer.

"Naw. I can't leave Buster Lee in his hour of need," she said, and headed inside.

⇒

Josephine had never committed a real crime before, so she couldn't imagine what Mama might say or do. But settled in the ole blue car and bouncing down the washed-out path, Mama didn't fuss or lecture or say *Mary Josephine Willoughby, what in the world were you thinking?*

Instead, Mama turned up the radio and rolled down the windows.

As they drove toward town, Josephine admired the rolling hills and puffy clouds and cows chewing cud in the pastures. There were little white churches and small country houses and fields with stalks of corn.

Her worries began to peel away. That was what good music and riding in the car beside Mama could do for Josephine sometimes.

In spite of everything, she was beginning to feel happy. After all, she loved going to the fabric store, and she love-*loved* seeing Miss Augustine and Lucas, too.

Everything was humming along, that is until the Barbra Streisand song started up with its *mmm-mmm-mmms* and *ooh-ooh-oohs*. They could put that song in the *Guinness World Records* book as the saddest song of all time.

Josephine sank lower in the seat. Suddenly, the breeze was much too hot.

"Jo, there's something I need to tell you," Mama said.

They sat at a red light near the fabric store, both of them quiet. The light went green, and Mama eased the car forward, then into a parking space in front of Fabric Delights and Other Notions. The windows were up now, the air conditioner turned on. Mama switched off the radio, and they sat with the car running.

It was coming. Josephine could feel the scolding ready to pounce.

"Miss Connie came by this morning to—"

"I *had* to do it!" Josephine's voice was very loud inside the car. "You don't understand, I *had* to!"

"Had to do what?"

Josephine opened her mouth to speak, and then she froze.

"Had to do what, Jo?"

Josephine shook her head. "Nothing," she replied.

"You look like you swallowed a toad."

Mama did not know. At least she didn't seem to know.

"Anyway, I need to tell you something. It's... well, I guess it isn't exactly bad news, considering how you feel about Happy World, but Miss Connie has a cousin coming the end of July. He'll be visiting for an extended period of time. There isn't space for him in Miss Connie's place, so... he'll be staying in number 13."

"With *us*?" Josephine asked, horrified.

"Of course not. He's taking over our place."

"Where will we go? We can't live in the empty trailers with spiders and snakes... and *squirrels*!"

Mama frowned. "Have you and Lisa Marie been playing in those abandoned trailers?"

Josephine shrugged.

"Goodness, Jo. Don't let me catch you doing that again."

"You didn't catch us. I told you," Josephine corrected.

Mama sighed. "What this means, Jo, is we'll have to move again. We were only renting month-to-month anyway, but..."

"I don't care," Josephine said. "I hate it there."

"We don't have to leave until the end of July, but with you and Lisa Marie becoming such good friends, I—"

"We're not *friends*." This came out mean-sounding. "Not real friends. Lisa Marie isn't what I had in mind."

"That's an ugly thing to say!"

Josephine scowled.

"This is difficult, I realize." Mama was angry now. "But it doesn't give you the right to be insensitive. Or mean-spirited. Lisa Marie has been nothing but—"

At this Josephine flung open the car door, jumped out, and slammed the door shut. Slightly off-kilter, she tripped toward the entrance of Fabric Delights and Other Notions, trying her hardest to think of something funny. Anything funny. She was desperate for funny!

Plain as day she imagined it then, that comedian Carol Burnett performing her famous Tarzan yell—*Ah-ah-ah-ah-ahhhh!* Carol Burnett was the funniest person ever, probably because of her happy childhood, Josephine decided.

Fabric Delights and Other Notions

Josephine was trying to stay focused on Carol Burnett's happy childhood as she entered the fabric store, which was an amazing place, with tall ceilings and bright lights and colorful fabrics. So many store clerks chattered and rolled out bolts for customers—silks and cottons and linens and everything in between.

The smell of dye made Josephine's nose burn and her eyes sting, but she didn't much mind. In fact, she felt a bit better at the sight of so many racks with buttons and snaps and zippers. There were tall tables with stools so you could look at books filled with pictures of dresses and jumpers and skirts and slacks *or* curtains and bedspreads and the sorts of things Mama made.

Plus, Miss Augustine was there, waving to them with both hands, her mouth stretched into a wide, happy-to-see-you grin. She was always real excited to see Mama and Josephine. Mama said it was because Miss Augustine didn't have children of her own, so Mama was like a daughter and Josephine was like a granddaughter.

"How are my girls?" Miss Augustine said, and swooped them both into a bosomy hug.

"We're fine," Mama said.

Miss Augustine looked at Josephine. "My goodness, you got big since the last time I saw you! Boy oh boy, have I got something to show you, honey."

"Is it a Barbie Pool Party set?"

"Jo," Mama said in her scolding voice.

Miss Augustine laughed. "No, sweetheart, it's not that. It's something way better. Come on, Jo. I b'lieve this'll put a right smart pep in your step."

Mama wandered off to the upholstery fabric section, and Miss Augustine led Josephine through the bright store and past the double doors with a big sign that said Employees Only. Josephine felt like a famous person going into the back like that.

Lucas was standing by an open door, smoking a cigarette. "Hey there, ladybug," he said.

"Hey, you ole stinkbug!" Josephine replied.

Lucas laughed. Miss Augustine laughed, too. "He is an ole stinkbug, ain't he?" Miss Augustine agreed, but everybody, even Josephine, knew Miss Augustine was sweet on that man.

"I'm fixing to show Jo some of the new fabric that was supposed to go to Price's Corner," Miss Augustine said.

"You takin' up sewing things like your mama?" Lucas asked.

"No way," Josephine said.

Lucas laughed and took another puff.

Even before Miss Augustine pointed out the fabric, Josephine knew which bolt it was—bright, sunny yellow with giant flowers all over.

"It's pretty, don't you think so?" Miss Augustine asked.

Josephine nodded and ran her fingers over the fabric. She couldn't believe how pretty it was.

"Tell her what happened," Lucas said, and stubbed out his cigarette.

"Well, a lady over in Price's Corner ordered this, sent me a check for it and everything, then changed her mind. Couldn't even be bothered to come pick it up! I been holding it awhile, thought maybe she'd change her mind again, because it's crazy to pay for something and then toss it. But I talked to her yesterday, and she said she is not interested. It's yours if you want it. Why, with this kind of fabric hanging in your new room, the sky is the limit. It'll get you writing all kinda good stories."

Miss Augustine liked to talk about Josephine's writing, bragging about how she'd be famous one day. Sad swooped in again and dug its claws into Josephine's heart. She hadn't written any new stories, which meant she would never be a famous writer. She wouldn't even be a writer nobody had heard of. And Mama wouldn't hang the fabric on her walls now, not with them moving again.

"What's the matter, sweetheart? You don't like the material?"

The ball of sad that was lodged inside Josephine came loose then, and she busted out crying. Mama's ruined inventory, the rinky-dink trailer, Molly Quiver and the way Helen-Dove sold her car and walked to work. That half smile on Buster Lee's face when Lisa Marie kissed him. And the hateful things Josephine had said just now in the car.

Happy World was a tragic place, and there wasn't anything Mary Josephine Willoughby could do about it. She didn't much like it there, but somehow she didn't want to leave it now, either. And then she thought about Lisa Marie squeezing her hand this morning and cried even harder.

"Lucas, take Josephine round to the drugstore. She'll feel better if she gets some of them fries. Don't you think so, honey?"

Josephine was too choked up to speak, so she simply nodded.

⊏⟹

While Mama and Miss Augustine had a business meeting, Josephine and Lucas walked over to the Reynolds' drugstore. They sat on twirly stools and ordered french fries and fizzy Coca-Colas. Lucas smothered the fries with ketchup and salt, the way Josephine liked. They didn't say any words to each other. They just ate and twirled and watched the skinny lady behind the counter make milk shakes.

When they were finished, Lucas bought Josephine a pink bubble-gum cigar, and they took a walk through town. Josephine was mostly too old for hand-holding, but because she liked how big and scratchy Lucas' hand was, she latched on to it and didn't let go.

⊏⟹

When they got back to the fabric store, Lucas sat down on the bench out front and lit up a cigarette. "You want to talk about what-all's the matter?" he said.

Josephine shook her head. She sat down beside Lucas and bit off another hunk of the pink bubble-gum cigar. She smacked the gum loud as she pleased and then blew a fat bubble.

"You don't like it too good over in Happy World," Lucas said.

"It's alright," Josephine replied.

"You don't have to pull my leg, ladybug. You can tell ole Lucas your troubles."

Josephine kept quiet.

"Want me to tell *you* a secret?" he asked.

Josephine nodded.

"I'm fixin' to ask Scarlett to marry me."

Josephine felt her eyes bug out. She stared at Lucas in horror. "What about Miss Augustine? I thought y'all were sweethearts?" She felt another breakdown coming on.

"Miss Augustine *is* Scarlett. You ain't fixin' to cry again, are you? You cry any more, I'm gonna have to go bowling."

Josephine sucked in some air and shook her head.

Lucas pulled a coin purse from his pocket and opened it. "Look what I got right here," he said, and took out a gold ring with a heart-shaped diamond.

Josephine's mouth dropped open, and the wad of gum fell onto the sidewalk. Lickety-split, she picked it up and popped it into her mouth again.

"Attaway," Lucas said. "Think she'll say yes?"

Josephine gave Lucas a hard once-over. There was a silent agreement between them to say honest things, and so Josephine said the first honest thing that came to mind. "You're old."

"Old people need love, too," Lucas replied.

Josephine nodded because this seemed true. She gave Lucas another once-over.

"What is it?" he asked. "What's wrong?"

"You have long nose hairs. If you expect her to say yes, you better clip those things."

Lucas laughed. "Okay. Anything else?"

Josephine looked back at him closely and held up two fingers. "Two things, actually."

"Fire away," Lucas said, and squared his broad shoulders.

"Why'd you say you'd go bowling if I cried again?"

Lucas grinned. "Aw, I'm going bowling anyways. Wednesday's my league night."

Josephine nodded.

"And the second thing?" he asked.

"Do you think I'm too old for toys now? My friend... *ex*-friend gave away her Barbies in third grade."

Lucas narrowed his eyes. "How old you gettin' to be now?"

"Almost eleven," Josephine replied.

He nodded and rubbed his chin. "Well," he said finally, "I'm fifty-nine, and I still play with toys."

"It's a serious question," Josephine scolded.

"And I'm giving you a serious answer. Lionel trains. I got every single one from when I was a boy. They're down in my cellar. If I go down there to tho some clothes in the washer, I fire 'em up. Spent many happy afternoons thataway."

Josephine squinted one eye. "Do you play with them or just look at them?"

"Both, I reckon."

Josephine smacked her gum, considering this.

"When we lose the kid in here"—Lucas tapped his chest—"we might as well turn out the lights, 'cause the party's over. You know what I mean?"

Josephine studied Lucas' face, the wiry eyebrows and deep lines. His forehead reminded her of the curvy furrows of a freshly plowed field. "You're gonna die," she said. "We're all gonna die."

Lucas nodded.

"We don't know when, but our hearts just stop beating," Josephine went on.

"It's a hard truth," Lucas agreed. "Look there, across the street."

Josephine gazed toward the men's department store. Pigg and Parsons, it was called. Three nicely dressed men were standing out front by a lamppost, chugging Coca-Colas and laughing. Telling jokes, if Josephine had to guess. A short, roundish man mopped his face with a handkerchief.

"They got stories that'd break your heart. Wouldn't know it to look at 'em, would you?"

"No," Josephine agreed.

"We all got them kinda stories, ladybug."

The short, round man was shaking his head and swiping at his eyes now. Laughing so hard he was crying.

"But there is sweetness in this life," Lucas said. "Look for it and you'll see it. You just got to look for it, Josephine."

Blowin' in the Wind

Mama and Josephine were quiet that afternoon. Josephine spent most of it doodling in her spiral notebook and making lists of what-all she and Molly would do together after the rescue: make Dip-a-Do flowers and play Operation and visit the art center downtown. They would be dressed in very smart outfits and pick out the same plaster-of-paris molds for their creations, and paint them in the same patterns, too.

Delia and Kitty would be there, of course, and want to sit at their table. However, there would not be room since Molly and Josephine were famous now, and also *extremely* popular.

In the other room was the *whirr-thump* of Mama's sewing machine, and outside the wind had kicked up. Josephine put two pillows under her knees and stared out the window. The sky was dark and thick with clouds, and the plastic buckets from number 10 were blowing down the washed-out path. "Good grief," Josephine said, "y'all ought to stop being litterbugs!"

Just then she heard Mama's footsteps, and then, "Jo! *Jo!*" Mama opened the door without knocking. "Get your raincoat.

If there's one place we don't want to be in a storm like this it's a trailer. We'll stay with Miss Connie till it's over."

The rain began to crash then, like marbles dropping from heaven.

Mama and Josephine huddled together under the umbrella, which turned inside out and wasn't any help. The washed-out path looked like a raging, muddy river now, and the ugly fake flowers Miss Connie kept in old whiskey barrels went skittering past them. The branches of the pine trees bent till they seemed ready to snap.

When Josephine and Mama reached the leasing office, the rain shut off as though a switch had been flipped. The sky went darker, then darker still. Spirals of black and green and purple loomed.

"Mama," Josephine whispered.

"We'll be alright, Jo," Mama said, and banged hard on Miss Connie's door.

Finally, Miss Connie yanked it open. She was holding Bob Barker and wearing something different today. Instead of the nightgown, she had on a blue chenille duster. In place of the zipper's pull tab was a red twist tie. Her head was a nest of tight curls, fresh out of rollers and not yet combed.

"What are *you* looking at?" Miss Connie barked.

Josephine flinched.

"Thank goodness you're home!" Mama said.

"Where *else* would I *be*?"

It occurred to Josephine then that the woman's voice was like an ax. Every time she spoke, it came down with a deadly *thwack!* Miss Connie was not the sort of person who was looking for the sweetness in this life, Josephine decided.

"It's too dangerous for us to be in the trailer." Mama

glanced toward the dark sky. "We'll need to stay with you." This was not a question.

Miss Connie clutched Bob Barker tighter and stepped aside to let Mama and Josephine cross the threshold.

"I wisht somebody had told me I was having a damn party!" *Thwack!*

The place smelled like cat pee and bacon grease and cigarette smoke, but Josephine kept her lips pressed tight and did not speak a word about it.

Junk was piled everywhere. Outside chairs were inside, and instead of Miss Connie's underwear hanging on the clothesline, her intimate things were clipped to the TV antenna. There were *TV Guide*s and half-filled Pepsi bottles with peanuts and cigarette butts floating inside. Josephine pinched her nose shut, but Mama gave her a hard frown, so she quit pinching it and breathed only through her mouth.

The cellar steps were rickety and without a light. Josephine thought of blind Mary Ingalls and how awful it must be to stumble around in the dark all the time.

"You okay?" Mama asked.

"No!" Josephine whispered.

On Redbud Avenue there was a nice storm cellar. A cellar that smelled like laundry detergent and Pine-Sol because that was where the landlady, Miss Nancy, kept the washer and dryer and cleaning supplies. Miss Nancy was sweet and used to buy Josephine nail polish at the Dollar Store on account of she never had any girl kids, only boys. Plus, Miss Nancy let Josephine dress her dogs, Oscar and Mayer, in doll clothes.

Josephine was surprised to see the residents of Happy World crammed like sardines in Miss Connie's dim, damp, cobwebby basement. Side by side they sat along the foundation.

Lisa Marie was cross-legged and tucked in tight between Granddaddy and Buster Lee. "We got us a party goin' on down here," she said, and waved at Josephine and Mama.

Guilt crawled into Josephine's throat then. She thought about what she'd said earlier, heard the words, loud as cymbals, crash inside her head: *We're not friends. Not real friends. Lisa Marie isn't what I had in mind.*

On the other side of Buster Lee was Helen-Dove, and they sat shoulder-to-shoulder. Helen-Dove was holding his left hand, but it didn't seem to Josephine like the romantic kind of hand-holding. It seemed more like the hand-holding of a person fixing to get a needle jab.

It occurred to Josephine then that Buster Lee was in actual, physical pain.

"This is a storm of mammoth proportions," Helen-Dove said.

"Surely is," Mama replied.

Sandwiched between a stack of mushy-looking boxes and a pile of Styrofoam mannequin heads was Hog, the motorcycle guy. Up close, Josephine could see his sideburns were thick as lamb chops, and the tattoo on his arm was a long-stemmed red rose beneath the name *Joella.*

"Hog right here." He tipped his leather cap at Mama and Josephine. "Nice to meet y'all."

Joella was sitting extra-close beside him, and she had feathers dangling off her earlobes. "Hey," she said.

"It's nice to meet y'all, too," Mama replied.

Next to the motorcycle couple were those real live hippies, beads and tie-dye and everything. The boy hippie strummed his guitar with long, delicate fingers.

The girl hippie's hair was in thick braids, and Josephine spied two clothespins still clipped to them. The girl rubbed her beach-ball-shaped belly in wide circles as if she were about to tell their fortunes.

The boy hippie stopped his strumming and said, "I'm Zeus." His face was young, and he wore wire-rimmed spectacles. In his left ear was a tiny silver earring.

"And I'm Mercedes," the girl hippie added. "This one here"—she smiled and gave her belly a pat—"is as yet unnamed."

"Congratulations," Mama said. "I'm Penny, and this is my daughter, Josephine."

"Hi," was all Josephine said.

"Don't just stand there. Y'all squeeze in somewhere," Miss Connie said. She yanked the string of a bare lightbulb, though it did little good, then plopped herself and Bob Barker onto a lawn chair.

Mama nudged Josephine to a grim corner, then took off her raincoat. She placed it on the floor and they sat down on it. Josephine tried not to think about the spiders that must be creeping around in this place, or possibly snakes and rats.

Outside, the wind roared and the rain pounded again. It occurred to Josephine that they might blow away—Miss Connie's small house yanked off its foundation, twisting in the air like in *The Wizard of Oz.*

Terrible things happen. It's just a part of life. Josephine squeezed her eyes shut, determined to get the thought out of her brain. And when she opened them again, Lisa Marie had come to sit beside her.

"Hidy," she said. "I brought cards. And my Snoopy flashlight." Lisa Marie propped up the flashlight and began to shuffle the deck.

A riffle shuffle, it was called. Some long-lost memory of

Josephine's dad surfaced. His fingers, skillful as a surgeon's, on the playing cards, the flutter and breeze as he maneuvered them, showing off for Josephine. He could cut the deck perfectly in half without even counting.

"Y'all play a game," Mama suggested. "It'll take your mind off the storm."

They played gin rummy and go fish and crazy eights. After a while, Zeus started strumming his guitar again and singing a song about "blowin' in the wind," which Josephine thought was clever, given the storm.

Thunder crashed and lightning crackled. The bulb dangling above their heads flickered, then went out. Everything stopped then—the strumming and singing. Even Josephine and Lisa Marie quit playing cards. The only light was the Snoopy one, but Lisa Marie turned it off to conserve the batteries.

"I ain't scared a bit," Lisa Marie whispered.

"Me neither," Josephine replied, though this wasn't true. She didn't much care for storms, and she especially didn't care for storms in Miss Connie's cellar. The news of moving was on the tip of her tongue, but she didn't tell Lisa Marie.

Not with Buster Lee looking pale and sick and holding on to Helen-Dove the way he was. Not with Lisa Marie's granddaddy seeming worn out and tired from his long days at Swan's farm. The part inside Josephine that'd felt so mean earlier evaporated.

They would not go back to Redbud Avenue. Josephine did not ask this question of Mama because she already knew the answer. Redbud Avenue was, as Miss Augustine said about so many things, *gone with the wind.*

After the Storm

When the storm was over, they climbed the rickety stairs and headed outside. Josephine thought maybe their trailers would be blown away, but other than toppled lawn chairs and rusty barrels rolling around and garbage strewn everywhere, things were more or less the same.

"Would you look at that!" Mama said in a whispery voice.

"What?" Josephine asked.

"I don't believe I've ever seen a sight more beautiful."

Josephine saw then what Mama was seeing. The green pine trees in back of the trailer park shimmered. The clouds parted and pillars of light stretched ladder-like from heaven. Beneath a brilliant rainbow were the folks of Happy World: Lisa Marie on one side and Granddaddy on the other, both of them helping Buster Lee back to number 17; Zeus strumming his guitar, and Mercedes patting her round belly; Hog giving Joella a piggyback ride, the pair of them giggling like leathery lovebirds; and Helen-Dove on the front stoop of number 7, her Mona Lisa face staring up at the wondrous sky.

"Hey, Mama?" Josephine said. "Is it all right if Lisa Marie spends the night with us? I'd like to have a friend stay over."

Mama raised her right eyebrow.

"Please," Josephine added.

"Fine by me," Mama replied.

Lickety-split, Josephine took off running toward Lisa Marie. "Hey! Want to spend the night at my trailer?"

Granddaddy grinned down at Josephine, and she noticed he had a truck-sized gap between his front teeth to match Lisa Marie's. "It's all right if you want to, shug," he said.

"You care if I go, Buster Lee?" Lisa Marie asked.

"Won't bower me none," Buster Lee said.

And then Josephine and Lisa Marie whooped and hollered like a pair of lunatics.

⊏⟹

Once the electricity came back on, Mama fixed Josephine and Lisa Marie Jiffy Pop popcorn, and she let them split an Orange Crush and stay up late playing Operation, a game *not* sold at the yard sale.

Josephine and Lisa Marie were making a racket, but Mama didn't seem to notice. She was too busy catching up on her sewing, matching bedspreads for some twin girls up on Moon Lake.

Lisa Marie started to yawn, and even though Josephine hated to admit it, she was getting sleepy herself.

Like she was some kind of mind reader, Mama stopped her sewing and said, "You girls go brush your teeth. It's way past time for bed."

Josephine picked up the pieces from the game and shoved everything into the box. "Good night," she said, and kissed Mama's smooth cheek, which smelled like Pond's cold cream.

"Good night," Lisa Marie said, and then she did something that surprised Josephine. She kissed Mama's other cheek.

Mama looked surprised, too. "Why, thank you for that, Lisa Marie," she said. "You're a sweet young lady, and I'm glad you and Josephine are becoming good friends." Mama did not look at Josephine when she said this, though Josephine knew exactly what her mother was thinking.

Josephine led Lisa Marie to her teeny-tiny bathroom. "Where's your toothbrush?"

"I didn't bring one. I can just use my finger," Lisa Marie said.

"Your finger?"

"Well, I can't use my big toe!" Lisa Marie laughed.

Josephine put a glob of Crest on Lisa Marie's finger. And then, as if she'd been named queen of good oral hygiene, she brushed her own teeth exactly as the hygienist had demonstrated during Dental Health Week.

"You shouldn't give plaque a ghost of a chance," Josephine said when she was done.

"You stole that line from Casper the Friendly Ghost. I seen that commercial."

Lisa Marie followed Josephine into the teeny-tiny bedroom. They climbed beneath the fresh sheets on Josephine's bed and lay side by side listening to the Happy World sounds: a car engine starting up; the thump of music; bottles being chucked into a metal barrel. Through the screen came the faint scent of wet grass mixed with cigarettes. Miss Connie on her nightly prowl with Bob Barker. Behind all this was another sound, distant and close at the same time.

Josephine sat up to listen. "You hear that, Lisa Marie?"

Lisa Marie propped herself on one elbow. "Hog likes to

pitch bottles in them barrels. He won't stop till Joella hollers at him."

"Not that. Between the bottles. Listen."

"Aw, yeah. It's just them keys stuck up in that tree."

The hairs on Josephine's arms stood at attention. "What keys?"

"It's a wind chime, 'cept the keys are tangled together, so it don't chime right. It's up in the swirly-gig tree. Now *you* listen. I got a secret I'm fixing to tell you, and you can't tell nobody, not even your mama. Swear on a stack of Bibles?"

The keys on Molly's desk. The one hidden in Josephine's shoe. Molly had made a wind chime. "The swirly-gig tree is the one with those fuzzy flower things, right?"

"Yeah. You swear it, Josephine?"

"Swear what?"

"You ain't even listenin', and I'm fixin' to tell you a secret."

"I'm listening."

"I'm nearly eleven, and I ain't never stayed the night with nobody. This is my first time."

"You're not scared, are you?"

"Naw. I ain't scared a bit. You've had a bunch of sleepovers, I reckon."

"A few," Josephine said. She thought about the last sleepover with Delia and Kitty. Mrs. Collingsworth forced Delia to invite Josephine, a fact Josephine would never have known, except Delia told her, just to be mean.

"I hope you're having fun," Josephine said to Lisa Marie.

"I am. I been having a real good time since you moved here. I don't know how I stood it before you came."

Josephine swallowed hard.

Soon Lisa Marie was snoring softly as Josephine lay still

and listened to the faint clinking of Molly's wind chime. Somewhere, beneath the same sky, Molly was sleeping. "But where?" Josephine whispered.

She waited.

She listened.

And then, as if it were written on the cool night air, the words unscrambled: *They don't love me, not really.*

Naysayers

The early-morning-after-a-storm sun shone through the thin curtain. Josephine's eyelids flickered open, and the words passed through her brain: *They don't love me, not really.*

She sat up gently so as not to wake Lisa Marie and tried to clear away the cobwebs of sleep. She recalled the friendship bracelet she'd seen in Molly's room, the foil one in a bag by itself. She'd been tempted to take it, but she hadn't, of course. Josephine touched the place on her wrist where it had been.

They don't love me, not really. Over and over she turned the words, trying to detect their true meaning. Miss Lake said stories had surface meanings and deeper meanings. Smart readers looked for deeper meanings.

They don't love me were sad words. But the *not really* part implied something more. These folks, whoever they were, wanted people to *think* they loved Molly, but Molly knew the real truth, the *not really* part.

Josephine thought of her dad. Months ago, he'd called from a pay phone on a Sunday night, right in the middle of

The Wonderful World of Disney. Josephine was only half listening until he said, "Guess where *I* am!" Before Josephine could guess, he said, "Memphis, Tennessee. A couple of weeks and I'll be sending you and your mama mink coats from Las Vegas."

But he hadn't sent them mink coats. He hadn't even sent them a postcard.

He doesn't love me, not really. These words had spikes on them.

Josephine glanced down at Lisa Marie, sprawled every which way and hogging the bed. Her hair was a mess of tangles, and her mouth gaped wide open. Her granddaddy loved her, and Buster Lee loved her, too. But what about her parents? Where were her mother and father?

Josephine was staring at the girl, trying to figure out this mystery, when something caught her eye. She stared harder, and then she got extremely close and stared some more. What she saw made her gasp.

Josephine crept out of bed and tiptoed into the other room. The trailer smelled like coffee and toast.

Mama had fabric laid out on the floor and a whole bunch of pins sticking out of her mouth. "Mornin'," she said, and pushed a pin into the fabric.

"Something's wrong with Lisa Marie." Josephine tiptoed over and whispered in Mama's ear.

Mama spit the rest of the pins on the floor. "Oh, my goodness!" She flapped her arms and jumped to her feet. "Oh, this is all I need!" she said, and flapped her arms again.

Josephine wondered if Mama might fly away.

⊂⟹

After a trip to Reynold's drugstore (for two lice combs) and another trip to IGA (for two large jars of mayonnaise), Mama and Josephine walked with Lisa Marie to number 17.

"Sorry about them bugs," Lisa Marie said. "I hope y'all don't catch 'em."

Mama scratched her head and tried to smile. She handed Lisa Marie the brown sack. "You remember what I told you. Think your granddaddy can help with this?" Mama asked.

"Aw, yeah. It's happened before," Lisa Marie said.

Josephine couldn't believe it. This was definitely *not* what she had in mind. Still, she felt sorry for Lisa Marie. She looked helpless. Not the least bit embarrassed, though, which Josephine thought was odd. If she'd been the one with bugs crawling in her hair, she would have died from mortification.

"All right. Well, we'd better get started then," Mama said. "If you need any help, you come get me. Okay?"

Lisa Marie nodded and disappeared inside the trailer.

⟹

The rest of the morning Mama spent combing out Josephine's hair, and it felt like monkeys were pulling it right out of her head.

"She's the one with bugs. Not *me*," Josephine pointed out.

"Yes, but they probably jumped on you in the night and laid their eggs. A week from now, you'll have them crawling all over if we don't take care of this today," Mama said.

Josephine didn't much care for being still, but she cared even less for bugs in her hair, so she tried not to wiggle.

"Didn't you think it was strange last night, Lisa Marie kissing you like she did?" The truth was Josephine didn't much care for other kids kissing Mama's cheek.

"That child has no mother. Maybe it was nice for her to be around females for a change. I sure hope her granddaddy can take care of her hair. Her head was crawling with those things."

"What happened to her mother?"

"I don't know, Jo. Maybe she left."

Like my dad the cad, Josephine thought, but didn't say.

"You've gone quiet," Mama said. She glopped on more mayonnaise and worked it through the strands. "Is that better?" She ran the lice comb through Josephine's hair again.

"A little," Josephine admitted. "But mothers don't usually leave their children."

"Mostly not." At this she turned Josephine around to face her. She looked right into Josephine's eyes. "Wild horses couldn't drag me away from you, Mary Josephine Willoughby, and don't you ever forget that."

Josephine nodded and turned around again. Mama continued combing.

"What if I was kidnapped? Then what would you do? Terrible things happen. You said so yourself."

"I don't like thinking about such things."

"Helen-Dove has to think about such things. She has to think of them every single day."

"The misery in that woman's heart must be almost too much to bear."

Like dragging around a bag of rocks, Josephine decided. A simile to write down in her yellow notebook. "We could help her look," Josephine suggested.

"Interfering in official police business is not a good idea, Jo."

"Helen-Dove sold her car to pay some officer to keep looking after the other ones quit. He got her money and didn't look hardly at all. Then Officer Frye took over. That's what Lisa Marie says. She says he looks for free, but he's just one person. Why aren't all the police out looking every day?"

Mama sighed. "I don't know."

Josephine hesitated, trying to decide if she should say what she was thinking. Finally, she scrunched up her toes inside the Tiger Paws and said, "I've got a funny feeling I'm the one who's supposed to find her."

Mama kept quiet.

"Brother Davis says everything happens for a reason."

"What's your point, Jo?"

"The reason for the fire and the reason for moving to Happy World and the reason for me getting Molly's shoes is I'm supposed to find her." And then she added, "So we can be best friends."

"That sounds like a Hollywood movie, Jo."

"Miss Lake says truth is stranger than fiction. And Lisa Marie believes if you have faith the size of a freckle, you can move mountains." Josephine's confidence wavered. This did sound more like a movie than real life, but it was too late to back down now.

Mama stopped to wipe the mayonnaise from the comb. "We'll ask Helen-Dove if there's anything we can do," she said.

"And if she needs you to drive her someplace to look, will you?" Josephine asked.

"Of course," Mama replied.

"What if it's far? What if it's in Timbuktu?"

"Well, we couldn't drive to Timbuktu because it's across the ocean, in Africa."

"What if I was across the ocean in Timbuktu?"

"I would find a way to get there, Jo."

"What if they said you'd never find me?"

Mama shook her head. "I wouldn't listen to the naysayers."

"Well, then I'm not listening to the naysayers, either," Josephine replied.

Something Horrifying

The following day Mama had an install at a swanky place called Moon Lake—big fat houses and cars and big fat boats, too. On the drive back to Happy World, Mama and Josephine listened to the radio, but they didn't sing along.

For one thing, Josephine could tell Mama was upset about the snooty lady and her bratty twins not liking the bedspreads much. And for another thing, the car was making a terrible racket, and whenever the car made a terrible racket, Mama got the worried kind of quiet.

When they reached the Happy World entrance, Mama stopped at the string of battered mailboxes and stuck her hand inside the one with the number *13* on the side. Quickly, she thumbed through the mail. "Nothing but bills and junk," she said, and handed the stack to Josephine.

Josephine liked looking through the mail. Sometimes the stuff Mama called junk was fliers advertising canopy bedroom sets or shiny ten-speed bicycles. "This one's from the IGA. They got Reese's Peanut Butter Cups, buy one get one free. And here's a phone bill and a—" Josephine stopped suddenly.

Hidden between the phone bill and the IGA flier was a shiny postcard with a photograph of a sunny beach and writing that said *Wish you were here!*

Josephine flipped the postcard over, but there was no message on the back, just a printed caption about someplace called the Emerald Coast and Helen-Dove's name and *Happy World Trailer Park, Glendale, Tennessee,* printed in neat handwriting.

"Where's the Emerald Coast?" Josephine asked.

Mama cocked her head to listen to the car's terrible racket. It was beginning to sound an awful lot like their refrigerator.

"Where's the Emerald Coast?" Josephine asked louder.

Mama blinked and frowned. "What is it, Jo?"

"The Emerald Coast. Helen-Dove got a postcard from the Emerald Coast."

Mama shook her head. "Don't go reading other people's mail, Jo."

"There's nothing to read." Josephine held up the blank card. "Whoever sent it didn't write anything."

"We'll leave it on Helen-Dove's stoop. The mail carrier must've put it in our box by mistake."

"It might blow away if we leave it on her stoop," Josephine said, though there wasn't a breath of wind today. The truth was she wanted to keep the card and study it for clues. Already she'd noticed the person who'd written *Happy World Trailer Park* used a funny-looking *a*. The small *a* in *Happy* was not a circle with a tail. It was the other kind of *a*, like Josephine saw in library books. A circle with a crook on top.

Mama stopped the car at number 7 and plucked the postcard from Josephine's hands. "Wait here," she said.

From the front seat, Josephine watched as Mama tucked the postcard into the heart-shaped wreath.

Number 13 was hot and stuffy, like living inside an Easy-Bake Oven. Josephine stood perfectly still in her bedroom and tried to imagine what it felt like in Florida. According to Delia, the place was hot as the devil's pitchfork, more like living in a *real* oven than an Easy-Bake one.

Josephine had always wanted to go to Panama City, mostly because Delia went there every summer and bragged about what-all she did on vacation—Miracle Strip Amusement Park and Silver Spike Petticoat Junction, where pretend cowboys had phony shoot-outs.

Josephine hurried into her play clothes and headed for the front door. "I'm going to run around with Lisa Marie," she called.

Mama poked her head out of the kitchen. "First you have to help with chores. I'm not taking chances with those lice." Mama was dressed in her cleaning clothes now, and in her hands were a roll of paper towels and a bottle of Windex. "Here," she said, and handed Josephine the bottle of blue liquid. "Get your toothpaste globs off the counter."

After the bathroom was finished, Josephine grabbed the bag of trash and hauled it to the green dumpster in back of Happy World. She was just about to toss it inside when she saw something horrifying. It was *so horrifying* that Josephine dropped the trash bag at her feet.

Slowly, slowly, slowly she backed away from the dumpster, then took off running.

Josephine banged open the door. "Mama! *Mama!*" She was panting.

"What is it, Josephine?" Mama had her hair tied back in a bandana now, and she was on the floor with a bucket and a sponge.

"Lisa Marie! Something terrible—" Josephine gulped for air.

"What on earth is the matter?" Mama dropped the sponge into the bucket, and dried her hands on her dungarees.

"I can't...It's so..." Josephine trembled.

"Show me," Mama said, and got to her feet.

"No!" Josephine ran around the tiny trailer, snatching all the thin, ugly curtains closed.

"Josephine, stop overreacting. Show me what it is." Mama opened the front door.

"The big green dumpster," Josephine whispered, and followed Mama outside.

Mama took Josephine by the hand and led her toward the dumpster. Flies buzzed around, and the smell was rotten. Just as they approached, a giant crow flew out of the top, and Josephine screamed.

"It's just a bird, Jo. Goodness gracious."

"It's *not* just a bird! Look in there if you don't believe me!" Josephine's legs were ready to run.

Mama peeked inside. "*Ahhhh!*" she hollered. "Oh, my! Oh, my goodness!"

"They scalped my friend!" Josephine yelled.

Mama clutched her chest and took some deep breaths. "Nobody scalped Lisa Marie. I guess they...well, they must've...Come on, we'll go see for ourselves."

⊏⟹

Mama knocked on number 17's door, and Josephine pressed close beside her.

It was Granddaddy who answered. "Hidy, Miss Penny. How you doin' today?" he said.

Mama wiped a bead of sweat from her forehead. "We just...came to check on Lisa Marie. You know, the situation and all."

"Aw, I took ker of that," Granddaddy said. He grinned his gap-toothed grin.

"Yes, well...Josephine went to take out the trash, and she—"

"You scalped my best friend!" Josephine said.

"Well, little lady, it's the only surefire way I know to get rid of them bugs. Lisa Marie, we got company," Granddaddy called over his shoulder.

There was the sound of the TV switching off, then Lisa Marie's bare feet on the floor. And there she was, blinking at Josephine with her big green eyes.

"Oh my," Mama said, and put a hand over her mouth.

"You *did* scalp her!" Josephine said.

"Guilty as charged," Granddaddy replied. "But them bugs is gone, ain't they, shug?"

Lisa Marie nodded, and it was the saddest nod Josephine had ever seen. For what seemed like a long time they just stood there, staring at one another.

Finally, it was Granddaddy who spoke up. "Y'all gettin' settled in good?" he asked.

"Oh, we're fine," Mama said.

"You need anything, holler, hear? I'm right handy with stuff, and Miss Connie...well, she don't keep up with much now that Tadpole's gone."

"Tadpole?" Mama asked.

"Miss Connie's husband. We all called him Tadpole on account'a he was so little. Good fella. He kept this place up real nice. Worked like a dog 'round here back in the day. Anyway, y'all let me know you need anything. Lisa Marie here has been right lonely with Buster Lee so sick." Granddaddy gave Lisa Marie a pat on the back. "It's nice for her to have your little girl to play with, and we wasn't fixin' to let bugs ruin a good friendship."

"Are you handy with cars, too?" Josephine asked.

"Jo, it's fine. Don't bother him with that."

Mama squeezed Josephine's shoulder, which meant for her to hush, but Josephine kept talking. "Our car is rattling something awful," she said.

"I fixed a car or two in my day. Know how to keep 'em runnin'. You got car trouble, Miss Penny?"

"Well..." Mama hesitated.

"I got plenty of time. I took off early today to see 'bout Buster Lee's doctor's appointment. I'll get my toolbox. Won't take no for an answer."

"You wanna run around?" Josephine asked. It was hard to look at Lisa Marie's bald head. Her hair had been dirty sometimes *and* it had bugs, but still it was pretty. With a bald head, Lisa Marie didn't seem like herself.

Lisa Marie shrugged.

"It won't do no harm to play now." Granddaddy smiled.

"Come on," Josephine said, and dragged Lisa Marie out into the sunshine.

Sweet Release

While Granddaddy was taking a look at Mama's car, Josephine and Lisa Marie headed to the back of the trailer park. Lisa Marie didn't gallop or hop on one foot or squawk like usual.

Josephine stopped at the mimosa tree and gazed up. At the very top was a wad of ribbon and a tangle keys. Judging by the height, Molly was an agile climber. "Think we could get that wind chime down?"

"I ain't got it in me to climb up there today," Lisa Marie said.

Josephine turned to look at the girl. She was sitting on a rock at the edge of the pine trees, staring at her dirty, bare feet. Her head was knobby and her ears stuck out. Josephine had never noticed her sticking-out ears before. She went to sit beside her.

"Why didn't you use that comb and the mayonnaise Mama gave you?"

Lisa Marie put her face in her hands.

"It doesn't look bad," Josephine lied.

Lisa Marie shot her a hateful look.

"At least you have a pretty face."

Lisa Marie scrunched her nose.

"I thought you were scalped dead when I saw your hair in the dumpster."

"I wish I was dead," Lisa Marie said.

"Don't wish that. Take it back!" Josephine scolded.

"I will *not* take it back."

Josephine looked toward the sky and hollered, "She doesn't mean it!"

Lisa Marie let out a mournful sigh. "Granddaddy says Buster Lee ain't long for this world. He says I got to get used to the idea of him being gone. Buster Lee's been looking after me ever since I was little. Th'other night he asked would I pray with him. And you know what he prayed?"

Josephine shook her head.

"He said, 'Lord, give me sweet release.' It means he's ready to go. I heard Granddaddy tell some lady at church how Buster Lee was lettin' go bit by bit every day. Yesterday he didn't even watch *Name That Tune*. I asked did he want to watch with me, but he shook his head."

Josephine didn't know what to say about Buster Lee. Every time Lisa Marie talked about him, she got a petrified feeling. At some point, she would have to tell Lisa Marie about moving, but how could she with the bald head situation and Buster Lee so close to dying?

Happy World was a sad place with sad problems. It would be good to leave. It would be awful to leave. It would be both at once. And maybe it would be like Redbud Avenue, memories following her wherever she went, reminding her of things. Reminding her of *people*.

Josephine studied the Tiger Paws. The rubber around the

edges was starting to fray, and the plastic end of one of the shoelaces was gone. Time was running out. Like that giant hourglass on the soap opera Miss Augustine liked to watch, *Days of Our Lives*. The sand was going, going, almost gone.

"Like sand through the hourglass, so are the days of our lives," Josephine said.

Lisa Marie looked at her. "Do what?"

Josephine closed her eyes and sniffed the air—once, twice, three times.

"What're you doing?"

Josephine had no idea what she was doing, just that Florida was on the tip of her tongue and fixing to jump off. "Florida," she said.

"We can't take Buster Lee to Florida. You ain't makin' sense."

"I mean Molly Quiver. She's in Florida. I think that's where she is. And sand is pouring through that hourglass, and we have got to do something before time runs out."

Lisa Marie sniffed the air. "I don't smell no Florida. I don't smell nothing but pine needles and mayonnaise. Your head smells like macaroni salad."

"I'm telling you that girl is in Florida." Josephine glanced at the shoes again. "Me and Mama got the mail today, and there was a postcard for Helen-Dove."

"What kinda postcard?"

"A picture of a beach. Beaches are in Florida. On the back it said the picture was taken someplace called the Emerald Coast."

"Sounds like *The Wizard of Oz* to me," Lisa Marie said.

"That's Emerald City, not Emerald Coast."

Lisa Marie frowned. "What're y'all doing with Miss Helen's mail?"

"The mail carrier put it in our box by mistake. It was tucked into an IGA flier. They're having a buy-one-get-one-free special on Reese's Peanut Butter Cups."

"I sure do like them candies," Lisa Marie said.

"Me, too," Josephine agreed. "Anyway, there was no letter or note or anything. Just Helen-Dove's name. *Helen-Dove Quiver* was what it said, and her address. Whoever wrote it made their *a*'s funny. Not the circle with the tail, but the other kind, like in books. You think Molly Quiver was the type to make her *a*'s that way?"

Lisa Marie shrugged. She picked up a blossom from the mimosa tree and ran her fingers over the feathery flower. "Hey, Josephine?"

"Yeah?"

"I ain't lived a day yet without Buster Lee in it?"

This was a question, but Josephine didn't have any answers. She put her arm around Lisa Marie's shoulders. "Try not to think about it. Think about...think about how nice it would be if we had some Reese's Peanut Butter Cups. Think about that instead."

26

Witchy Eye

Just as Josephine and Lisa Marie emerged from the pine trees, a patrol car bounced up the washed-out path. Bug-eyed, the girls looked at each other.

"Run!" Josephine said, and they both shot off in opposite directions.

Josephine hid behind a clump of pokeweed in back of number 7. Across the path, Lisa Marie squatted behind number 17. Josephine motioned her over, but Lisa Marie frowned and shook her head.

Duck-like, Josephine crept toward the front of Helen-Dove's trailer. She crouched behind a rusted metal barrel and watched as Officer Frye got out of his patrol car. His face was shiny and serious, and she wondered if it felt strange to be a Black man in a trailer park of only white people.

His uniform looked much too hot for this time of the year—long-sleeved shirt and pants and heavy shoes. A glittering badge. A gun.

Josephine's heart began to pound. He had bad news, she realized. She could see this as he got closer. He looked heavy.

Not heavy on the outside. On the outside, he was lean, probably from catching so many bad guys. This heaviness came from within.

He gripped his officer's cap tighter, then stuck it on his head. He went out of Josephine's sight line, but she could hear his big, heavy feet on Helen-Dove's stoop. His big, heavy fist knocking on Helen-Dove's door.

Josephine squeezed herself into a ball and shut her eyes. Again, she saw the keys and the cheerful, flying pigs, and the zigzags on Molly's white teeth. *Don't let her be dead.*

"Officer Frye!" Helen-Dove said as if sounding an alarm.

Josephine squeezed her toes hard inside Molly's Tiger Paws.

"What's happened?" she asked.

"Got a lead from Pickersgill early this morning. I tried calling, but—"

"Phone's been shut off," she said flatly. "Pickersgill?"

"I can't say for sure it was your Molly, but the description was close enough that it aroused suspicions."

Josephine let out a sigh of relief.

"Where was she exactly? Who saw her?"

There was a pause, and then, "Some nurses at the emergency room."

"The emergency room? The emergency room!"

"Raylene, or someone fitting her description, showed up and caused a commotion," Officer Frye continued.

"What do you mean *showed up*? Who took Molly to the hospital?"

"Again, this is hearsay, but according to the sergeant, it was a neighbor. And then Raylene, or whoever this person was, showed up and pitched a fit. Said they didn't have the right to examine a child without permission."

"What's wrong with Molly? Is she hurt?"

"They left before anybody got a look at her. Does Molly have any medical conditions?"

"Not unless they've done something to her with that snake oil nonsense!"

At the word *snake*, Josephine motioned Lisa Marie over, and this time she sprinted across the path, and the girls scootched close together, listening.

"You said you couldn't be sure. Why do you think it was Molly?"

"That sergeant I spoke to, his wife works in billing at the hospital down there. That's how this information made its way to me. The scene in the emergency room had everybody riled up. But what made me drive out here today was... well, his wife told him that one of the nurses told her..." He cleared his throat.

Josephine thought she might bust wide open if he didn't hurry up and finish this long story.

"Told her *what*?" Helen-Dove said, sounding impatient herself.

"The woman who came to get Molly, if it *was* Molly... well, she was wearing sunglasses, and when she took them off—"

"Witchy eye," Helen-Dove said.

A peeping sound came out of Josephine then, and Lisa Marie clamped a hand over her mouth.

"Maybe it wasn't your mother-in-law. Coincidences happen."

"Raylene is my *former* mother-in-law," Helen-Dove corrected. "I have something to show you."

"The postcard," Josephine whispered. "She's gonna show him that postcard."

Lisa Marie pressed a *Be quiet* finger to her lips.

Just then Hog started his motorcycle. The sound exploded into the air and what followed were a series of rumbling, mechanical growls. By the time the racket died down, Officer Frye was getting into his patrol car.

⊐⟶

When he was gone, Josephine and Lisa Marie went to sit in a patch of green. "We missed half of what they said because of that dumb motorcycle," Josephine complained. "She must have showed him that postcard. Don't you think?"

"Maybe," Lisa Marie said. Her eyes were faraway and sad again.

Josephine plucked a fistful of white clover and began knotting the flowers into a necklace. Finally, she tied the ends together and held up the long chain. "This is for you," she said. Lisa Marie leaned forward, and Josephine dragged it over her head.

"You're good at making these," Lisa Marie said.

"I know it," Josephine replied. "We have to find out where Pickersgill is. This afternoon when Mama gets done with her work, we're gonna beg her to take us to the library. Practice putting on a good begging face. Let me see it."

Lisa Marie made a begging face to beat all begging faces. It was pitiful and sweet at the same time.

Miss Mona Button

With the Moon Lake project finished, Mama was delighted to take Josephine and Lisa Marie to the library. They didn't even need to use their begging faces.

"I can't think of a better place to spend a sticky summer day, but first y'all need to wash up and change your clothes. And, Lisa Marie, you have to ask your granddaddy."

"Ain't nobody gonna say no to this," Lisa Marie assured them, and off she went, lickety-split, back to number 17.

Josephine and Mama were fixing to get in the car when Lisa Marie showed up again a few minutes later.

Like a peacock, she strutted up the washed-out path. If it hadn't been for her bald head, Josephine might not have recognized her.

Lisa Marie was wearing a dress, and it was frilly and fluffy and white and it stuck way out from her legs. It had ruffles around the collar and ruffles around the puffy sleeves and a giant sash she hadn't bothered to tie.

Josephine was fixing to say *We're not going to any beauty*

pageant, but Mama gave her a stern look, and said, "Get in the car."

Lisa Marie shoved Josephine out of the way. "I call shotgun!" she said, and scrambled into the front seat.

"That's *my* seat!" Josephine said.

"Not anymore." Lisa Marie stuck her tongue through the big space between her teeth.

"Lisa Marie is our guest," Mama said, so Josephine climbed into the back. "Lisa Marie, you look mighty pretty today. Doesn't she look pretty, Jo?"

Lisa Marie looked silly in such a fancy dress. And her white shoes were scuffed, and she wasn't wearing socks. Everybody knew you didn't wear fancy dresses to the library, and besides, this one looked dirty up close, but Mama gave Josephine a stern look in the rearview mirror, so Josephine said, "I guess so."

"How about after the library we get some ice cream over at the DQ?" Mama offered.

"I'm flat broke," Lisa Marie said.

"Oh, it'll be my treat. Your granddaddy probably saved me a fortune fixing my car."

"Then I'll get the banana split!"

"You never let *me* get a banana split," Josephine complained, wishing now that she was going to the library by herself.

"You girls can share a banana split. How about that?" Mama suggested.

"Split a banana split!" Lisa Marie said, and laughed bigger than the joke was funny.

⊏⟹

The library was quiet and cool, and it smelled thrilling, like books and floor polish and the faintest hint of Miss Mona Button's perfume. Miss Mona Button was the head librarian, an elegant lady, with salt-and-pepper curls styled just right and pretty clothes and colorful Lucite bracelets that made soft clacking noises when they knocked together.

"Well, if it isn't Mary Josephine Willoughby, a Gold Star Reader!" Miss Mona Button said, and waved to them. "Who've you got with you today?"

Josephine hesitated. Lisa Marie hadn't washed up the way Mama told her to. At the corner of her mouth was the strawberry filling from this morning's Pop-Tart and above her lip a stain of Nestlé's Quik.

"She's got *me* with her!" Lisa Marie shouted.

"Shush!" Josephine scolded.

Miss Mona Button stuck out her hand, and the row of shiny bracelets clacked together in the nicest way, but Lisa Marie just stood there.

"Shake her hand," Josephine demanded.

"Oh, that's alright, she doesn't have to," Miss Mona said just as Mama came through the double doors.

"Sorry, Miss Mona, I had to feed the meter, and my change purse spilled out all over the sidewalk. How are you today?" she asked, slightly out of breath.

"I'm doing splendidly. Fine patrons coming and going."

"Summer reading in full swing, I guess?" Mama said.

"Oh, yes, that and they like to come in here to cool off." Miss Mona winked. "It's my strategy to get Glendale reading." She swept her salty-peppery hair away from her face and beamed at them.

Mama placed the books they were returning on the counter. "I hope these aren't late."

Miss Mona opened the back cover. "They are right on time. How'd you like *By the Shores of Silver Lake*, Josephine?"

Josephine shook her head. "It was sad. I want to check out a Pippi Longstocking again."

"May I make another suggestion?" Miss Mona asked.

Josephine was dying to ask where the books with maps were kept, but she only nodded.

"Judy Blume has a new book I think you'll like. The protagonist is about your age, and I happen to have two fresh copies."

"What's the title?" Josephine asked. Usually, she could tell whether or not she might like a book based on its title.

Miss Mona smiled and said, "*Blubber.*"

Lisa Marie let out a barky laugh, and some library patrons turned to stare at them.

"This is a *library!*" Josephine said. "You have to be quiet."

"*You* have to be quiet!" Lisa Marie replied, and smacked Josephine on the arm.

Mama stepped between them. "Lisa Marie, you don't have a library card, is that right?"

"Naw, I ain't got one," she said.

Josephine cringed. Words like *ain't* belonged in a place like Happy World, but here, *ain't* and *naw* and *yeah* and *huh* were embarrassing.

Josephine frowned at Lisa Marie and was horrified to see she had the end of her untied sash in her mouth. It was wet with slobber now, and she was making sucking noises.

"I'll get you fixed up," Miss Mona said. "*And*, for every

child who signs up for a library card today, we have a Gold Star Reader goodie bag, too."

"How can she be a Gold Star Reader if she's never checked out books?" Josephine asked.

Miss Mona looked at a loss for words.

"She's on her way now, isn't she?" Mama said smoothly.

$$\Longrightarrow$$

For a while Josephine and Lisa Marie browsed the preteen magazine section, but as soon as Miss Mona Button got busy with another customer and Mama disappeared behind a row of shelves, the girls walked over to the world atlas.

"Look at this!" Lisa Marie said, and grabbed the book roughly.

"Stop! You'll tear it!" Lisa Marie was plucking Josephine's nerves like banjo strings today—*pluck-pluck-pluck*.

Lisa Marie chewed the end of her sash and said, "How we ever gonna find Pickersgill in this thing?"

"Quit chewing your sash. Here, let me tie it. Turn around."

Lisa Marie spun around so hard Josephine caught a glimpse of her flowered underpants.

"You want the fine patrons seeing your underwear?" Josephine steadied Lisa Marie, then tied the bow extra-extra tight so it wouldn't come loose.

"I can't breathe good," Lisa Marie complained.

"It'll loosen up in a minute," Josephine said, and she directed her attention to the giant book of maps. Sure enough, there was an index. "These are towns and cities," Josephine explained.

Lisa Marie was dragging her heels across the floor and making long, black scuff marks on the white tile.

"Stop doing that. You'll get us in trouble." Josephine ran her finger down the page. "Here are all the *H*'s. We need *P*'s."

Lisa Marie barked out a laugh again.

Josephine glared. "What *is* the matter with you? You're acting like somebody who's never been anywhere."

"I ain't been anywhere. I'm just trying to have a little fun."

Josephine found the listing for Pickersgill, U.S.A. "It's the only place called Pickersgill in the country."

Lisa Marie peered over Josephine's shoulder, and they stared at the numbers next to the listing: 30°31N, 87°54W and 315 and F-11.

"Longitude and latitude." Lisa Marie bumped Josephine out of the way. She flipped to page 315 and traced her fingers over the map. "There it is. See?"

Sure enough, beneath Lisa Marie's dirty fingernail was a tiny dot of a town called Pickersgill. "How far is it from here?"

"You got to measure it with the key." Lisa Marie held her thumb and finger close together and moved them down the page. "Eight hours, give or take," she said.

Pickersgill was at the tip of Alabama, a sliver of land sandwiched between Florida and Mississippi and on a body of water called the Gulf of Mexico.

"Girls, what are y'all doing way over here?" Mama asked, startling them both.

Lisa Marie blinked and Josephine blinked. And then Lisa Marie said, "We're planning us a vacation, Miss Penny. We're wantin' to go to the Gulf of Mexico."

Mama peered over them to look at the map.

"How long will it take to get there?" Josephine asked.

Mama studied the map, and just as Lisa Marie had done,

she measured the distance with her fingers. "Eight hours. There's a key," she said, and began to demonstrate.

"Told you so," Lisa Marie said. She smiled up at Mama.

"You can figure miles and calculate time, adjust it according to the speed of a car."

This was Mama's tricky way to get them doing math problems, and Josephine did not want to do math. In that moment, she wished she'd never heard of any kidnapping. The whole thing was impossible. Josephine thought of last summer and Redbud Avenue and Miss Nancy's begonia-filled patio.

Mama had been out with Lucas on a complicated install, so Josephine stayed with Miss Nancy. They sat on a quilt, eating heart-shaped peanut butter sandwiches and drinking white grape juice from real teacups. Josephine had never heard of Molly Quiver then. She'd never sneaked inside her bedroom or walked in her shoes.

Suddenly there was a hard stomp on Josephine's toe, and a red bulb of anger bloomed inside her chest.

"Ain't that what I been tellin' you, Josephine?" Lisa Marie was giving her an *Agree with me* look.

Mama squinted one eye. "I've got sewing, girls. Pick a book, and we'll stop at the DQ."

As they browsed the children's section, Josephine thought about the kids living on those pages—Mary Lennox and Sara Crewe and Birdie Boyer. By the end of their stories, everything was mostly figured out.

Josephine trailed her fingers along the spines of books. Somewhere between sections A and L, she fell into her imagination. Instead of dwelling on *how* they would get to Pickersgill and wrestle Molly from a witchy-eyed granny, she skipped ahead to the happily ever after. It was a pleasant, daydreamy feeling, that is until Lisa Marie opened her mouth.

And *burped*.

Lisa Marie burped loud enough for it to echo throughout the entire library.

And then Lisa Marie said, loud enough for the fine patrons to hear, "That'uz a good'n, Josephine!"

Drama at the DQ

Josephine and Lisa Marie watched while the teenager behind the DQ window made their dessert: a banana cut in half and ice cream and strawberry syrup and chocolate syrup and whipped cream. The teenager was about to put nuts on it, but Lisa Marie hollered, "We don't want them nuts!" so she stopped and put a few extra maraschino cherries on top instead.

With two spoons Josephine and Lisa Marie dug in, and they didn't even have a spoon war over the ice cream because the banana split was plenty big for both of them. With each bite Josephine felt the teensiest bit better.

Plus, they were the only folks in the DQ this time of day. There were no patrons around to see Lisa Marie chew with her mouth open or wipe the chocolate on her arm instead of the napkin.

"Oh, look, Jo!" Mama said. She pointed out the window. "It's Delia and Kitty. You haven't seen those girls since school let out."

"Who's Delia and Kitty?" Lisa Marie asked with her mouth full.

Josephine set down her spoon. She wiped her mouth on the paper napkin. On the tile floor was a dead fly, and Josephine thought how the good feelings of the banana split had died, just like that fly.

A shiny red convertible was tucked in the parking spot right next to Mama's sad blue car. The top was down, and propped on the back of its white leather seats, looking like a pair of beauty queens in a Fourth of July parade, were Delia Collingsworth and Kitty Hawkins.

Delia and Kitty wore matching outfits, and their hair was fixed the same way—side ponytails with red, white, and blue ribbons. Worst of all, they had their arms around each other's shoulders, and they swayed back and forth.

Josephine took a good, hard look at Lisa Marie. Her mouth and arms were covered in chocolate, and her napkin was perfectly clean. Her bald head was bumpy, and her ears stuck out. The tacky white dress had a new stain now, strawberry syrup. "If I eat one more bite of this split, I'll pop like a tick," Lisa Marie said. "It sure was good, though."

"I'm glad you liked it, Lisa Marie," Mama replied. She wiped the ice cream off the table and threw the container and their napkins into the trash. "Come on," she said. "Let's go say hello."

The next thing Josephine knew Mama was nudging them out the door and toward the red convertible.

"You seen a ghost or what?" Lisa Marie said, but Josephine didn't answer. She just stared straight ahead and pretended not to know Lisa Marie.

"Hi there!" Mama called, and waved with genuine excitement. Mama had gotten to know Mrs. Hawkins at some of the room parties in Miss Lake's class. They'd decorated bulletin boards together and planned class parties, except twice Mama couldn't attend because of last-minute installations, which meant Mrs. Hawkins had to take over Mama's role as head room mother.

"Well, hey there, Penny! It's so nice to see you." Mrs. Hawkins smiled a white-toothed smile and flipped her sunglasses onto her head.

"Looks like you girls are having fun in that pretty car!" Mama gave Josephine a glance and motioned for her to come say hello.

"Oh, it's brand-new and we're out for our first spin," Mrs. Hawkins replied. "I just figured out how to get the top down. Had to look in the owner's manual, didn't I, girls?"

Delia and Kitty nodded like their heads were connected to a string. Delia was smiling the way she always did when grown-ups were around, a perfect angel smile. Except Josephine knew Delia was not a perfect angel. If Delia stubbed her toe, she said swear words. And once she'd told Josephine a secret about helping Randy, her big brother, put toilet paper in their neighbor's trees.

"Y'all have plans for Fourth of July?" Mama asked.

"We're going to the country club," Delia piped up. And then Josephine noticed Delia's and Kitty's matching earrings, little red strawberries with gold leafy stems.

"They have an impressive display of fireworks, or so I hear," Mrs. Hawkins said. "I hope it doesn't rain."

"Oh, that sounds nice. The weather's supposed to be good." Mama gave Josephine a nudge. Josephine still hadn't said hello. She was too busy looking at Delia and Kitty, who were gawking at Lisa Marie.

"Hidy," Lisa Marie said to them, and grinned her gap-toothed grin.

Josephine knew what those girls were staring at—Lisa Marie's bald head and her stained dress and her scuffed shoes without any socks. Josephine wished a giant hole would open in the DQ parking lot and swallow her up.

Lisa Marie's bow had come untied, and she was sucking on it again.

Josephine couldn't stand this situation a second longer. The red bulb of anger that'd bloomed back at the library was blistering her insides now. "Stop chewing that!" she snapped. She remembered something Miss Augustine said about folks who smacked their gum too loud. "You look like a cow chewin' its cud!" And then Josephine added, "A *bald* cow."

Lisa Marie's big green eyes went bigger and her face turned red.

"Josephine!" Mama said.

Delia and Kitty exchanged horrified looks and pressed their elbows into each other. Mrs. Hawkins' pink lips weren't smiling any longer.

Josephine couldn't back down now. She had to keep going. "I thought you had sewing to do, Mama? I thought you were in such a big fat hurry to get home."

"All right, young lady, that's quite enough." Mama squeezed Josephine's shoulder. "I'm so sorry. Somebody is clearly having a bad day. I hope y'all have a nice Fourth of July. It was good to see you girls. I just love those matching outfits."

"Thank you," Kitty and Delia singsonged like a pair of goody-goodies, which they most certainly were not.

Lisa Marie didn't want to sit up front on the trip home. Instead, she sat in back, and Josephine sat up front, except it didn't feel good. In fact, everything felt terrible. They weren't even out of the DQ parking lot when Josephine heard sniffling sounds coming from the backseat.

"It's alright," Mama said in her gentlest voice. With her left hand on the steering wheel and her right arm stretched over the seat, Mama held Lisa Marie's hand, and like that they drove back to Happy World Trailer Park—*Dandiest Little Place on Earth!*

A Dangerous Place

When they arrived at Happy World, Lisa Marie scrambled out of the car in a hurry and took off toward number 17. She didn't say thank you for the trip to town or for the banana split.

"She left her library card." Josephine pointed to the back-seat. "And the book and the Gold Star Reader goodie bag, too,"

Without a word, Mama grabbed these things from the car and carried them inside. Josephine watched as she switched on the sewing machine and went straight to work.

Not even the sewing machine's gentle *whirr-thump* made Josephine feel any better, so she went to her room, changed into her play clothes, and put on that sad Donny Osmond record.

Over and over, she sang along to "Are You Lonesome Tonight?"

Yes, she sure was lonesome, except it was daytime. Delia and Kitty were off doing something really fun together. Probably shopping downtown or swimming at the country club. Mama and Josephine had driven past the country club lots of times on the way to clients' houses. The water was sparkling blue and there was a high dive and a low dive, and even better, a curvy slide. From the road you could hear kids squealing and splashing, and it was the sort of torture that made Josephine ache head to toe.

These things were terrible to think about, but even worse was picturing Lisa Marie in that dark trailer with poor sick Buster Lee.

⇨

After supper and a shower and writing a dumb story about Delia and Kitty moving to California and never being seen or heard from again, Josephine switched off her light and lay in bed listening to Happy World sounds: Zeus strumming his guitar; a car door slamming; the volume of someone's TV turned up too loud.

Mama was in the bathroom—toilet flushing, spigot on then off, the medicine cabinet door opening with its squeaky sound and then a *click* when it closed again. Josephine would bet a million bucks Mama was putting Pond's cold cream on her face this very second.

Soon everything was quiet and dark. The wind and strumming stopped. Josephine was finally drifting off when something made her eyes snap open. Very carefully, she listened. Her heart beat faster, then faster still, and she felt stifling hot under her covers. She kicked them off and scrambled onto her knees to peek out the window.

Way up the road, lights flashed and a siren moaned. Closer and closer the sound came until Josephine could see it: an ambulance. She watched the ambulance pull into the Happy World entrance, then switch off its siren. There were only the flashing lights now as it jounced up the washed-out path toward number 17. Doors flung open and medics tumbled out.

Mama came into Josephine's bedroom and sat on the end of her bed.

"I guess it's poor ole Buster Lee," Josephine said. "I see Hog and Joella and Zeus. Miss Connie's out there in her night-gown, with rollers in her hair. Granddaddy is starting his pickup."

Mama didn't even tell Josephine to quit being nosy.

"They're loading him in the back," Josephine went on. "It's leaving now. Granddaddy's truck is following along." When everybody went back to their trailers, Josephine shut the curtain and crawled under the covers again.

"You okay, Jo?" Mama asked, and tucked her in too tight.

"Maybe a miracle will happen tonight. Buster Lee could wake up and feel good again. Jesus brought that dead guy back to life. What's his name?"

"Lazarus," Mama said.

"I remember that story. Jesus cried and Lazarus came back to life." Josephine was doing her best to hang on to these thoughts. She was doing her best to look for sweetness in this life.

"Jesus wept, that's true."

"If Jesus can do that, he can take care of Buster Lee."

"I don't think that'll happen, Jo. That's why . . . I was very disappointed in you today. Lisa Marie has a hard life. I know sometimes she doesn't know her manners, but she doesn't have anybody to teach her those things."

Josephine did not want to think about Lisa Marie's hard life. Thinking about her hard life only made Josephine feel worse about what she'd done. The awful look on Lisa Marie's face had tortured her all afternoon and evening. "I've got a hard life, too," Josephine pointed out.

"We have not had an easy time of it lately, that's true, but I didn't just shave your head. And I'm not sick with cancer. And I don't leave you in this trailer day in and day out with nothing to do. We have some fun sometimes, don't we?"

"Sometimes," Josephine agreed, then added, "But sometimes I'm bored to death."

Mama sighed. "I love you with my whole heart, Mary Josephine Willoughby, even when you're awful."

"I love you with my whole heart, even when you're awful," Josephine replied.

"What am I going to do with you?"

Josephine thought for a minute. "You could let me get my ears pierced. We could get Lisa Marie's ears pierced, too. That might make her feel better."

"An apology will make her feel better, a proper and *heartfelt* apology," Mama said firmly.

⇨

For what seemed like forever and a day, Josephine flopped around in her *bo-ING!*-y bed. She turned this way and that. She tugged the covers up to her chin, then kicked them off again. She thought about Molly Quiver. She thought about Buster Lee smiling with half his face. And she remembered Lisa Marie's sad expression at the Dairy Queen.

The Fourth of July

The next morning at breakfast Mama was tilting her head and studying Josephine like she was a hard math problem. "How'd you sleep, Jo?" she asked.

Josephine shook her head. "This place is creepy at night. I'm glad we're leaving soon."

"We're here until July thirty-first. Plenty of time for you to take care of the task at hand." She put her nose into her coffee cup, then took a deep sip. "I've finished the pillows for Mrs. Morrison's living room. I thought we'd ride over there this morning and drop them off."

Josephine shrugged and took another bite of soggy Cheerios and sliced banana.

"It's the Fourth of July. We could stop and get some sparklers. I thought I'd make a cake. You want to decorate it with blueberries and strawberries and whipped cream?"

Josephine sipped her grape juice.

"Are you upset about Buster Lee?" Mama asked.

Josephine nodded.

"How about we ask Lisa Marie to come with us on our

errands? She can help with the cake. Might take her mind off her troubles. And give you a chance to apologize. You won't feel better until you apologize, Jo. Suffering like you are means you feel bad about what you did. It's your conscience talking to you."

"It's you talking to me," Josephine said. During the sleepless night, Josephine had thought up all kinds of excuses for why she'd said such awful things. "It's not my fault. She was the one sucking on her bow and—"

"Not another word. Accept responsibility for your actions."

"But she's not—"

"I *said* not another word." Mama tapped her coffee cup with a freshly painted fingernail. "You'll apologize, and tonight we'll grill out hamburgers. We'll have cake and light the sparklers. Now put your dishes in the sink, and if you're going to ask Lisa Marie to come with us, you'd better head over now."

Josephine sat in her chair. She did not move.

Mama stared hard at her.

"Fine! I'll ask her!" Josephine snapped, and went to her room to change out of her pajamas.

⊏⟹

Josephine was knocking hard on Lisa Marie's door when Granddaddy's truck pulled up. She waited on the porch while he switched off the ignition and climbed out. His head was bowed like he was praying.

"Hi. It's me," Josephine said, so as not to startle him.

"Hidy, Josephine," Granddaddy said. "How you doin' this morning, shug?"

"Fine. How's Buster Lee?" she asked.

The door snapped open and Lisa Marie appeared, wearing what looked to be an old man's undershirt.

"Well? Where's he at?" This time it was Lisa Marie who pretended not to know Josephine. She didn't even say good morning. "Is he fixin' to come home today?"

"I'm afraid Buster Lee has gone to be with the Lord," Granddaddy said. "He ain't suffering no more."

Lisa Marie's mouth tugged downward. She blinked. "Not like 'is. He can't go thissaway. Me and him had it all planned."

Granddaddy gave her a sad look and shook his head.

"But I was gonna sing him out of this world and into the next. He wanted that song 'In the Garden.'"

Josephine waited for Lisa Marie to cry. Seemed like Granddaddy was waiting for her to cry, too, but then Lisa Marie surprised them both by taking in a deep gulp of air. Finally, she said, "Well? Where are we gonna bury him at, then?"

"I don't know, shug. We'll deal with that later. Right now, I need to get some shut-eye. You girls be quiet. Okay?" Granddaddy climbed the porch steps and squeezed past them. He gave Lisa Marie a pat on the back, then went inside.

Lisa Marie sat on the porch and Josephine joined her. It was a little like sitting in a jungle because the plants had grown so tall. Bees buzzed. The air smelled like heat and grass and tomatoes so fat they were starting to split wide open. In the way distance, a Bush Hog roared.

Josephine thought about Buster Lee's half-a-face and that handkerchief he used to wipe his mouth. She pictured him watching *Name That Tune* and winning the Golden Medley. "I'm sorry!" Josephine blurted out. "I'm sorry I was so ugly to you! I'm sorry I said you were a bald cow. You're bald, but you're not a cow. You don't look anything *like* a cow. And I'm sorry about Buster Lee. I'm really, *really* sorry about him."

Lisa Marie rubbed her head, which was starting to get

some stubble. She stuck her nose into the tomato plant and inhaled.

Josephine waited. Inside her head she said a prayer. *Please* was the prayer, and then, *Please-please-pretty-please, let Lisa Marie still be my friend.*

Lisa Marie stopped smelling the tomatoes and looked into Josephine's face. "I reckon Buster Lee has gone to the sweet by and by on the Fourth of July."

Josephine nodded.

"And you know what else?"

Any second Lisa Marie was surely fixing to tell Josephine to get lost forever. She braced herself for this unpleasant news. "What else?" Josephine asked.

"I'm glad I got you here with me. I got a good friend in you, Josephine. A mostly good friend anyways."

Josephine knew this wasn't true. She only knew she wanted it to be true. Very badly, with her whole heart, she wanted to be a good friend to Lisa Marie.

Cool Whip

Lisa Marie went with Mama and Josephine to run errands, and this time both girls sat in the backseat together. Mama had the radio on WKRN, but Josephine didn't sing along. She didn't much feel like singing now that Buster Lee was gone.

Lisa Marie didn't sing, either, not even when Mama switched to the country station. Instead, Lisa Marie stared out the window and looked like the saddest girl Josephine ever saw.

As they waited at a red light, Josephine noticed a giant bus in front of the Greyhound station. It hissed and popped and roared off up the street. As it passed by, Josephine caught a glimpse of the people inside. "They're leaving the driving to Greyhound," she said.

Mama glanced at her in the rearview mirror. "What?"

" 'Leave the driving to Greyhound.' It's on the commercial. Those people on that bus are leaving the driving to Greyhound."

Mama gave Josephine a puzzled look, but said nothing.

"Leave the driving to Greyhound," Josephine whispered to herself.

Mama pulled into an empty space right in front of Fabric Delights and Other Notions. "Girls, this is going to be a quick stop. I just need to pick up some fabric that was on back order. Miss Augustine has the day off today, so we're not going to take up much of her time," she said, and they got out of the car and went inside.

$\Longrightarrow$

Josephine expected Lisa Marie's eyes to go wider and greener at the sight of the fabric store, but she stood near the door and didn't say a single word. Miss Augustine showed off her diamond engagement ring, but Lisa Marie didn't even look at it. Miss Augustine asked Josephine to be a junior bridesmaid in her wedding and said Lisa Marie could keep the guest register if she wanted to, but Lisa Marie just stared at the floor.

As they got ready to leave, Miss Augustine picked up the giant jar of buttons that sat near the cash register. "Lisa Marie, would you like a jar of buttons?" she offered.

Ever so slightly, Lisa Marie's chin quivered. "I don't know what I'd do with them," she said, and a single tear slid down her cheek.

"I guess we'd better be going," Mama said, and then she took hold of Lisa Marie's hand and led her to the ole blue car. Just before Lisa Marie climbed into the backseat again, Mama hugged her hard and gave her stubbly head a gentle rub.

$\Longrightarrow$

After the fabric store errand, they headed to Mrs. Morrison's to drop off the pillows. Lisa Marie didn't seem to notice Mrs. Morrison's poufy blond hair or the fancy house with its long, winding driveway or the swimming pool or tennis court.

All this quiet was making Josephine think more and more about Greyhound buses and where they went. *Pickersgill, Alabama, maybe?* She imagined herself on one of those buses. Next to her on the imaginary bus sat Lisa Marie, the pair of them off in search of Molly Quiver.

And then they were heading home again. Lisa Marie on one side and Josephine on the other. In between them was Molly Quiver, smiling the whole way home. They took turns asking her questions about her life as a kidnapped girl, and Josephine wrote it all down in her yellow notebook. When the newspaper printed the story, the headline read BEST FRIENDS FOREVER.

"We have to stop at the IGA to pick up some things for our supper," Mama said, and Josephine snapped out of her daydream.

⊂⟹

In the store, Josephine and Lisa Marie followed along behind Mama while she dropped things into the cart. Lisa Marie kept sniffling and wiping her nose on her arm and not talking, which plunged Josephine deeper into her imagination.

Josephine wondered what Greyhound buses smelled like and if they had snacks. She considered how she would fill the hours of travel and what-all she might notice while gazing out the window.

Miss Lake said even the most ordinary moments in our lives *metamorphosed* us. She'd written the word in her elegant handwriting on the chalkboard. *Metamorphose* was the "challenge word" on a vocabulary test, and Josephine had gotten it wrong.

At the checkout, Josephine and Lisa Marie studied the

rows of candy while Mama put their things on the belt—hamburger meat and buns and ingredients for a flag cake, plus a box of sparklers.

The checkout lady, a hunched woman with a pair of giant glasses perched on the end of her nose, smiled at them and said in a booming voice, "Boy howdy, somebody's having a party tonight!"

Josephine turned to face her. "We're making a flag cake," she said.

The woman nodded approvingly and replied, "Are you and your big brother gonna decorate it?"

Josephine frowned.

"Jo, here's a quarter. Y'all go ride the pony out front while I settle up," Mama said.

"I don't want to ride no pony," Lisa Marie said when they were out of the store. She slumped on a bench and stared at the parking lot, which had a wavy look to it on account of the heat.

Josephine settled beside her. "You don't look like a boy," she said.

"Don't matter if I do. Who really cares? *Huh?* Who?"

"You just have a bald head is all," Josephine tried, but Lisa Marie didn't answer.

Josephine sighed and stared at Bucky, the phony pony. Next to Bucky was a pay phone with a directory that dangled from a metal cord. Behind the store's plate glass window, Mama stood talking to the cashier and grocery bagger, a teenage boy with knobby elbows.

Josephine was reminded of something else from her fourth-grade classroom: connect-the-dots worksheets. On rainy days when they couldn't go out for recess, Miss Lake put on records and let them do worksheets. Hard ones, not the baby kind.

She started to connect the dots in her head.

Bucky. The quarter in her pocket. The directory. A pay phone.

Metamorphose.

Josephine stood and walked over to the phone. She picked up the directory and searched through its yellow pages. Compared to the world atlas, the phone book was easy as pie to manage. She found giant, italicized letters that said *Go Greyhound and Leave the Driving to Us!* with a phone number below. Josephine glanced at Bucky again, then pushed the quarter into the slot and dialed the number.

"Greyhound," a man answered.

So easy. A piece of cake, really. "How much is a ticket to Pickersgill, Alabama?" she asked.

"Hold on," the man said, and set the phone down with a smack.

Josephine glanced at Lisa Marie. She had her head in her hands now and was rocking back and forth.

The man came on the line again. "Nearest station's Mobile."

Josephine had no idea what this meant, but she said, "Okay."

"One-way or round-trip?" he asked.

Mama was pushing the cart toward the automatic doors. Any second they would swing open and she would be outside, wondering who in the world Josephine was calling on a pay phone. "Round-trip," Josephine said.

"Hold on," he replied.

Closer and closer Mama came. Just as the doors opened

and the grocery-store air wafted out onto the sidewalk, Josephine was saved by a container of Cool Whip. It seemed to leap right out of the cart, and Mama stooped to pick it up.

"Round-trip is twenty dollars," the man said.

At this, Josephine hung up and raced over to Lisa Marie. Her heart was pounding, and she realized she'd left the change, fifteen cents, inside the coin slot.

Mama wheeled the cart over to them. "Y'all didn't ride Bucky?" she asked.

Josephine shook her head.

"Well, then where's my quarter?"

A lie pushed past Josephine's lips. "I lost it," she said.

Splurge

A s they drove through town, Josephine's insides churned. She'd hung up on someone. She'd used Mama's quarter for a phone call instead of a pony ride and then told Mama a lie. Part of her felt like she was a girl about to run away.

No, she would be running *to*.

Metamorphose.

Getting words wrong on a vocabulary test was a sure-fire way to remember them forever. She knew the definition now: *change or cause to change.*

And there were the connect-the-dots again. Run to the shores of Alabama. Find Molly Quiver. Bring her home.

Hovering along the edges of this daydream was Redbud Avenue and the emerald-green sofa and the lovely crape myrtle outside her bedroom window, its heavy, pink blooms swaying in a breeze.

And then Josephine's imagination was on the Greyhound bus again, roaring back to Happy World, with Molly Quiver sitting beside her.

The girl in the school picture had come to life. She was laughing and telling wild stories, stories better than Pippi Longstocking even. Everyone on the bus was looking over their seats and leaning across the aisle to hear the harrowing tale.

Josephine was so lost in her head she didn't notice when Mama turned into the Rose's Discount parking lot. "I have a plan!" Mama said, and shoved the gearshift into Park. "As Miss Augustine likes to say, this ought to put a pep in your step, Lisa Marie. Come on, girls!"

⊏⟹

At the toy section, Mama made a wide sweeping motion, and smiled like those ladies on the *Let's Make a Deal* game show. "I want you girls to pick a toy. Ten dollars each."

Lisa Marie rubbed her nubby head. "Ten dollars?" She rubbed her head again.

"Mrs. Morrison gave me a generous tip this morning." Mama patted her pocketbook. "Go on and splurge."

"Splurging is my favorite hobby," Josephine replied, and wandered off by herself toward the Barbie aisle.

Shelf after shelf of shiny packages—oodles of outfits and Barbie's Country Camper and Barbie's Dream Boat and a Barbie Pool Party set. Longingly, Josephine gazed at them. Her Barbie carrying case was under her bed at home: four Barbies, two Skippers, and a lone Ken. She hadn't touched them since moving to Happy World. Even before Happy World, Josephine hadn't played with them much.

Last summer, Mama offered to make stylish outfits for Josephine's and Delia's Barbies. "No thanks," Delia replied. Back in Josephine's room, with the door closed, Delia screwed up her face and asked, "You don't still play with them, do you, Josephine?"

Josephine continued to the next aisle. She studied boxes of Pet Rocks and Spirographs and Hasbro Lite-Brites. Finally, she stopped and said out loud, "As a matter of fact, I do still play with them!"

She raced back to the Barbie aisle, plucked the last Pool Party set off the shelf, and hurried to find Lisa Marie.

⊃⟹

Lisa Marie was over by the for-real baby toys. She was pushing a Fisher-Price corn popper up the aisle, and it was making an embarrassing ruckus. Josephine tapped her on the shoulder. "Did you pick something?"

Lisa Marie shook her head and put the corn popper back on the rack. As if in a daze, she ventured over to the automotive section.

"You don't want anything from here," Josephine said gently.

"You never know," Lisa Marie replied, but then she drifted back to the toys again.

Lisa Marie squeezed stuffed animals and bounced balls. She picked up boxes, studied price stickers, then set them down. She examined bicycles, touched every banana seat and tasseled handlebar, but those cost way more than ten dollars.

"There you are, girls!" Mama said, coming up the aisle. "Did you find what you want?"

Josephine nodded. Lisa Marie glanced down at her battered creek shoes and shook her head.

"Not to rush you, sweetie, but I do have groceries in the car," Mama said.

Finally, after what felt like forever and a day, Lisa Marie said, "I think I want this Slip 'N' Slide. I seen it on the commercial, and it looks fun."

Mama smiled. "That's a fine idea. And how about we find you a pretty bathing cap to match your swimsuit?"

"I ain't got no swimming suit."

"You swim in your *panties*?" Josephine asked, horrified.

Mama frowned. "Well, then I guess we'll be getting you a swimsuit *and* a bathing cap. Come on," she said, and off they went to the preteen department.

⟹

Lisa Marie chose a baby blue suit with red ties on the side. And instead of a bathing cap, she wanted a stylish floppy hat, because she could wear it any old time, not just for swimming.

"That's very sensible of you, Lisa Marie. I'm all for being sensible, especially when it comes to money," Mama said.

At the word *sensible*, another connect-the-dots dot rolled into Josephine's brain. Twenty dollars.

Twenty dollars was a round-trip ticket to Mobile, Alabama, which was almost to Pickersgill, or so Josephine figured.

A *sensible* girl would save the money.

Josephine glanced at the Barbie Pool Party box. On the splashy front was the pool with shimmering blue water and the ladder and diving board and slide. It came with a small floating lounge. *It's the sunny, FUN thing to do!* the caption read, and the Barbies looked like they were having a fabulous time.

"Well, girls, looks like we're ready to go," Mama said, and headed toward the checkout.

Josephine trailed behind Mama and Lisa Marie. Twenty

dollars would buy the round-trip bus ticket, but Josephine wasn't about to ask Lisa Marie to make such a sacrifice. Not after the Dairy Queen. And certainly not after Buster Lee.

Ten dollars was enough for a one-way ticket. Surely if Josephine could get to the shores of Alabama, she could find her way home again.

⊏⟹

At the checkout Josephine watched Lisa Marie place her new things carefully on the belt. Her precise movements made Josephine's heart squeeze tight.

"Hey, Mama?" Josephine said.

"Yes, Jo," Mama replied without looking at her.

"I don't want this."

Mama turned to face her then. "What?" she asked.

"Do I get to keep the ten dollars if I don't get this today?" Josephine held up the box.

The cashier, an older lady with hair the color of woodsmoke, raised her eyebrows in surprise, and the belt stopped moving.

Mama frowned. "But you've wanted one of these for—"

"I'm too old now." These words were prickly as a cocklebur.

"Are you sure, Jo?"

"I can have the toy restocked. Not a problem," the cashier said.

"I'm sure," Josephine replied, and handed the woman the box.

The Barbie on the floating lounge chair had her hand in the air, and she seemed to be waving goodbye. Goodbye to Josephine, who would soon be leaving on a Greyhound.

Goodbye to Josephine's childhood, which she would abandon right here in the checkout line at Rose's Discount.

⊏⟹

Josephine crawled into the backseat of Mama's hot car. Her heart was heavy, and she felt a blister beginning to bubble on her right heel. Lisa Marie clutched her shopping bags and stared out the window. On her head was the floppy hat, its brim so low Josephine couldn't see her face.

It was a quiet ride until Lisa Marie broke the silence with "Me and Buster Lee used to go to the creek. He took me fishing, too. Last summer we went fishing a whole lotta times. That was before...you know."

"Before he got cancer in his face?" Josephine said.

"Yeah. And we seen *Mary Poppins* at the Sunday matinee. *Chitty Chitty Bang Bang*, too. And Buster Lee made fudge. He made the best fudge you ever tasted. He knew just the way to stir it so it didn't get stuck to the pan. And he could whistle. That man could whistle like a bird."

Goodness and Mercy

There was a red checkered tablecloth with matching cloth napkins and candles and a jelly jar with fat blue flowers in water. The cake, which was on the counter, was the prettiest thing—Cool Whip for icing and blueberries and strawberries to make it look like a real live flag. Mama had even unplugged the refrigerator so they could eat their supper in peace.

There were juicy burgers with soft buns and lots of ketchup. Pork and beans and potato chips and crunchy ice-berg lettuce and sweet tea to drink.

"Leave room for dessert," Mama urged.

Josephine didn't answer.

"You're mighty quiet this evening."

Still, Josephine did not respond.

"Give Lisa Marie some time, Jo. She's had a hard day. And I'm surprised you didn't want the Barbie Pool Party set. You only get to be a child once, you know."

"I'm almost eleven," Josephine pointed out.

"Eleven is still a child. All I'm saying is try not to rush through life."

Josephine shrugged. Mama had given her the ten-dollar bill to keep, and she'd tucked it inside the sleeve of the "Are You Lonesome Tonight?" record.

All afternoon she'd been considering how one second Buster Lee's heart was beating and then it wasn't.

"You want to talk about Buster Lee?" Mama asked. Sometimes that woman was a mind reader.

"Does he get the other side of his face back? And does he go straight to heaven, or have to wait, like at the doctor's office?"

"I don't know, Jo."

Josephine frowned. "What does Brother Davis say about this kind of stuff?"

"You're looking for exact answers to impossible questions. Brother Davis doesn't know these things, either."

Josephine bit into a potato chip and Mama took a sip of sweet tea.

"Want to know what I say to myself whenever my heart is heavy?"

Josephine blinked, waiting.

"When I'm weary of considerations, and life is too much like a pathless wood..."

"Do what?"

"It's a poem, Jo. I memorized it in high school, but I can only remember snatches of it now. 'Birches,' it's called. Normally, I'm a pragmatic, precise sort of person. A seamstress has to be that way. But with matters of the heart, or maybe the soul, I think the great poets..." She patted her chest and bit her lip.

"What about the great poets?" Josephine pressed.

"Oh, I don't know, Jo. We go to church and we listen to

Brother Davis, but I think poetry comes pretty close to defining the meaning of life."

"I don't get it," Josephine said.

"The Twenty-Third Psalm is another good one. 'Surely goodness and mercy shall follow me all the days of my life.' The whole time at our yard sale, I kept repeating those words under my breath. 'Goodness and mercy, goodness and mercy.'"

"He'll hate it if he has to wander around heaven with half his face. He hates for people to see him like that."

Mama placed her hand on Josephine's. "We leave our earthly bodies behind so they aren't a burden to us any longer."

"You mean at the cemetery."

"That's right, but Buster Lee's spirit is all around us."

"Sounds like Casper the Friendly Ghost to me." Josephine wasn't satisfied.

"Well, I'm afraid that's all I've got in the way of philosophy. Robert Frost and the Twenty-Third Psalm." Mama sighed and went to plug in the refrigerator.

⊂⟶

Outside, Josephine wandered around Happy World. She slipped behind trailers and spied on folks. Hog and Joella cooked ribs on the grill, and Zeus and Mercedes hung red, white, and blue tie-dyed T-shirts on the clothesline.

Josephine spied longest on the old couple who lived in number 10, the trailer with the plastic buckets and broken mop handles. They were never around much, at least not when Josephine might see them. According to Lisa Marie, they cleaned businesses at night and slept during the day. This evening they wore matching red checkered shirts and took turns hand-churning ice cream, which made Josephine like them instantly, since hand-churned ice cream was better than anything you could buy at the store.

Josephine was scared to spy on Miss Connie. Whenever Josephine and Lisa Marie got into stuff and Miss Connie saw them, she hollered, "Y'all go on away from here! Git now!" like they were a pair of stray dogs instead of girls. Still, Josephine pressed onward to the leasing office.

The Tennessee flag was flapping on its pole, and Miss Connie's underwear was flapping on the clothesline. A giant bra hung out there, too, and Josephine wished like anything Lisa Marie could see it so they could laugh their stupid heads off.

She was just about to skip on back to number 17 and try to snag Lisa Marie's attention, but something pink caught her eye. Just beyond the smudged glass of the leasing office stood the old woman. Her white hair was every which way and the skin on her pale arms practically glowed.

Any second the ax would come down on Josephine. *Thwack!* She took a baby step closer.

Miss Connie was holding Bob Barker, smiling down at him, rocking the yellow cat, like he was her bundle of joy.

"Josephine! Jo-se-*phine*!" Mama's voice pierced the silence.

Miss Connie stopped rocking and stared at Josephine.

It felt like the moment just before those gazelles on *Wild Kingdom* get eaten by lions. But then the strangest thing happened. Without knowing she was going to do it, Josephine waved to Miss Connie.

Even stranger, Miss Connie waved back.

Screaming Banshee

Hog and Joella stacked cinder blocks to use as a launch pad, and after it was dark, they set off fireworks. Colorful ones and noisy ones. Josephine liked the colorful ones best. Everyone cheered and clapped and oohed and aahed. Even sad Lisa Marie squealed a time or two.

Zeus played "This Land Is Your Land" on his guitar, and the Happy World folks sang along, their faces tilted toward the night sky.

Josephine couldn't help but glance over at number 7. Helen-Dove's lights were on, and the air conditioner was purring.

"Y'all stand back," Hog warned, and lit another Roman candle. It sizzled and crackled, then shot a ball of fire high into the air. Lickety-split, without Mama or Lisa Marie noticing, Josephine raced toward number 7 and knocked softly.

As she waited, Josephine noticed the geraniums had wilted. She reached into the clay pot to check the soil. Not recently watered, she noted, just as the door squeaked open.

"Hi," Josephine said, and removed her hand quickly from the pot.

Helen-Dove nodded. Beneath her eyes were dark half moons.

"We made a flag cake, and that couple"—Josephine tried to decide how to describe them—"the ones that talk with their hands, they churned ice cream."

"Jewel and Rufus," Helen-Dove said. "Signing, it's called."

"Oh," Josephine replied. "Buster Lee, well, he..."

"Yes, I heard," Helen-Dove said as another ball of fire shot skyward. It streaked the heavens with golden glitter. "Josephine, I'm weary tonight and not up for talking."

Helen-Dove's cheeks were hollow. Her brown hair had been pulled into a tight ponytail, and it made the lines in her face deeper.

Josephine felt nervous under the woman's gaze, but she continued. "Buster Lee...he...he...made a scrapbook for her."

"A scrapbook for who?"

Scrapbooks were about happy things, events a person actually wanted to remember. "Not really a scrapbook. He saved the news clippings from when Molly was..."

Helen-Dove made a face like she thought Josephine was crazy.

"He thought Molly might want to see that people were looking for her."

"Of course we're looking for her," Helen-Dove said sharply.

But you're not *looking for her*, Josephine wanted to say.

There was another explosion of fireworks, and then a smattering of silver stars floated gracefully back to the earth.

Josephine took a deep breath and pressed on. "How did Molly write her *a*'s? Did she write them like this?" Josephine wrote on the air with her finger—a circle with a tail. "Or, like this?" She made the other type of *a*. "That postcard from the Emerald Coast, it was in our mailbox by mistake. I was noticing the *a*'s."

Helen-Dove was frowning at her. "You really do beat all I've ever seen. Does your mother know you're over here pestering me with questions?"

From the top of the television set, Molly gazed at Josephine. *Keep pestering*, she seemed to say.

"Do you remember how she made her *a*'s?"

A sharp shriek of something Hog called a screaming banshee made Josephine and Helen-Dove flinch at the same time. "I detest those things." Helen-Dove took a step backwards. "I have to go, Josephine. I'm not up for company tonight. This racket makes me jittery."

She moved to shut the door, but stopped suddenly. A look passed over her face as if Buster Lee's ghost had just floated by.

Josephine turned to see a pair of white headlights coming up the washed-out path. In a matter of seconds, Officer Frye was getting out of his patrol car and walking solemnly toward the trailer.

Helen-Dove shooed Josephine away with an irritated flip of her wrist and motioned Officer Frye inside. She shut the door with a firm *whump*.

The Happy World crowd broke up then, their ragtag celebration cut short by whatever was happening inside number 7. And there was no way to *know* what was happening, either. Just that the Quiver trailer was eerily quiet, the sort of quiet that felt louder than any screaming banshee.

Junkyard

Weeping may tarry for the night, but joy comes in the morning." Brother Davis was always saying this, but joy did not come in the morning.

Sweat came in the morning.

In spite of the fan, sweat rolled down the sides of Josephine's face and pricked the backs of her knees and the crooks of her arms. It made her itch, so she lay perfectly still on top of the covers and studied the water-stained ceiling. She prayed for *help*.

But there was no answer. Buster Lee was gone forever, and even though Josephine didn't want to admit it, Molly Quiver might be gone forever, too.

At this thought she sprang from the bed and grabbed the "Are You Lonesome Tonight?" record. She slid off its sleeve and removed the ten-dollar bill. Someone had marked on it with blue ink. *Bill*, it said, and Josephine wondered if whoever had written this meant *Bill* the person or *bill* meaning money.

People didn't run off and get on a bus without a plan. For

Mama's projects, she started with sketches. Sometimes she spent hours on that part. And then she measured again and again and again. Every stitch was perfect, or she ripped it out and started over. But Josephine didn't have time for perfect. The clock was ticking, its giant pendulum swinging in the direction of doom.

Mama knocked, startling Josephine. Quickly, she slipped the money back into the record sleeve just as her mother pushed open the door.

Mama was dressed in a stylish jumpsuit the color of Kentucky bluegrass, large gold hoop earrings, and platform-ish shoes.

"Why're you dressed like *that*?" Josephine asked.

Mama glanced down at herself. "Does it look ridiculous? Tell me the truth."

"You look like Phyllis from *The Mary Tyler Moore Show*. She's the most stylish one," Josephine pointed out.

"Thank you," Mama said. "That's exactly what I was hoping for."

"We can't go anywhere today. I've got things to do," Josephine said, but already she could feel where this was heading.

Mama smiled. "We have an appointment for what is potentially a very nice account."

"No!" Josephine protested.

"This'll be fun, Jo. And it'll take our minds off the sadness around here."

"Appointments are never fun."

"A new boutique just opened downtown," Mama said, ignoring Josephine. "The owner wants me to jazz up the dressing rooms. Something 'hip and sophisticated' was what she said, so I need to look hip and sophisticated myself. When it's over maybe we can window-shop. Get some ideas for your school clothes. I'll have to get started making them before long."

Josephine's brain fixated on the word *downtown*. The bus station was downtown.

"Put on one of your church dresses and wear your white sandals."

Josephine could not very well run around the shores of Alabama in a church dress. "My church dresses have puffed sleeves. I'm too old for puffy sleeves."

"Your blue dress has capped sleeves," Mama pointed out. "Come on, Jo. Don't give me a hard time about this today. Just—"

"Capped sleeves are the same thing," she protested.

"Capped sleeves are not the same thing, which is why they're called capped sleeves."

Josephine held her ground.

"Oh, good grief, Jo. Wear whatever you want. I don't have the energy to argue," Mama said, and shut the door.

⊐⟶

In no time they were in the ole blue car heading down the washed-out path. They'd nearly reached the highway when Josephine spotted Helen-Dove walking along the edge of the blacktop. No lunch bag, Josephine observed, and no purse or thermos, either. The light blue smock and dark navy pants hung loose on her skeletal frame.

"We have to give her a ride," Josephine said.

"I was thinking the same thing." Mama pulled over, and Josephine cranked down the window. "We're going right by

Cameron Mills," Mama called out. "It's no trouble to give you a lift."

Helen-Dove stared at them as if she'd forgotten who they were.

"Really, no trouble," Mama insisted.

Helen-Dove nodded, and Josephine clambered over the front seat and into the back.

While Mama drove, Josephine stared at Helen-Dove's neck. She was sweating, and loose strands of hair were glued to her skin. Everything about her was worn out and washed up and tragic. To look at her, even the back of her, gave Josephine a pain in the heart.

Mama seemed to sense Josephine was burning up with questions. She glanced in the rearview mirror, and ever so slightly shook her head. But how could you get answers if you didn't ask questions?

"Why was Officer Frye here last night?" Josephine heard herself say.

Mama tapped the brakes lightly. "Jo, that's—"

"He's leaving town," Helen-Dove replied. "Moving. Wanted to tell me in person."

Mama drove even slower down the highway now, and cars and trucks went roaring impatiently past them. "He won't give up looking?" Mama said.

Helen-Dove stared at her lap, a turtle gone back inside its shell. Her silence sounded like giving up. Her silence sounded like Molly Quiver had nobody looking for her.

"But what about Pickersgill?" Josephine asked, realizing in that instant she'd tattled on herself for eavesdropping.

Helen-Dove turned around in the seat. Josephine wanted

to avert her eyes, but instead she held the woman's gaze for a second and something shifted between them.

"What's this Pickersgill place I keep hearing about?" Mama glanced at Josephine in the mirror again.

"Raylene and Ray, they move around quite a bit. Pickersgill used to be a sweet spot for them. Lord knows why. It's nothing but abandoned railroad tracks and cottonmouths."

Josephine frowned at the description. Cottonmouths were snakes, *poisonous* snakes.

"Raylene and Ray?" Mama asked.

"My ex and his *lovely* mother."

Josephine could tell by the way she'd said *lovely* Raylene was anything but.

The light turned red again.

"He wanted to name Molly 'Ray Raylene' when she was born. It was the one time I put my foot down. That man could charm a bird out of its wings. And there's hell to pay if you don't agree with him."

"Hell to pay?" Mama asked.

"Ray is the kind of mean that leaves no bruises, not that you can see. The master of insidious evil. I told Molly a hundred times never to get in the car with him, especially if I wasn't around. Their visits were to be supervised. Who knows what sort of story Ray told her."

"What do you mean *story*?" Josephine asked.

Helen-Dove turned to look at her again. "The lie kind of story. The your-mother's-decided-she'd-rather-you-live-with-me kind of story. Or..." She stopped talking for a second, then added, "Or, the your-mother-is-dead kind of story."

A rush of cold air whooshed through Josephine.

They don't love me, not really. Molly wasn't talking about friends from school. She was talking about her father. And grandmother.

"That's his brand of mean," Helen-Dove said, and turned around again.

They were nearing the Cameron Mills factory, and on the roadside marquee were the words RIP Buster Lee Green. We miss you at the Mill!

Happy World Trailer Park—*Dandiest little place on earth!* was nothing but tragedies. One right after the other. It was like a junkyard, but instead of wrecked cars, there were wrecked people.

"You can let me out on the edge of the highway. I'll walk the rest of the way," Helen-Dove said, but Mama flicked on her blinker and drove up to the large double doors where other smock-wearing folks were headed inside.

"That sign about Buster Lee makes it real, doesn't it?" Helen-Dove remarked. "What a good soul he was." She pushed open the door. "Thank you for the ride," she said, then glanced back at Josephine. "And thank you, Josephine."

"Me?"

The corners of her grim Mona Lisa mouth lifted ever so slightly. "For caring," she said.

Flights of Fancy

That man could charm a bird out of its wings. This is what Josephine was thinking as Mama pulled into a parking space in front of Flights of Fancy, a pink storefront with a black and white striped awning. A sign was painted to look like a tangle of flowers, and on either side of the door were two giant urns with petunias so pink they hurt Josephine's eyes.

"What's this place again?" Josephine asked.

Mama switched off the ignition and dug through her purse to find her compact. She tilted the rearview mirror. "A new boutique. Like I told you." She patted her face with the powder puff.

Normally, Josephine would've been excited to go inside such a fancy store, but her brain was far away on this tragic morning. *Find Molly Quiver,* she ordered herself. *Bring her home. Have a best friend.*

But what if Molly Quiver wasn't interested in being best friends? What if she didn't like Josephine the same way Delia and Kitty hadn't liked her?

Mama closed the compact with a snap and dropped it into

her purse. "The owner wants privacy curtains for the dressing rooms, but that front window could use some dressing."

"What about Helen-Dove?" Josephine asked.

"I agree, it's upsetting, Jo, but Helen-Dove went to work this morning. We're working people. It's what we must do."

"It's what we must do," Josephine repeated. *It's what I must do.*

"When Helen-Dove gets home, we'll talk about what she needs, okay?"

Josephine nodded. A Jawbreaker-sized lump had lodged in her throat. Working people didn't take time off. They worked and slept and ate and worked some more. There was no time for sick folks or missing children.

On the heels of this realization, Josephine felt another one coming on: She would go searching for Molly Quiver. She would find her. And if they didn't become friends . . . knowing Molly was found would be enough.

⊂⇒

Bells jangled over their heads as they stepped inside Flights of Fancy. The place smelled so strongly of perfume it made Josephine sneeze a big, slobbery sneeze.

"Goodness, Jo, cover your face," Mama said, and opened her purse. She handed Josephine a tissue.

"That's a used one!" Josephine protested.

"It's not used. It's crumpled. Now hush, I mean it." Mama pressed a finger to her lips.

"Good day! Welcome to Flights of Fancy," the woman said. She came from the back of the store and walked toward them in a great sweeping motion—head high, arms swinging. Her chin was long and pointy. Her body was long and pointy.

In fact, Josephine thought she looked like an extremely tall arrow.

"I'm Chrissy Love," the woman said.

Chrissy Love wore a shiny black pantsuit and shiny black shoes and a crisp white shirt with a necktie. She was dressed like a man except she slung her long hair in Cher-like fashion.

"I'm Penny Willoughby," Mama said, "and this is my daughter—"

Josephine let out another enormous sneeze. Like the previous one, it'd snuck up on her and, unfortunately, landed all over Chrissy Love.

Mama stared at her in horror.

"Sorry," Josephine said, and wiped her nose with the tissue.

"Well, *that* should fortify my immune system for a while. Come along with me, darling. I have a place designed especially for children." Chrissy Love made a motion for Josephine to follow.

There was a cluttered storage room with naked mannequins and cardboard boxes and a small office with a giant lamp shaped like a woman's leg, with a stocking and a high heel and everything.

"You'll have a marvelous time in the fresh air," Chrissy said, and pushed open a door. Josephine stepped out into what appeared to be the backstage of downtown—cinder block walls and gray gravel and a giant dumpster. "Your mother and I will finish in a bit," Chrissy said, then shut the door firmly.

There was a tiny metal table and tiny metal chairs and a tiny square sandbox with a faded canopy over top. Chrissy Love's "place designed especially for children" was terrible. On any other day, Josephine would've been horrified, but this morning she was grateful.

Josephine glanced at the Tiger Paws and thought of the long journey ahead. Miles and miles on a bus. More miles on foot. A jolt of fear shot through her, and another feeling came along behind it. A mix of calm and sad. She thought of Buster Lee's fist in the air and the way he'd smiled with only half his face. Josephine knew she should be with Lisa Marie in her hour of need. She wanted to hold her dirty hand, but that wasn't possible. She could not be two places at once.

"When I get back from Pickersgill, I'll make it up to you."

If you get back from Pickersgill, replied a doomy voice inside her head.

The journey of a thousand miles begins with just one step. Miss Lake sometimes said this when Josephine talked about wanting to be a famous writer. She'd never understood what walking had to do with writing, but now she did.

You started. You kept going.

Departure

In just a few brisk steps, Josephine was standing on the stage part of downtown again. It was a lively scene, with cars and people and lampposts and parking meters. To her left was Pearl's Good Eating Place, and to her right, like a miraculous beacon, was the Glendale bus station.

Josephine began to walk faster. For fear her courage would leave her, she ran. Much too quickly she darted across the busy street, and a driver blared his horn. *"Heeeeyyy you!"* he hollered out the window.

Still, Josephine kept going until she found herself in the bus loop. She stopped to catch her breath and stared up at a giant Greyhound. MIAMI, said the sign in its window.

⇨

It was dimmer inside the building, and though the windows were massive, their panes were strangely opaque. There were long wooden benches and vending machines and pay phones with bifold doors for privacy. People checked large signs for arrival and departure times. Something told Josephine to blend in, to behave as though she'd taken a bus by herself dozens of times.

Over the loudspeaker came a man's grumpy-sounding voice. "Bus 117, bound for Miami, leaves in ten minutes," he said, and the speaker clicked off again.

Josephine waited. Maybe his next call would be for Mobile, Alabama, but a few seconds later, when the loudspeaker crackled to life, he only said, "Ethel Tull to lost and found."

Josephine wandered over to the departures sign and gazed up. Plain as day she saw it: MOBILE, ALABAMA—DEPARTURE TIME—11:55 AM.

In the middle of the station was a round booth encased in glass. Josephine realized then that the grumpy-sounding man sat inside the booth. He was dressed in a light blue uniform. People walked up to the booth and came away holding tickets.

Maybe ten dollars wasn't enough money, after all. Maybe almost-eleven-year-olds weren't permitted to purchase tickets. She hadn't thought to ask this when she called from the IGA pay phone, but there was only one way to find out.

For what seemed a very long while, she stood, waiting. Finally, she knocked on the glass, and the window slid open.

"Yeah?" he said, frowning down at her.

Putting on her most pleasant face, Josephine smiled at him.

"What do you want?"

Josephine tried to think how to say it.

He moved abruptly to shut the window.

"Wait!" she said. "I have to get to Pickersgill, Alabama." The man had a lot of chins, and his nose was dotted with beads of sweat. "It's in the sandwich part of Alabama. The part between Mississippi and Florida."

"Gulf Coast," he said. He slipped on a pair of black glasses and swiveled his chair. A giant map hung on the wall near his desk, and he traced his fingers along its surface. "Line goes far as Mobile."

Josephine nodded. "How far is it from there?"

"Mobile to Pickersgill?"

"Yes, sir."

He studied the map again. "Looks to be about thirty miles."

A knife of scared sliced through her. She'd never walked anything close to thirty miles. "I need a ticket," she heard herself say.

The man gave her another hard look. "Round-trip or one-way?"

She'd heard what the man said when she called from the IGA. Round-trip was twenty dollars. "One-way," she replied.

He swiped the sweat from his nose on his shirt sleeve and stared at her.

It was coming, the question about her age, the question that would bring her plan to a screeching halt.

"How old are you?" he said.

"The ticket's not for me. It's for my mother." There was her answer.

The man yanked off his glasses and scowled.

"It's *for* my mother," she said again, firmly this time.

He shoved the glasses back on his face and scanned the room, looking for a woman who might be Josephine's mother.

"She doesn't have time to buy her own ticket. She's working today, over at Chrissy Love's Flights of Fancy. I'm her errand girl."

He glanced toward the ceiling and let out a sigh. "Departure date?"

"The sign over there said 11:55 a.m."

"Your mama wants to leave today?"

Josephine nodded.

"You going with her?"

Josephine shook her head. "She has business in Alabama. *Important* business."

Without a word he punched something into a machine, and it spat out a ticket. "That'll be $9.95," he said.

Josephine slipped off her shoe and pulled out the ten-dollar bill. It was slightly damp on account of her warm foot. She unfolded it and smoothed it out and placed it on the counter.

$$\Longrightarrow$$

Eleven-fifty-five was time enough to chicken out. Two whole hours. Two whole hours was time enough for second thoughts and third ones and so on. Two whole hours was time enough for the ticket guy to see Josephine waiting around the bus station. Soon, he would figure out what was what. Maybe he'd even call the police.

Josephine took a drink of water from the fountain, then went out into the hot summer sunshine to find a bench.

At least she was dressed cute today. Cuteness always helped with stressful situations. Instead of a church dress, she'd worn a blue scooter skirt and a sleeveless cotton top with a Holly Hobby appliqué. The Tiger Paws were good and broken in now, comfortable for walking, but still nice looking.

Look sharp, feel sharp. Miss Augustine said this sometimes, and Josephine felt a sudden tug of missing the woman. And she missed old Lucas, too. *Don't think about them,* she told herself.

Her thoughts turned to Happy World. Lisa Marie was

picking out a casket for Buster Lee today, and he'd be stuck in that thing for all eternity, his body at least. This thought gave her the heebie-jeebies.

Tired of so much thinking, Josephine studied the bench she sat on. The green paint was rubbed off in some places, and people had written things: *Call 615-749*-scribble-scribble-scribble-scribble *for a good time.* "How's anybody supposed to know what number to call if you scratch it out?" she whispered.

$\Longrightarrow$

Josephine was getting bored. And restless. Her Tiger Paws itched to move. She wanted the bus to *leave*.

But there was a higher purpose in her discomfort. Brother Davis was always talking about higher purposes. Somewhere on the other end of Josephine's long bus ride and walk was Molly Quiver.

I'm coming for you! Josephine pushed this message out into the universe, which was when she heard the sound of someone calling.

"Josephine! Jo-se-*phine!*"

Lucas' blue van sat in the loop. Josephine would've recognized that van anyplace on account of the big yellow letters and buzzing bee. And then Josephine saw something else that surprised her. It was Miss Augustine in a polka-dot dress, and she was running fast toward Josephine.

She swept Josephine into her arms and said, "Oh thank you, Jesus!" The hug was soft and a little sweaty. "Where have you been? Where have you *been?*" She let go of Josephine and gave her a serious stare. "Your poor mother is searching high and low for you! You scared us to death!"

Miss Augustine's cheeks were red and her eyes were red, and Josephine could tell she'd been crying. She opened her mouth, but no words came out because she couldn't tell Miss Augustine the truth and she couldn't tell Miss Augustine any lies, either.

Lucas honked the horn and hollered out the window. "Y'all come on! I'm blocking traffic."

Behind him was a Greyhound bus, and in its window was a sign that said MOBILE.

38

A Polaroid Picture

On Saturday morning, in the quiet of her bedroom, Josephine dressed for the funeral, then went to stand at the bathroom door to watch while Mama did her routine.

Josephine liked all the makeup faces. There was the eyelash-curler face and the mascara face and the rouge face.

Mama leaned in close to the mirror and smeared on lipstick. "Are you prepared for today?" she asked when she was finished.

"Delia's grandmother died last year, and she looked like something out of *Daughters of Satan*. That's what Delia said."

"*Daughters of Satan*?" Mama looked skeptical.

"A horror movie. Randy took her."

Mama shook her head disapprovingly. "The casket will be closed. You won't see any dead bodies. Hold your breath." She sprayed Aqua Net on her hair, then fanned away the fumes.

"Why do people even have funerals? It's so creepy. A dead person in a box?" Josephine shuddered at the thought.

"It's a way of honoring a person's life. It shows the family that people care." Mama poufed the sides of her hair, then sprayed more Aqua Net.

Josephine thought about Buster Lee's vacant room. The *Farmers' Almanac* calendar on the wall, stopped at last November; his neatly folded clothes; the cluster of amber-colored pill bottles. "What happens after the funeral?"

"We're gathering at the Greens' trailer for a potluck." She put the cap on the hair spray, then folded her arms. "I still can't believe what you did yesterday, Jo. Don't ever do anything like that again. Do you hear me?"

"I was only gone for an hour."

"Closer to two hours," Mama corrected, "and it felt like two days. I mean it, Jo."

"The whole town was looking for me. Molly's been gone nearly a year and—"

"This is a day to honor Buster Lee."

"I can think about Molly, too. You can't control my thoughts."

Mama sighed. "You're right about that. You look very pretty today, Jo." Mama bent to smooth out the fabric. "This material was a good find. Try not to get anything on your dress, hear?"

Josephine glanced down at the coral-colored fabric, a lightweight cotton with pastel butterflies printed on it. The cut was Josephine's favorite—a princess cut, they called it. Sewn into the side seams was a smart-looking tie belt. In spite of the fact that the Tiger Paws didn't match, Josephine decided to wear them anyway.

"Maybe this afternoon you and Lisa Marie could set up the Slip 'N' Slide. *If* she's feeling up to it. Now run tell Helen-Dove we're about ready to go."

⇒

As Josephine made her way to number 7, she couldn't help but think where she might be today if she'd gotten on that bus bound for Mobile.

Just yesterday, Molly Quiver had felt closer, like Josephine was getting warmer in a game of hot and cold. Now the girl seemed as far away as Patricia Hearst. Even with the entire country looking for the missing heiress, nobody had found her yet, either.

Josephine raced up the porch steps to number 7, knocked lightly on the door, and waited. She glanced around at the sad state of things. The heart-shaped wreath was sun-faded. The geranium was down to its last bloom, and even that one was nearly dead. She put her ear to the door and listened, but everything was quiet.

She knocked, harder this time.

Mama's ole blue car started up, and she stuck her head out the window. "What's the matter, Jo?"

"She's not home."

Mama got out of the car and knocked for herself, but Helen-Dove wasn't home.

"It's unlocked," Josephine said without thinking. Guilt crept into Josephine's cheeks. "I mean," she backpedaled, "I'm just guessing. If I had a kidnapped daughter, I'd never lock my door. What if Molly came back and—"

"I get the picture, Jo." Mama put her hands on her hips and glanced around. "Maybe she rode with the Greens. It's too far for walking. We're all liable to have a heatstroke in this weather. Come on," Mama said, and they got in the car again.

They were nearly to the Happy World entrance when they spotted Helen-Dove down by the mailboxes. She was dressed in the usual drab work slacks, but instead of her smock, she wore a white sleeveless blouse. Even from a distance, Josephine could see she'd stitched flowers down the front of it.

Helen-Dove stood so still she resembled a statue. "Why's she standing in the road?" Josephine asked.

"Goodness," Mama said, and shoved the gearshift into Park. She hurried out of the car and down the path, stumbling slightly in her green wedge heels.

A dust cloud rose in the distance and there was a loud grinding of gears. Josephine pushed her way out of the car and shouted, "Y'all get out of the road!" Helplessly she watched as Mama pulled Helen-Dove to safety and a janky pickup rattled on past, leaving in its wake a thick plume of dust.

Judging by her tragic expression, bad news had come by way of the mail truck. Josephine crossed her fingers and walked slowly toward them.

"Are you sure it's her?" Mama had lifted her sunglasses and was studying something clutched in Helen-Dove's rough fingers. A tattered envelope and a Polaroid picture, Josephine saw on closer inspection.

The girl in the photo wore a ratty-looking striped sweater, its neck stretched out and misshapen. Her pants were baggy, and her hair was an odd shade of not-quite-red-and-not-quite-brown. It hadn't been brushed. *Or* washed. On her tiny face was a pair of tinted glasses.

"They've ruined her beautiful hair. She hardly looks like my child."

"What's it say there?" Mama pointed to smudgy black ink at the bottom of the photo.

Helen-Dove squinted. "I can't read it."

"Look at the postmark. Where's it from?" Mama instructed.

Helen-Dove turned the envelope over. "Mobile."

There was no return address, Josephine noticed. And Helen-Dove's name seemed off somehow. The *D* in *Dove* was bold. Someone had gone over it several times with ink.

"It's one of her awful tricks," Helen-Dove said.

"Tricks?" Mama asked.

"Raylene. She's the devil, that woman. She loves to send something, give me signs, get me hopeful, but then—" She shook her head. "They'll disappear, run off someplace else. Probably they're long gone by now. That's what she wants. Me to go looking someplace they've already left."

"But why?" Mama asked.

"A game of cat and mouse. Have me go chasing after them, wasting time and money to no avail." Helen-Dove's thin face was creased with anguish. "What makes people act so awful?"

Josephine was studying the envelope as if it were a treasure map. Above the *i* in *Quiver* was the tiniest of stars, hardly visible, yet it seemed to be winking at her. "She's trying to save herself," Josephine said.

Helen-Dove was shaking her head, and Mama was chewing on the end of her sunglasses, both of them lost in thought.

"It's Molly," Josephine said, more forcefully this time. "It's not that Raylene person. Molly's trying to save herself." Josephine had no idea how she knew this, just that the words tumbled out of her mouth like dice on a game board, haphazard and by chance.

Mama and Helen-Dove were staring at her now.

Josephine poked the tiny star. "This means something. I don't know what, but it has a purpose."

Mama and Helen-Dove exchanged one of those annoying looks between adults.

"This is exactly what I mean about Raylene," Helen-Dove said. "This is the reaction she wants."

"No," Josephine said. "It's Molly, not that grandmother person. We have to go." Josephine felt desperate. "I'm serious, we have to leave right now! We can't go to the funeral. We don't have time!" she insisted.

"*You* are not going anywhere," Mama said firmly.

Josephine narrowed her eyes, first at Mama, then at Helen-Dove.

"That's enough, Jo," Mama said.

Josephine tugged the envelope and photo from Helen-Dove's grip. "Look at it," she pleaded. "The star, it's a sign! A code. Molly does those. Codes, I mean." She held up the photo. "She's almost eleven. I'm eleven, almost, and I would try to save myself. Molly looks like the type of girl who would try, too. I bet she's smart. I bet she's capable."

Helen-Dove was frowning and tilting her head in a way that seemed to indicate something fuzzy was coming into focus.

Josephine held up the envelope and pointed to the address. "See the *D* in *Dove*? It's bold." Josephine was figuring things out as she went. "And the *r* in *Quiver*. It's a pattern. The *a* in *Happy* is fancy, but the rest of the *a*'s, in *Trailer* and *Park* and *Glendale*, they're plain old circles with tails."

*Helen-**D**ove Quive**r***
Happy World Trailer Park
Number Seven
Glendale, Tennessee 38401

"D-r-a-g-n-o. Or...D-r-a-g-n-zero..." Josephine tried sounding out the letters, but they made no sense.

There was the distant coo of a mourning dove, and the *vroom* of a truck out on the main highway. Josephine's eyes stayed locked on Helen-Dove's, and she saw it then, a flicker of recognition.

"Dragon!" they said at the exact same time.

Josephine's heart quickened, and there was a roaring in her ears. "It's her. It's Molly, I know it."

Helen-Dove seemed alive suddenly, like she'd gone from half-asleep to wide-awake. "It's a story I made up," she said. "I used to tell it to Molly when she was little. The dragon breathed stars instead of fire."

Josephine looked at Mama, who seemed unconvinced. "It's her," Josephine said firmly.

Mama checked her Timex. "Let's get on to Buster Lee's service. After it's over we'll put our heads together and come up with a plan." She slid the sunglasses onto her face again.

Helen-Dove did a most unexpected thing then. She hooked her arm through Josephine's, and like that they walked back to the ole blue car.

39

Pretty Please

After the service Mama and Helen-Dove and Josephine headed over to number 17, along with everybody else from Happy World—Hog and Joella and Jewel and Rufus Mooningham and Zeus and Mercedes. Bowls and Pyrex dishes and Tupperware containers lined the narrow kitchen counter: fried chicken and fried okra and macaroni salad and stewed potatoes and pinto beans and corn bread and chess pie and a Jell-O ring with peaches trapped inside, plus tea to drink.

Granddaddy had the air conditioner cranked up, so even though it was crowded in the trailer, everybody had cooled off, which was a good thing since they'd stood so long in the scorching heat. News played on the TV, but it was turned down low. Even with only the pictures, Josephine knew Walter Cronkite was talking about Watergate and Richard Nixon and Vietnam. Patricia Hearst's father was offering a fifty-thousand-dollar reward for her rescue!

"Want to Slip 'N' Slide?" Josephine asked Lisa Marie, who was pushing everything around on her paper plate.

Lisa Marie shook her head.

"There's a Spin Art under my bed. We could do that, except the paint might be dried up now."

Lisa Marie didn't answer. She just got up and put her plate in the trash can and left Josephine sitting in a room crowded with grown-ups. Josephine was dying to talk about Molly, but everyone was telling stories about Buster Lee.

Eventually, it was Helen-Dove who changed the subject. "I have to do something about Molly, and I have to do it quickly," she said, and the room went quiet. "There was an envelope in the mail this morning, and it makes me think she might be in Alabama, near Mobile."

"You can borrow my truck," Granddaddy offered. "I'd take you myself, but I can't miss another day's work."

"I'm too jittery for driving," Helen-Dove said. "Besides that, I let my license expire. Couldn't afford to renew it. Without a car, there didn't seem to be any need..." Her voice trailed off.

"We could take my van," said Zeus, combing his long beard with his thin fingers. He looked at Mercedes, and she gave her beach-ball belly a pat.

Jewel and Rufus Mooningham talked with their hands, then Rufus tugged a twenty-dollar bill from his wallet and held it out for Helen-Dove to take.

"I can't accept your hard-earned money. And you can't go anywhere, Zeus, not with Mercedes about to deliver any second, but I appreciate the generosity."

Josephine was practically boring a hole through Mama, but Mama was just sitting there, wringing her hands and not offering to help like she'd promised.

"Well, between the lot of us we ought to be able to figure something out," Hog said. "Me and Joella's fixin' to take a road trip down that way with our motorcycle club, if that helps any." Hog pointed to a patch on his leather vest that said TOOTSIE ROLLERS. "We could do some checkin' on your behalf."

"Have the authorities been alerted about this latest development?" Zeus asked. "Was there a postmark on the envelope? Have you called Officer Frye yet?"

"One question at a time, honey," Mercedes scolded gently.

Helen-Dove shifted in her chair. She set her glass of tea on the floor beside her. "Officer Frye doesn't know anything about this. He relocated."

"Relocated?" Joella asked.

"To Washington, D.C."

"Aw, naw," Hog said. "For good?"

"He was accepted to Howard University. He's getting his degree in political science."

"Why, he's a good fella," Granddaddy said. "Don't seem like the type for politics."

"That's why he wants to study political science. Thinks maybe he can right some wrongs."

"Rock on," Zeus said approvingly.

Helen-Dove extended the Polaroid, and one by one the Happy World residents shook their heads and clucked their tongues at the dramatic change in Molly.

"Bet you a nickel they got one'a them police scanners," Hog said. "You catch wind of a lotta things 'atta way. Any blip of nonsense and you'll hear somebody mouthin' off about it. It's entertainin' if you ain't got nothin' better to do."

At this Joella rolled her eyes. "There's always something better to do," she said firmly.

The picture made its way around to Josephine, and she stared at Molly's face. This was not the same girl as the one in the frame on Helen-Dove's TV. Everything about her looked different. Josephine tried to imagine what it must've taken for Molly to sneak this picture and mail it.

She glanced around the room—IGA sacks for curtains, a sofa with stuffing coming out of the arms, flimsy paper plates instead of real dishes. Taped to the brown paneling were the pages of an old calendar, pictures of tractors mostly.

A shameful memory crept into Josephine's brain. Last summer. Sitting in the way-back seat of Mrs. Collingsworth's station wagon, a seat that faced backwards instead of forwards. The smell of Necco wafers and suntan lotion. They'd stopped for gas, and parked at the pump behind them was a clunker of a car. It rattled and sputtered and stank of burning oil.

"Uck, poor people," Delia said casually, and dropped another Necco wafer onto her tongue. "They're like a disease or something."

A man was struggling to get the hood open, and a woman sat in the front seat looking hot and forlorn, a small girl on her lap.

"Get a job," Delia said, and then burst into a fit of laughter. She jabbed Josephine to join in.

Josephine hesitated. As always, she felt the sharp divide between Delia and herself. A real house versus a rented apartment. Store-bought clothes versus homemade ones.

Josephine had almost taken the high road, but with the second jab, slightly more painful than the first, she'd echoed Delia's words loud enough for the man to hear. "Yeah. Get a job!"

Now Josephine was sitting on the worn linoleum floor of number 17, studying the residents of Happy World.

Every single person in the room had a job. The people in that clunker car probably had jobs, too. Worked harder than Delia's dad, Josephine would guess. Delia said all he did was smoke cigars and prop his feet on a polished desk at some downtown office.

Delia's mother's only job was getting her hair fixed twice a week and leaving long lists for the cleaning lady.

Josephine got to her feet and smoothed out her dress. She raised her hand because she couldn't think how else to get everyone's attention. One by one the Happy World heads swiveled in her direction. "I need to say something," she began. "And what I need to say is..." She glanced at Mama, whose eyes had a pained look. "We'll take you to Mobile, Alabama."

This was the time for Mama to chime in with *Of course we're happy to drive you*, but the trailer was bloated with an uncomfortable silence.

"I know you're busy with your work," Helen-Dove said. "I understand that pressure. I can see why none of y'all would want to get mixed up in this mess. Could be a ruse."

Mama studied the crocheted ring on her finger. Mercedes shifted on the sagging sofa, and beneath her a spring groaned. Ever so gently Hog tapped the floor with his motorcycle boot until Joella touched his leg, a sign for him to stop.

"Maybe it's not a ruse," said Mama finally. "Maybe there's something to that dragon business."

Lisa Marie appeared in the doorway then. She'd changed out of the frilly white dress and into her usual cutoffs and Dr Pepper T-shirt with the Popsicle stains. Her mouth was pulling down sad, and her eyes were puffy and red. "What dragon business?" she asked.

Mama glanced at Josephine. "Turns out I have some time

on my hands. I won't be doing the job at Flights of Fancy after all."

"I'm coming with you!" Josephine said.

Mama frowned. "Of course you're coming. I don't intend to let you out of my sight!"

Granddaddy cleared his throat. "Well, I reckon if y'all are gonna do this, you better let me get another look-see under that hood. Check the tires, too. Probably want to replace that belt I jerry-rigged. When's the last time you had a oil change?"

"Six months ago. Or so," Mama said.

"Well, it won't cost you nothin'," Granddaddy assured her. "Consider it my contribution to a good cause."

Rufus Mooningham took out that twenty-dollar bill again. He said something with his hands, and then offered the money to Helen-Dove. This time she took it. "Thank you," she said, and made a sign with her hands, too. Both Rufus and Jewel smiled, maybe because having somebody talk to them in their own hand language made them happy.

"So, it's settled?" Mama asked.

Josephine's brain was giving her that tugging feeling again, like she'd forgotten something. "Can Lisa Marie come?"

"Where y'all fixing to go?" Lisa Marie asked.

"It's fine with me if she comes." Mama was looking at Granddaddy now, waiting on his reply. "It'll give Josephine some company for the long car ride."

"They're gonna take Miss Helen down to the shores of Alabama, see if maybe they can find Little Bit and bring her home. You want to go with them, shug?"

Lisa Marie hitched her bony shoulders. "Who's gonna be here with you?"

"I'll look after myself. I b'lieve it might do you good to get away from here. Give me a chance to get caught up at Swan's farm." Swan's farm was where Granddaddy worked, and Josephine had seen him lots of nights coming home hot and dirty and plumb wore out.

Josephine ran to where Lisa Marie stood. She got down on her knees and squeezed Lisa Marie's hands. "You're my very best friend and you've got to come! Pretty please with sugar on top!"

40

Swisher Sweets

By the time Mama's car was up to snuff for the drive—the old belt replaced by a new one that had to be ordered and took days to come in—and Mama and Helen-Dove had studied maps to decide exactly where they were going, a whole week had dragged by.

Josephine was beginning to think they might never set out on their trip, but finally, the departure date arrived. She could hardly believe it. After all this time, all the long, hot nights staring out her window, exhausting her brain trying to figure out where Molly Quiver might be, Josephine was about to find out.

Hopefully.

That morning, Josephine woke up before the sun and peeked out from behind the thin curtain. Birds stirred. The needles on the pine trees made swishing sounds. Josephine loved it when the trees made swishing sounds. She checked her suitcase again. It was neatly packed with scooter skirts and cute tops. Her yellow pajamas were in there, too, and a bathing suit, plus hair bobbles in lots of colors.

The previous night Mama put some things in a bag to keep

Josephine and Lisa Marie occupied during the long car ride—the potholder weaving kit, playing cards, a Baby Tender Love coloring book, plus a big box of sixty-four Crayola crayons with a built-in sharpener. There were pipe cleaners in the bag, too, because Mama always said you could have a lot of fun with pipe cleaners, *if* you used your imagination. And, of course, she would bring her yellow spiral notebook.

Josephine put on her navy scooter skirt with the strawberry appliqué and a cute white top with piping around the collar, then went to fix herself breakfast.

She was eating Rice Krispies when she heard a sound that was *not* snap-crackle-pop. "What was that?" Josephine whispered. She put down her spoon and went to the door to open it the tiniest crack.

"Ahhh-*grrr*-ha-aaa!"

Josephine frowned.

"Ahhhgrhaaaa-ahhh-grrr-haaaa-eeek-ahhhgrhaaaa!"

Bob Barker? she wondered. Sometimes the old cat made sounds like a baby crying. Josephine waited. Josephine listened. Josephine prayed there wasn't some new catastrophe about to befall the residents of Happy World. A kidnapping and a death were more than enough to handle.

And then...

"Ahhh-gr-haaaa!" and "Help *meeee*! Somebody help *meeeee*!"

"Definitely not Bob Barker," she said, and slammed the door. Lickety-split, Josephine shot through the trailer to the back room where Mama was still asleep. She pounced on the pull-out couch, shook Mama hard, and said, "Wake up!"

Mama blinked and rubbed her eyes. "What is it, Jo?"

"Somebody's hollering! The bad kind of hollering! Not somebody playing around."

Mama yawned and stretched and hoisted herself off the couch. She tugged on her duster and slid her feet into fuzzy pink slippers.

Josephine grabbed Mama's hand and dragged her to the living room. "Listen," she said, and opened the front door, but there were only the pleasant morning sounds of *cheep-cheep-cheep* and *tweet-tweet-tweet*.

"Those are just birds, Jo. Go back to bed. It's still early."

Josephine held tight to Mama's arm. "Wait," she said. "*Listen.*"

Mama was in the middle of a yawn when there was another ghastly howl. "Goodness!" she said, looking wide-awake.

"Somebody's fixing to die out there!" Josephine said.

Mama shut the door and leaned against it. She gave Josephine an *I haven't had my coffee yet* smile.

"*Why* are you smiling?" Josephine put her hands on her hips.

"It's Mercedes, Jo. Those sounds mean she's in labor."

Josephine had heard all manner of terrible things about babies being born. Delia used to talk about such gross stuff at recess until Miss Lake told her that was not appropriate conversation for the classroom *or* the playground.

"Zeus and Mercedes wanted to have their baby at home," Mama went on. "I think it's very interesting. Do you have any questions?"

"Definitely not," Josephine replied. She and Mama had already had that talk once before, and Josephine didn't intend to have it again. "Mercedes ought to get herself to a hospital. Maybe they can give her an aspirin."

Mama laughed. "I suspect it's too late for the hospital. And an aspirin wouldn't begin to touch that kind of pain."

Josephine clamped her hands over her ears. "I don't want to know anything else!"

"Fine." Mama smiled and went to put on a pot of coffee.

Josephine poured some fresh Rice Krispies over top of the now-soggy ones and switched on the radio.

Mama lowered the volume and said, "I don't know about this trip, Jo. I couldn't get to sleep last night for worrying about it." She leaned against the counter and took a sip of coffee.

"We made a promise," Josephine said firmly.

"I know, but my number one job is to make sure you're safe."

"It's Helen-Dove's number one job to make sure Molly comes home."

Mama tilted her head. "So, we're really doing this?"

Josephine swallowed a clump of cereal. "Yep," she said just as there was a knock at the door. "I'll get it," Josephine said, and slid off the chair.

Mama headed down the hallway to get dressed, and Josephine opened the door.

"Hidy!" Lisa Marie pushed her way into the room. She was wearing her new blue bathing suit and floppy hat. "Granddaddy went to gas up y'all's car right quick." She dropped a paper sack on the floor. "Look what-all I brung," she said, and pulled everything out.

Josephine took inventory: ragged cutoffs, stained Dr Pepper T-shirt, holey creek shoes, ripped underwear, fluffy white dress, and one of Buster Lee's undershirts.

"What about a toothbrush?" Josephine asked.

"I can just use my finger," Lisa Marie said. She wadded up her clothes and stuffed them into the sack again.

The things in Josephine's suitcase were freshly washed and ironed and folded neatly so nothing wrinkled. Her panties, a brand-new pack Mama had picked up at Rose's Discount, were discreetly tucked in the side pouch so they didn't accidentally fall out and embarrass her to death. The toothbrush and toothpaste had a special case so as not to leak all over her outfits, and the travel-sized matching hairbrush and comb set were sealed in a plastic bag so they wouldn't snag her clothes.

Mama had done these things for Josephine, and whenever they got to where they were going, she would open the suitcase and her clothes would be crisp and smart looking. She couldn't imagine wearing Lisa Marie's wadded-up mess in public. Also, she couldn't imagine being seen with someone wearing that wadded-up mess.

"Cat got your tongue this morning?" Lisa Marie said. Her whole face beamed with what Josephine could see was real excitement.

It would be awful not to have a mother, Josephine thought just as Mama came into the room.

"What do you think, girls? I made these culottes out of an old skirt." The culottes were bright orange, and Mama wore a matching sleeveless blouse. Her hair was tied with a colorful scarf, and dangling from her earlobes were the tiniest turquoise butterflies.

"I think you're the prettiest lady I ever seen," Lisa Marie said.

"Me too," Josephine agreed.

"Hey! Mercedes had her a baby boy," Lisa Marie announced, "and I'uz the first person to see him. Other than some old woman in there bossing everybody around."

"What about Zeus?" Mama asked.

"Aw, he was sitting on the floor with his head between his knees."

Mama looked concerned.

"He's fine. He only passed out once," Lisa Marie explained.

"Are you sure it's a boy?" Josephine had been hoping for a girl.

Lisa Marie nodded. "He ain't big as nothin'."

"The midwife let you in the room?" Mama asked.

"Naw. I'uz peekin' in the windows. I ain't never having a baby. No way!" She grinned her gap-toothed grin, and suddenly Josephine didn't care what Lisa Marie wore on their trip. She was just glad to have her company.

$$\Longrightarrow$$

By nine o'clock Mama, Helen-Dove, Lisa Marie, and Josephine were pulling down the washed-out path in the ole blue car, which had some new parts inside it now. Granddaddy and Zeus were smoking cigars outside number 15.

Mama stopped to say congratulations, and Josephine stuck her head out the car window. "What's his name?" she called.

"Zephyr." Zeus smiled proudly. "It means gentle breeze."

"Can I hold him when we get back?" Josephine asked.

"Of course!" Zeus said.

Granddaddy slapped Zeus on the back, and said, "Ain't nothin' in this world better than a new baby!"

A washing of striped bed sheets flapped on the line. The summer air was filled with the scent of Swisher Sweets cigars.

And for once Happy World Trailer Park really did seem like the dandiest place on earth.

Getting There

Mama wasn't kidding when she said it was a long way to the sandwich part of Alabama. It was a *super*-long way, but Josephine and Lisa Marie were good at occupying themselves. They dressed Josephine's Barbies in cute outfits, and sang to the radio—a little bit of country and some rock 'n' roll. "Band on the Run," which Josephine loved, and "Lucy in the Sky with Diamonds."

When Dolly Parton came on, Lisa Marie sang "Jolene" all by herself. Helen-Dove clapped and shouted, *"Bravo!"* and Lisa Marie got red in the face and grinned from ear to ear.

For lunch, they stopped at the Camellia Roadside Park, a sliver of grass with a weathered placard declaring its name. There were two picnic tables, but there wasn't another traveler in sight, save for a hopeful crow perched on the rim of a garbage can.

All was quiet as they ate the bologna sandwiches Helen-Dove had brought along and Ruffles potato chips and grape Nehi drinks, which were good and cold because they'd been packed on ice.

Yesterday, Miss Augustine and Lucas had delivered a Tupperware container filled with Miss Augustine's world-famous tea cakes, sugary cookies with hard chocolate frosting on top. "For your road trip," Miss Augustine said, and opened the container to show them. Circles of sweet-smelling goodness were neatly layered on waxed paper.

Lucas had pulled Josephine aside and pushed a twenty-dollar bill into her palm. "Your mama won't take this. She's too stubborn, but you take it, hear? In case of an emergency," he said.

It was a hot day, but not unbearably so, and Josephine and Lisa Marie sat elbow-to-elbow. Josephine was glad for Lisa Marie's presence, and it didn't bother her, not even a little, that Lisa Marie was dressed in nothing but her new bathing suit and the floppy hat and her bare feet.

Maybe it was the tea cakes and the company. Or the hope that Molly Quiver might soon be found. Whatever it was, Josephine knew what Lucas meant when he'd said there was sweetness in this life. She saw signs of it everywhere. The flowers stitched on Helen-Dove's blouse and the brightly colored scarf tied around Mama's shiny hair. The way Lisa Marie's big, floppy hat kept brushing against Josephine's cheek.

Sweetest of all was the picture in Josephine's imagination: Molly Quiver joining them on the trip home.

Lisa Marie let out a sturdy burp and said, "I think my belly might bust!"

Josephine glanced at Mama, who exchanged a look with Helen-Dove.

"'At'uz a good'n," Lisa Marie said, and smacked her flat stomach.

Helen-Dove spoke up then. "Lisa Marie, I think this trip is the perfect opportunity to work on your manners."

Lisa Marie looked confused. "What manners?"

"What manners is exactly right," Helen-Dove replied. "Lisa Marie, you can't go through life burping at the table in the presence of company. You hold that sort of thing in when other people are around."

Lisa Marie opened her mouth to protest, but Helen-Dove shook her head. "And when you've had enough to eat, you say, 'I have had enough, thank you very much.' No one wants to hear about you busting. It's disrespectful to the people around you."

Lisa Marie's green eyes went larger and she glanced at Josephine. "I reckon I've had enough of them tea cakes, thank you very much," she said softly.

"You are more than welcome," Mama replied. "I'm delighted you liked your meal. Now let's get our things together and be on our way."

⊃⟶

In the afternoon Josephine and Lisa Marie thumb-wrestled and played the hand-slapping game until Mama said they had to quit because it was too distracting. There were multiple rounds of go fish and old maid. When Lisa Marie grew tired of cards, she wove a potholder and Josephine made up stories, except she had to tell them out loud because writing in the spiral notebook while riding in the backseat made her want to upchuck.

After a while they grew quiet again. Lisa Marie drifted off to sleep, and Josephine's head began to fill with worry. Exactly *how* would they locate Molly? Exactly *what* would they do if this Ray person was dangerous? The words *insidious evil* brought to mind the red guy on the can of deviled ham. He had a tail and horns and a pitchfork even.

When Josephine couldn't keep these thoughts to herself any longer, she leaned over the seat. "Mama?"

"Yes, Jo," Mama replied.

"What will we do when we get there? I mean steps, like 1-2-3?"

Helen-Dove stopped her stitching and glanced back at Josephine.

"How will we know where to look?" Asking such questions made Josephine nervous, mainly because she feared nobody had answers.

"You want the honest truth?" Helen-Dove replied.

Josephine nodded.

"It's a let's-get-there-and-see situation."

Josephine settled back in her seat and stared out the window at the changing landscape—green pastures and rolling hills and pine forests and thick scrub. Stretched out before them was a monotonous ribbon of yellow-lined asphalt with its occasional heat mirage or clump of grisly road kill. The rhythm of the tires on the highway made Josephine's eyes grow heavy.

Sharks

"Girls, wake up. We're here," Mama said softly. She gave Josephine a nudge.

Josephine pried open her eyes, and Lisa Marie stretched and groaned out a sleepy-sounding "Where are we?"

"The Gulf of Mexico! We're at the Gulf of Mexico!" Josephine squealed. They flung open the doors and took off running.

"I ain't never been to the beach before!" Lisa Marie hollered as their feet pounded the earth. "Buster Lee said he'd take me, but we never did go."

"Well, you're here now!" Josephine shouted. The sand made running difficult, so Josephine stopped to take off the Tiger Paws.

"Told you not to wear no shoes at the beach!" Lisa Marie shouted over her shoulder. She beat Josephine to the water's edge by a long shot.

Josephine took her time crossing the rest of the warm sand. Miss Lake said writers had to take everything in, especially stuff they'd never seen before. The sky was vast and the water was vast and the sand was vast. So much vastness made Josephine feel smaller than normal. It filled her with wonder and awe and some terror, too.

"Ain't it amazing?" Lisa Marie said.

Josephine nodded and wriggled her toes in the soft, sugary sand. The color of the blue-green water was something to behold, and Josephine tried to think how she might describe it in her notebook.

"I ain't never been nowhere much." Lisa Marie sighed.

Delia was always bragging about where-all she'd been, and it made Josephine feel stupid. "Me neither," Josephine confessed. "We went to Point Mallard Park one time. And Davy Crockett. And the Great Smoky Mountains last summer."

Gentle waves lapped the shore and white foam swirled over the tops of their feet. Lisa Marie reached for Josephine's hand. She shut her eyes and said, "I get this terrible pain in my heart sometimes. Squeeze hard as you can."

Josephine squeezed Lisa Marie's hand with all her might.

"Use both hands," Lisa Marie insisted.

Josephine squeezed until her own hands hurt. "Is that hard enough?" she asked.

"I think so," Lisa Marie replied, and Josephine let go.

⊂⟹

Josephine changed into her swimsuit, and the girls splashed and dove and swam. They floated on their backs and stared at the sky. After a while Helen-Dove coaxed them out of the water by hollering that sharks tend to roam in the early evening.

For supper they feasted on the chicken Joella had fried for them, and the peach turnovers Mama had made for the journey. As the sky began to turn dark in earnest, they packed up their things and settled into the car again.

Helen-Dove studied the map and told Mama where to turn. They passed through the city of Mobile, a pretty place filled with shops and restaurants and churches. On the outskirts of town, they took an exit and continued down a twisty-turny two-lane highway.

"Are you sure this is it?" Mama asked. "There wasn't a sign to speak of."

"I'm sure," Helen-Dove said, her voice heavy with dread.

Several miles off the main highway was a single roadside marker: PICKERSGILL 12 MILES. Josephine peered over the seat at the odometer and watched as the miles ticked off. She waited to see if she felt a hot or cold feeling about Molly's whereabouts, but the truth was she just felt scared.

"This is it, in all her Pickersgill glory," Helen-Dove said, and leaned closer to the windshield, which was coated in bug guts. "Lord knows I never wanted to come back here."

Josephine didn't much blame her. To the left was a boarded-up gas station and to the right a billboard that said REPENT OR THE DEVIL WILL GET YOU! The words were written in bright red letters, and next to them was a devil with a tail and horns and a pitchfork. Josephine shuddered.

"This place is right scary looking," Lisa Marie said.

Mama continued onward. Parallel to the worn highway was an abandoned railroad track, its weedy banks littered with beer cans and food wrappers. Josephine would've bet a million dollars those swampy ditches were loaded with cottonmouths, too.

Lisa Marie leaned her head against the closed window and began to hum the hymn she'd meant to sing for Buster Lee: "In the Garden."

Helen-Dove switched on the overhead light and spread a map across her lap. "The motel ought to be around here somewhere," she said. "I just need to get my bearings straight. This is a place you try to forget, not remember."

For every house with a lamp switched on in the front window, there was a sagging building with its roof caved in. They passed what looked to be a pile of rocks with a historic marker that read McNALLEY SCHOOL, FOUNDED 1819.

"There it is!" Helen-Dove pointed. "Howell Road. Take a right."

Mama turned right and just around the corner was a small cluster of yellow lights. A grocery store, Josephine saw as they grew closer, and a pair of fireworks stands. The signs indicated a rivalry: GET YOUR CIGARETTES CHEAP! and GET YOUR FIREWORKS CHEAPER!

"There's the motel up there," Helen-Dove said.

Mama pulled into the gravel parking lot. A massive eighteen-wheeler occupied most of the space and beside it sat a dusty station wagon with a flat tire.

"Look," Lisa Marie said, and pointed.

The flickering neon sign read _HELL MOTEL.

"At least God's got a sense of humor," Helen-Dove said. "Come on, let's get checked in."

Josephine exchanged a wide-eyed look with Lisa Marie, who shook her head slightly and made the motion of slitting her throat.

The Shell Motel

There was brown shag carpet in the motel room, and a pair of dingy-looking beds, plus a cot for Lisa Marie. Between the beds was a small table, and hanging above it, a lamp made to look like a cluster of orange grapes. Josephine had never in her life seen orange-colored grapes. Worst of all, the room had a faint odor that was somewhere between Lysol and dirty feet.

Still, they were tired from the long drive, and after everyone had washed off the road dust and salt water, they settled in for the night. Mama and Lisa Marie, even Helen-Dove, drifted off to sleep, but not Josephine. Josephine's brain would not shut down.

A pair of shoes. A postcard. A Polaroid picture. Officer Frye and the word *Pickersgill*. Change the *g* to a *k* and you had *Pickers*kill.

Josephine rolled onto her side and drew back the curtain. She stared at the flickering ‿HELL MOTEL sign. Molly Quiver was out there. One thing led to another. Warehouse mice had chewed the wires that caused the fire that led them here. Like a tightrope walk, one wrong move could lead to disaster.

One misstep and your whole life was changed forever.

Eyes and Ears

Josephine and Lisa Marie awoke the next morning to find Mama and Helen-Dove already dressed.

"What're we doing?" Josephine asked. She was groggy, and the sun, which streamed hot and bright through the window, made her grouchy.

"We're getting up and out," Helen-Dove said. She looked thinner than ever, and it seemed the slightest wind might blow her over.

Lisa Marie stretched her arms high above her head and yawned out, "I'm starving to death!"

"We're all hungry, Lisa Marie. We'll have peach turnovers in the car." Mama pointed to something on Helen-Dove's neatly made bed. "You should get dressed," she said.

Lisa Marie's sleepy green eyes were suddenly alert. "What's that?"

Mama smiled. "It's your new dress."

"For *me*?"

"For you," Helen-Dove assured her. "You've outgrown that fluffy white thing, so Miss Penny made you something stylish.

And you won't be running around the trailer park getting it dirty, either. It's for special occasions only."

Josephine stared. Laid out on Helen-Dove's bed was a cream-colored smock dress in a soft cotton cheesecloth. The bodice had clever tucks and short set-in sleeves. On each of the deep front pockets was intricate stitching, a bouquet of flowers in vibrant colors, Helen-Dove's handiwork.

"We collaborated," Mama said, and smiled at Helen-Dove. "Now you girls get dressed so we can go."

"Where we going to next?" Lisa Marie asked.

"Church," Mama said. "We'll explain more in the car. Now y'all hurry up!"

The dress Josephine brought to wear was her blue one with the bumblebees, entirely too babyish next to Lisa Marie's stylish new one. Mama was staring at Josephine. It was the *Check yourself* stare.

Josephine snatched up her clothes and went into the bathroom. She shut the door behind her. Ever so slowly, she tugged off her pajamas and yanked the bumblebee dress over her head. "She's a poor girl with a new dress!" she hissed at her reflection. "Why can't you be nice?"

Josephine leaned in close to the mirror and breathed out a circle of fog on the glass. There were too many freckles spattered across her nose. At the corner of her mouth was a speck of last night's toothpaste. Her teeth were crooked.

It was as if the bees on her dress had come to life; they buzzed around the tiny bathroom, pollinating Josephine's head with hateful ideas: *What if Mama likes Lisa Marie better now? What if deep down she'd rather have her for a daughter?*

The way Josephine acted sometimes, she couldn't much blame Mama. "You have got to be happy for Lisa Marie," she whispered, and flung open the bathroom door. Much too loudly, she shouted, "You sure do look pretty today, Lisa Marie!"

Lisa Marie rubbed her stubbly head and grinned. "You look pretty, too, Josephine. You always look pretty," she said.

Josephine's compliment was phony, but Lisa Marie's was genuine. Mama cut Josephine a side-eye, as if to say *Why can't you be more like Lisa Marie?*

⊏⟹

The parking lot of the First Assembly of the Divine Resurrection was overflowing with cars. There were so many cars, in fact, that Mama had to park along the roadside.

"You really think she's here?" Josephine asked.

"Hard to say where she is," Helen-Dove replied. She stared out the window at folks ambling past—women with babies on their hips and men taking last drags off cigarettes before stubbing them out with their pointy-toed shoes. "But where there's a crowd of believers, you're liable to find Ray and Raylene trying to scam them somehow."

"So, what's the plan?" Mama asked. "Are we sitting together?"

"I'm not going in just yet," said Helen-Dove. "I want to look around out here first. Plus, I have to lay low. Better to take them by surprise."

Mama eyed the girls in the mirror. "Perfect behavior. Understand?"

"I ain't gonna burp, Miss Penny. Not dressed like 'is."

Helen-Dove turned around then. Her face was serious in a way that made Josephine shrink back in her seat. "I trust you won't burp *or* do anything else to draw attention to us," she said firmly. "We have to be all eyes and ears, but not too obvious about it, either. We want to blend in. And you girls must notice everything, and I do mean *everything*."

They got out of the car then, and Mama, Lisa Marie, and Josephine headed toward the front doors of the small white church while Helen-Dove waited behind.

Josephine couldn't help but glance over at Lisa Marie. She did look cute. In fact, she looked fashion-model cute. The soft cream color of the fabric was perfect for Lisa Marie's skin tone. And at the last minute, Mama had given Lisa Marie her green wedges to wear, which made her tower over Josephine.

Even the short hair seemed stylish today. Lots of models and actresses were wearing pixie cuts lately. Josephine had seen pictures of them in magazines.

⊏⟹

Inside the church, people greeted one another. Old women fanned themselves with programs, and folks scooched over to make space for those just arriving. Children bounced around in the pews, and babies squawked. Mama nudged Josephine and Lisa Marie into the last row, and a few heads swiveled in their direction.

After several restless minutes, the choir director raised her arms, and the audience stood to sing the opening hymn, "Softly and Tenderly."

During the sermon, Josephine read the program cover to cover. There were lots of names on the sick list, but she could tell by the sound of them—Gladys, Buford, Clovis, Agnes, Imogen, Mildred—they were all old folks.

Like hours, the minutes ticked by, and it grew steamy with bodies pressed so tight together. Josephine's legs were sweat-stuck to the pew, and she could feel dampness on her neck and down her back. Next to her Lisa Marie began to squirm, and even Mama, who normally sat so still in church, kept crossing and uncrossing her legs.

There was the chance they'd dyed Molly's hair again, so Josephine studied the hair of every single person. A few rows ahead was a red-haired girl, but even from a distance, Josephine could tell it was the real kind of red hair, not the type from a bottle.

Then the preaching was over, and the choir started thundering "Go Tell It on the Mountain." The preacher, a puffy, red-faced man with a voice like a bassoon, offered the benediction. Doors flung open, and the crowd spilled out into an Alabama boil.

Mama leaned in close and whispered, "Study. Every. Face."

They rose, the three of them working their way through the throng of people dressed in hats and suits and shiny shoes. With each face that wasn't Molly's, Josephine's heart sank lower.

☞

They were quiet on the drive back to the Shell Motel. Josephine knew better than to mention that she was hot and tired and starving to death. A wretched Helen-Dove stared out the window at the scenery whizzing past.

Back in the motel room, trails of moisture trickled down

the walls as if the room itself were perspiring. Helen-Dove disappeared into the bathroom.

Josephine could hear her turning the water on then off and blowing her nose. "She's crying," Josephine said quietly.

Mama ignored the comment and switched on the air conditioner. It made a gurgling noise, then sputtered out puffs of musty air.

"I want to wear this dress every day for the rest of my life," Lisa Marie said, and did a twirl.

"Now is not the time for twirling," Josephine snapped. "Don't you know anything?"

"I know you're right hateful sometimes. I sure do know that," Lisa Marie said, and did another twirl.

"Now is not the time for arguing," Mama said. "You girls get yourselves changed and then pack up."

"You mean we're leaving? We're giving up?" Josephine said.

Mama glanced toward the bathroom and pressed a finger to her lips. "We're not giving up, Jo, but hotels cost money, and it's nearly checkout time."

Lisa Marie stepped out of her dress and stood before them in nothing but her pink underwear. For some reason this was more irksome than the twirling. "You think we want to see you naked as a jaybird?" Josephine said.

"I ain't nekkid as no jaybird," Lisa Marie said.

"You are—"

"Girls, stop. That's enough," Mama said. "Both of you get changed so we can go."

A tide of panic was rising inside Josephine now, and it threatened to knock her over. "But what about Molly? What about—"

"Helen-Dove is in charge here, Jo. Not you. Not me. And we will do whatever she asks us to do, but we can't afford to stay at the Shell Motel for a second night. We'll look for someplace cheaper. Now do as I said and get changed."

Josephine snatched a clean outfit from her suitcase, and since Helen-Dove was still in the bathroom, she crouched between the wall and the bed to dress.

This trip was not going as planned. They hadn't found Molly Quiver. They didn't even have any clues. And now they had no place to stay, either. These thoughts were chewing up Josephine's insides like locusts—*crunch-crunch-crunch.*

"Please tell me we're not sleeping in the car tonight," Josephine said when she was dressed.

Just as she asked this question, Helen-Dove emerged from the bathroom. She gave Josephine a look that meant she was getting on everybody's nerves. Josephine hated that kind of look. She got those looks from Miss Lake sometimes when she asked questions before she was finished giving directions.

With a noisy clatter, Mama hoisted her bag off the luggage rack and said, "I'll get us checked out and meet you in the car, Helen. Come on, girls, let's go."

$\Longrightarrow$

The motel office was nothing but a little bitty place with some dusty fake plants and a gumball machine stuffed with colorful squares of sugar.

"Here are some pennies, girls," Mama offered before Josephine had a chance to ask.

Josephine and Lisa Marie took turns stuffing pennies into the slot and cranking out gum so stale it made their jaws ache.

"Dude called for you this morning," the front desk clerk said to Mama.

Josephine quit her gum-smacking and turned to look at the woman. Not a full-fledged grown-up, Josephine realized, more like a teenager, with a stringy blond ponytail and creasy blue eye shadow and the letters *P-E-A-C-E* tattooed down her arm.

"For me?" Mama asked, surprised.

"I told him y'all were out. Church, I figured, since it's Sunday. Name was Hog." She smiled at this, and Josephine could see a large chip in her front tooth.

Lisa Marie's cheeks were puffy now from so much gum. "Hog's our neighbor," she said, and a trickle of sugary spit rolled down her chin.

"What did he say?" Mama asked.

"He said him and this chick, Jonelle or Jolene or—"

"Joella," Josephine offered.

The clerk made a clicking sound with her teeth and gave Josephine a thumbs-up. "Yeah, that was it, Joella. Anyways, he wanted me to tell you they were over in Fontelle Beach at the Gull Cottages and Campgrounds. Said they were maybe bookin' after a while, though. They're with some biking club called the..."

"Tootsie Rollers," Josephine said.

"That's it." She made another clicking sound.

"What time did he call do you think?" Mama asked.

The clerk turned to look at a sunburst clock hanging on the wall behind her. "Couple hours ago, maybe more."

Mama's hopeful expression faded slightly. "How far is it to get to... where did you say again?"

"Fontelle Beach. Twenty minutes or so."

Mama handed over a few bills and took the receipt. "Thank you very much," she said. "Come on, girls, we have to hurry."

"Keep on truckin'," the clerk said, and flashed them a peace sign with her PEACE arm.

Blasphemy

Fontelle Beach was easy to find on the map, but Gull Cottages and Campgrounds was tricky to locate in person. Signs with the paint peeling off were the only bread crumbs to guide them down the single-lane dirt road with overgrown trees and scrub. It was a swampy sort of place that seemed ideal for alligators.

"There!" Helen-Dove said. "That might be it there." She pointed to a driveway that had a fat mailbox with a wooden seagull propped catawampus next to it.

Mama eased closer, then stopped the car. "Think I can get my car in there without getting stuck?"

Helen-Dove rolled down the window and leaned out to check. "You'll be alright," she said.

Mama was just about to give it a try when there was an explosion of noise, a rumbling so loud it made the leaves on the trees tremble. Josephine clamped her hands over her ears and waited for an earthquake to split the ground beneath them.

"It's the Tootsie Rollers!" Lisa Marie shouted. She lowered

her window and thrust herself out as far as she could, and Josephine did the same.

Just then a whole parade of chocolate-colored motorcycles thundered past—each bike more slicked-up than the one before it. The chrome was Hollywood shiny and on the handlebars were bright red speed tassels. The men and women wore black leather outfits and steely-toed boots.

"Hog! Joella!" Lisa Marie shouted when she spotted them.

Mama honked the horn, and Hog eased his bike out of the long line.

When the rest had driven on past and the racket died down, Hog cut his engine. For a few bewildering seconds, the Happy World residents stared at one another—Hog and Joella and Helen-Dove and Lisa Marie and Mama and Josephine. It was a strange thing to see people you knew from one place show up in another.

Finally, Mama said, "How on earth did y'all know we were at the Shell Motel?"

"Not many places to stay 'round here," Hog replied.

"We got us a couple of phone books and started calling," Joella added, and gave Hog a nudge. "Go on," she said, "tell 'em."

"I got a better idea," Hog said. "Y'all look hungry. Pull in the driveway. We'll discuss this stuff over Miss Coralina Collier's world-famous pork ribs."

⊏⟹

The miserable heat clung to them, and there were bugs, swarms of noisy, skittering, biting bugs with wings. The saving grace at the Gull Cottages and Campgrounds was a large screened porch with a pair of massive ceiling fans.

When the Happy World friends were settled around the picnic table, Helen-Dove said, "Y'all know something, so tell me what it is."

Josephine hoped they were about to hear good news, but judging by Hog's and Joella's worried faces, that was not the case.

Hog cleared his throat. He looked at Joella, then back at Helen-Dove. "Me and her don't normally go to church. Don't nobody on these bike trips go to church. Not while we're traveling anyways."

"What's that got to do with anything, Hog?" Helen-Dove asked.

"Hurry up. Get to the point," Joella said.

"Well, this time we'uz riding with a new couple. Wanda and Larry is their names. Wanda, she's the wife—"

"Hog, please," Helen-Dove said. Her thin fingers were on her throat now.

"Anyways, Wanda, the wife, she wanted to go to a service this morning. She was especially interested to hear some good singin', being she's a singer herself. They was a meeting up the road a piece. Not in a actual church, just some old office building they painted a cross on the front of. Anyways, Larry carried Wanda there early this morning. Figured he'd drop her off, then take a ride into—"

"We think Wanda might've met that Raylene person," Joella interrupted. Her words crashed onto the table like a lump hammer.

Helen-Dove's mouth opened but no sound came out.

"Keep going, Hog," Joella said.

"Right off Wanda realized it was a holy roller church. Not really her style, but since Larry was already gone, she didn't have much choice but to stay. She set next to some old lady, and they got to talkin'. Said the woman was right friendly, but she had a floaty voice that was sort of irritatin' to listen to."

Helen-Dove's fingers squeezed tighter on her throat.

"Said she was in the life insurance business and asked did Wanda have life insurance."

Wanda said they had insurance aplenty and didn't want no more. The woman went on to say her granddaughter was sick lately, and she'd come to pray for her. Wanda said the woman was right pitiful with her floaty voice and one of her eyes being..."

Josephine leapt from the table. "Witchy! It's *her*!"

"Jo, sit down," Mama scolded.

"But—"

"Sit!" she said.

Helen-Dove wrapped her arms around herself and began to rock gently back and forth on the bench. "Go on and tell me the rest."

"'Cloudy eyes' was how Wanda put it," Joella said. "Cloudy as a stormy day."

Josephine wanted to spring into action—take off in the ole blue car and find this Raylene person's house and break down her door. But she could see by the stillness in the grown-ups' faces this wasn't going to happen. Except for the sound of pots and pans banging inside the kitchen, there was quiet. "Well? What're we gonna *do*?" Josephine asked.

Helen-Dove sighed and glanced around the table. Her eyes moved from Hog to Joella to Mama to Josephine. "It takes one to know one," she said at last.

"What do you mean?" Joella asked.

"A con artist. A scammer. A fleecer. A flimflammer. Lots

of words for what Ray and Raylene do." Helen-Dove cast her eyes downward. "For what *I* used to help them do."

The hot travelers shifted uncomfortably, waiting for Helen-Dove to continue.

"We had quite a racket going. Raffles and tent revivals and snake oil. Any sort of thing where you could make money for doing mostly nothing. *Intangibles*, Ray called them. Holy water from the Jordan River, which actually came from our faucet. We were all criminals, but I was the only one who ended up doing time."

Doing time meant a person had gone to jail. Josephine stared at Helen-Dove's pretty brown hair and tiny hoop earrings, which Josephine hadn't noticed until now. Nothing about her looked criminal.

"I was a teacher," she went on.

At this Josephine's mouth dropped open.

"An educated person. When I met Ray, he was supplying T-shirts for a school fundraiser I was leading. He was charming and charismatic and handsome." She waved off the memory as if shooing a fly. "Anyway, what I did, *I* did. I take responsibility for my actions. I lost my license and was permanently banned from the McCracken County school system on the grounds of embezzlement. This was a long time ago, back in Kentucky."

Questions piled high in Josephine's brain. "What about Molly? What happened to her while you were in the...you know..."

Mama shot her a look, but Helen-Dove didn't seem fazed.

"Molly was with Ray and Raylene. She was a good prop for their scams, and they did their best to poison her against me until I got out. We were just starting to find our footing again. Molly was doing well in school. The past seemed to be fading...." Helen-Dove's voice trailed off.

Mama looked angry. Her face had the same sort of expression she wore whenever an auto mechanic tried to jack up prices, or the butcher gave her a gristly cut of meat. "And you chose not to tell me any of this?" she asked.

Hog shifted uncomfortably on the bench, and Joella frowned and bit her lip.

"I paid a heavy price for my crime. More than likely, I'll be paying for it the rest of my life," Helen-Dove said.

"I would like to have known the whole truth," Mama said.

"Would you have driven me down here if you did know?"

"That's not really the point, is it?" Mama replied.

"I'm sor—"

"Don't apologize if you don't mean it," Mama said sharply.

Helen-Dove took a shaky breath and continued. "Ray and Raylene don't want to invite any sort of trouble, not while they're present at least. The trouble comes after they've left town, when folks realize they've been scammed. Large gatherings are gold mines at first."

"Easy access to people, that right?" Hog asked.

"Exactly. Churches especially. Ray always said if folks would believe in the resurrection, they'd believe just about anything." At this Helen-Dove glanced at the ceiling. "Blasphemous, I realize."

Josephine studied the faces around the table. Mama's expression had gone unreadable, but Hog and Joella looked sympathetic enough. Lisa Marie was staring at the alligator salt and pepper shakers as if they had started to dance across the checkered tablecloth.

"What're you thinkin' we ought to do next?" Hog asked. "Me and Joella, we'll help you any way we can."

"I think we ought to go to this church tonight. My guess is they'll have a healing service, which means only the truly desperate people will attend, a magnet for the likes of Ray and Raylene." Helen-Dove looked at Lisa Marie and tilted her head slightly. "Think you could be an actress for me, Lisa Marie?"

"Do what?" she replied, still gazing at the alligators.

"Look at me, Lisa Marie. This is important."

"What is?" she asked, her green eyes gone alert.

"I need you to play a very important role tonight. Be an actress, Oscar-winning, like that Tatum O'Neal. Think you can do it?"

Josephine felt as though she'd been jabbed with a fork.

"It wouldn't require much," Helen-Dove continued. "You'd go down to the altar so the preacher can bless you. You'd have to pretend to be sick. Like Buster Lee was sick."

"Brother Corey laid his hands on Buster Lee a time or two. Didn't do no good."

"Well, you aren't really sick, so it won't matter," Helen-Dove said. She turned to Mama. "Would you be willing to help? You drove us this far, what's the sense in turning back now?"

"The sense in turning back now is preventing disaster," Mama said stiffly.

"Penny, I'm sorry if you feel misled, but you'd do anything for Josephine, right?"

"Of course. And I'd do anything to keep her out of harm's way, too."

"I understand that. I just need to see this through."

Mama sighed an exasperated sigh. "What can I do?"

"Pretend to be Lisa Marie's mother."

"Fine," Mama said.

Josephine was trying to hold her tongue. She was trying to control her feelings. She was doing her best not to act like a baby, but somehow the words slipped out of her mouth anyway. "But *I'm* her daughter."

"And?" Helen-Dove said.

"Well, if *I'm* her daughter, and she's my actual mother, I should play the part." Josephine did not look at Lisa Marie when she said this.

"That makes sense," Helen-Dove agreed.

Something about her calm reaction felt like a trap.

"Lisa Marie looks the part," Helen-Dove went on. "But, if you don't mind shaving your head, you'll do just fine."

Josephine touched her hair, which Mama had braided in pigtails that smelled faintly of Gee, Your Hair Smells Terrific. "Lisa Marie can do it," she said, and sank lower on the bench.

"Ribs is 'bout ready," Miss Coralina Collier called through the window. "Y'all better get ready, too."

"We're more than ready," Hog assured her. "Sure smells good!"

Josephine didn't have a part to play. Josephine would be a useless puzzle piece that didn't fit. She stared at the checks on the tablecloth and tried to steady herself.

"Josephine?" Helen-Dove said.

Josephine glanced at her.

"While your mama and Lisa Marie are at the altar receiving a blessing, you'll sit in the pew and pretend to be a sad sister. Nothing too over the top, okay?"

Josephine nodded. This was a sympathy offer. She'd sat the bench in peewee basketball enough times to know when she wasn't wanted.

"I'll be scanning the congregation the whole time," Helen-Dove went on. "If y'all are compelling enough, every pair of eyes will be on you. Especially you, Lisa Marie."

"I can get me some attention when I want it," Lisa Marie boasted.

"My guess is if Raylene and Ray are in the area, they'll show up."

"What about Molly?" Joella asked. "Think she'll be there?"

Helen-Dove squeezed her hands together. "I don't know. Could be Ray and Raylene will use Molly to hoodwink folks. Or, maybe Molly's really sick. Skeptics are the first ones to turn to the Lord in times of desperation. Trust me, I know."

"Your girl's fine," Hog assured her.

"What can we do?" Joella asked.

"You two make sure you're in the vicinity in case we need some backup."

"I'm gonna be an actress. Ain't it something?" Lisa Marie said, and then she beamed like she'd just been crowned Miss America.

46

The Sound of Someone Weeping

The unbearable heat gave way to a downpour. Trees swayed, lightning flashed, and the sky turned a moody shade of blue. Josephine sat in a soft armchair in one of Coralina Collier's minuscule guest cottages and pretended to be just fine with all the hubbub.

Judy Blume's *Blubber* was parked right in front of her nose, but the truth was she'd been on the same page for half an hour, stewing in her pot of misery.

In the bathroom Helen-Dove had finished dyeing her soft brown hair a jet-black color and was now snipping her waves into a shaggy mullet. Mama, casting aside whatever reservations she'd felt earlier, had taken on the job of makeup artist. And the truth was, Lisa Marie really did look terminally ill.

Beneath her green eyes were faint smudges of blue eye shadow, and on her face was foundation the unhealthy color and texture of chalk dust. She'd even insisted on shaving her head again. "Truly sick folks go completely bald, not stubbly!" she said, though when she made a move to shave her eyebrows, Mama intervened.

Miss Coraline Collier's plain gray house dress hung loose on Mama, and she'd scrubbed every trace of makeup from her face. She'd also Dippity-doed her hair so that it looked unwashed, then pinned it tight to her head with bobby pins. Mothers of sick children didn't have time to care for themselves, was her reasoning.

From behind her book, Josephine observed and tried to feel absolutely nothing, but like bumper cars her emotions kept smacking into one other. To prevent herself from saying anything mean, Josephine swore on her life not to speak at all. Not for the rest of the night and maybe not for the rest of the trip.

⇒

Along about five o'clock, they drove to another rundown town called Foggy Bottom, the same place that Wanda person had gone to church earlier in the day. Normally, Josephine and Lisa Marie would've bounced around the backseat and joked about the name Foggy Bottom, but this evening they were quiet.

Lisa Marie said she had to pretend to be sick all day if she was to play a sick girl tonight. And Josephine didn't say anything because she was keeping her vow not to talk.

Most of the Foggy Bottom storefronts were empty, Josephine noticed as Mama drove slowly down the street. There was a coffee shop–luncheonette, but it was closed since it was Sunday night. A dress boutique looked like maybe it was still in business, though the pair of mannequins in the front window had fallen over, one with her pants down around her ankles.

"Goodness," Mama said. "It's practically a ghost town."

The Sacred Garden of Gethsemane Church was in an office building, just like Wanda'd said. Someone had strung lights on the striped awning and painted a giant cross on a plate glass window. The rain had stopped, and the streets were mostly dry, thanks to the awful heat. Outside, a crowd of people waited for the doors to open.

"Circle the block," Helen-Dove said, and ducked low in the passenger's seat. "I don't want anyone seeing us together."

Mama did as she was told and stopped a good distance away at a vacant lot. Helen-Dove moved to open the door.

"I don't like the idea of leaving you here by yourself," Mama said, glancing around.

"I'll be fine," Helen-Dove assured her. "Try to park close. It'll seem strange if you park too far away with her being so sick." She glanced back at Lisa Marie, whose head was lolled to one side. "You're very convincing," Helen-Dove said as she got out of the car.

Mama's hands gripped tight on the steering wheel as she drove through town a second time. There was an empty spot diagonal from the church, and she pulled into it. "We stick together," she said, then switched off the ignition. "We stick together, except for when Lisa Marie and I have to go to the altar. Or however they do things here." She turned to face them. "Right?"

Lisa Marie peeped out a weak yes, but Josephine didn't utter a single word.

"Jo?"

Josephine only stared at her mother.

"You're not gonna answer me?"

Josephine shook her head.

Her mother's face shifted from irritated to angry. She

squinted one eye. "You've been a teapot ready to shout all afternoon." She pointed a finger at Josephine. "You wanted to come here, remember? We're in this now, for better or worse, so don't spoil the plan, hear? Come on, Lisa Marie," she said, and pushed open the car door.

Their pace crossing the street was irritatingly slow, but Mama seemed to be going on Lisa Marie's theatrical instincts now. Behind them Josephine did her best to avoid rolling her eyes. Already, she could see folks turning to stare.

Lisa Marie wasn't just playing the part of a sick girl; she *was* a sick girl. Putting one shaky foot in front of the other. Terribly weak and yet strong at the same time. In spite of herself, Josephine felt a surge of admiration.

⊏⟹

Gethsemane was nothing like Josephine's Methodist church back home. There were no pews or stained-glass windows or red carpeting. There wasn't a real pulpit, just a small wooden platform with a plain podium and a microphone. No piano or pipe organ, either, though there were hymnals and programs placed on each folding metal chair.

Mama directed them to a row toward the center of the room—Mama on one end, Lisa Marie in the middle, and Josephine on the other side.

Before the minister began speaking, he took a deep gulp of water and mopped his sweaty face with a handkerchief. The service was one without fanfare or drama. Still, Josephine's heart pounded as if she'd just run around the block. Beside her, however, Lisa Marie looked perfectly serene. A sick girl resigned to her suffering and maybe even her untimely death.

Lisa Marie rested her head on Mama's shoulder, and

Mama fanned her with the program. To Josephine's knowledge, her mother had never been on any stage, but she played the role of a distraught caregiver convincingly.

When it was time to sing, Josephine was the only one from their group who stood. She didn't dare turn to look for Helen-Dove. Whatever retail business had previously existed in this space, they'd neglected to remove the cheerful door chime, and each time it went off, Josephine flinched as though pierced by an arrow.

Any second Molly Quiver might come through the door. Would they even recognize her? Maybe Molly wouldn't show up. Maybe the flimflammers had moved on to some other town.

After what seemed a painfully long time, the sermon was over. Mama was visibly tense now, and Lisa Marie had closed her eyes and was so still and stiff Josephine wondered if she hadn't up and died during the service.

Any second, they'd do the call to the altar, and at this thought, Josephine began to tremble. To steady herself, she scratched a mosquito bite on her calf with the heel of her shoe. When that didn't work, she picked at a scab on her elbow, but the nervous feeling only grew worse.

"Bring your woes to the altar," the preacher finally said. Mama gave Lisa Marie a slight nudge. "Give your troubles over to God!"

People began to make their way to the front of the room— a tall, skinny boy with casts on both arms; two elderly women in wheelchairs with younger women pushing them along.

"It's time," Mama whispered.

Josephine feared she might twitch right off her seat. Her jerky movements were surely visible now—hands, legs, even her lips. Mama gave her a look, then gently tugged Lisa Marie off her chair, and the pair of them made their way to the front.

Watching them, Josephine's shaking subsided, and in its place was the sudden urge to laugh. It was nerves, she knew. She'd done this very thing in a class spelling bee once, burst out laughing, unable to continue.

It was the weird kind of laughing people did when they knew they weren't supposed to laugh, but the harder Josephine tried to suppress the urge, the more forceful it became. The entire miserable scene felt like a Carol Burnett comedy skit.

"There is nothing like the love between a mother and her child!" the preacher said, his voice louder now as he put his hands on either side of Lisa Marie's bald head. "Give them strength in their bond to one another, Lord." His voice warbled slightly, and Josephine came undone.

A strange choking sound escaped her mouth, and a few heads turned her way. She had to get out of there! Out of her seat and down the aisle she flew. She pushed open the door, and the chime sang merrily.

Alone on the sidewalk now, Josephine's need to laugh was miraculously gone.

Above her the twinkle lights swayed on a salty breeze, and beyond that an eye-shaped moon stared down at her reproachfully.

Hush, the breeze seemed to say. *Listen.*

A Laffy Taffy wrapper skittered and scraped down the sidewalk, and then Josephine heard it: the sound of someone weeping.

The End of the Sidewalk

The crying was intermittent, like a song trying to break through static on the radio. Josephine began to walk. Listening and stopping, stopping to listen, she followed the sound. There were buildings on either side of the street, one with a barber's pole, and it occurred to Josephine that Foggy Bottom had once been a bustling place.

A piercing cry sprang from the darkness in front of her, and Josephine froze. Which direction to turn, she couldn't decide. Away from misery or toward it. Mama's words rang inside her head: *You wanted to come here. For better or worse, we're in this now.*

Toward it, she decided, and began to walk faster.

Some distance ahead was a road that intersected Foggy Bottom's main street—a hurricane evacuation route. Josephine had noticed the sign earlier when they were looking for a parking space.

Stick together. Mama's words clanged like a gong, but Josephine kept going. Now and then she darted into darkened doorways to keep from being seen.

Still a safe distance away, she tucked herself behind an empty newspaper stand and tried to see past the darkness. There were no more buildings beyond this point; it was as if the town had simply given up growing.

A dark-colored sedan was parked on the other side of the highway, hidden amidst overgrown scrub.

The crying ratcheted up a notch. A deep-sounding raw pain, not unlike Mercedes in the throes of giving birth.

The car's interior light switched on, and Josephine squeezed herself into the tightest of knots. There was a crease in the bumper and a dent that made the door hang sadly askew.

The congregation was singing. Judging from the volume, it was the closing hymn, a tune Josephine recognized:

> *Leaning on the everlasting arms,*
> *What have I to dread, what have I to fear?*

An anchor seemed to weight Josephine to the spot. The word *help* passed through her brain, but not over her lips.

And then came a woman's voice from the car. She was shouting over the crying. "Stop that nonsense! You stop it this second!"

Something terrible was happening. Something terrible was happening and nobody was doing anything about it. There was nobody to do anything about it, except for Josephine.

The interior light switched off again, and the engine rumbled to life.

The woman's angry voice and the crying mixed oddly with the hymn singing now. Every nerve ending in Josephine's body pulsed out warning signals. *Stay put. Wait for a grown-up.*

But soon the car would drive away, and whoever was trapped inside it would surely be on the highway of wretchedness. This thought unstuck Josephine, and she inched slightly forward.

Timing was everything. Break out running too soon, and the driver could swerve past her. Too late, and she'd be left staring at taillights. And if the car went in the opposite direction, all would be lost.

The sedan stalled, and it seemed the driver was deciding which way to go. *This way, toward me,* Josephine prayed.

And then, by some miracle, the car began traveling in Josephine's direction.

She took off running then, a plan taking shape in her head. She would bang the glass and grab the passenger's side door handle. Seeing her chance to escape, Molly would fling herself out of the car, and together they would run. The image was so sharp Josephine could practically feel Molly's sweaty palm in her own.

The car accelerated. *Bang the glass. Grab the handle.* Josephine stumbled, and the timing seemed to go haywire. The car sped up, and—strangely—everything slowed down.

Sweet Details

Mary Josephine Willoughby lay in the road, and Joella knelt beside her. "It's going to be okay, Josephine. Isn't it funny how our names sound alike?" Joella peeled the hair off Josephine's sticky face. "I think we were meant to be good friends, don't you?"

Josephine didn't answer. She didn't much feel like talking after being hit by a car. When she closed her eyes, Josephine was back in Happy World, walking among the tall pine trees, gazing up at the light glinting through the needles. There was the soft, spongy feeling beneath her feet and a deep fragrance of summer.

Josephine blinked up at Joella and thought about how she had extremely wide nose holes. *Collect details like seashells.* It was Miss Lake's voice now, and she was clutching her silver whistle. Mama stepped in and pressed her soft cheek against the back of Josephine's hand. The Singer sewing machine *whirr*ed and *thump*ed.

"I'm going to call for help. Just keep still, honey, and don't move, okay? Hey! *Hey!*" It was Joella again. "Help! We need help over here!"

There was shouting, and like a balloon, Josephine's head seemed to be getting bigger and bigger. A few curious faces peered down at her.

"Y'all step away from that child! Let her mama in."

"What happened? Oh, Jo, what *happened*?"

There was scared in Mama's voice and scared on her face, but Josephine did not feel scared in the least. She was too busy with details. The firmness of the street, the comforting hands, the kind faces.

"Somebody call for an ambulance!" Helen-Dove shouted.

"What am I gonna do with another one gone?" Lisa Marie sobbed.

Josephine closed her eyes again, and then, as if pushing off the edge of a pool, she gave in to the leaden desire to sink.

Meeting Jesus

When Mary Josephine Willoughby woke up, she was in a room with white walls and bright white lights. Standing over her was a man dressed in white, too. "Am I dead? Are you Jesus?" she asked him, reading his name tag.

The man smiled down at her. "It's pronounced *hay*, like horses, and *Seuss,* like *Green Eggs and Ham.* I'm Dr. Jesús Pérez, and you are very much alive. You're at the hospital."

"I was run over by a car," Josephine told him.

"Yes, you were," he replied. "I've been taking care of you. You have a concussion and a lot of stitches. Want to see the stitches?"

Josephine shook her head. She'd been walking, then running, then... *here.*

"My head is hurting," Josephine said. This doctor was handsome, and he reminded Josephine of someone who might be on TV. "Are you sure I'm not dead?"

"You are alive, I promise. Your mother stepped out to finish up some paperwork."

So many questions pinged inside her head, yet Josephine didn't want answers just yet.

"Hold still, and I'll go and see if I can find your mother. Okay?" Dr. Pérez replied, and before Josephine could ask him anything else, he was gone.

Her achy mind began to wander over to the imagination department. Mama and Josephine had moved back to Redbud Avenue with their precious things in the apartment just as before. A hot day in the backyard, eating a Snack Pack pudding and playing with Miss Nancy's tiny dogs. Curled up on the green velvet sofa watching *Family Affair* reruns.

Stick together. Act sad. These were Josephine's only instructions, yet she had failed.

"Jo? Oh, Jo, I'm sorry I wasn't here when you woke up." Mama stood over her.

Josephine didn't speak. If she tried to talk, she'd burst out crying. Besides, she'd been having a pleasant time pretending she was back on Redbud Avenue.

Mama leaned in close and kissed Josephine's cheek. "I love you," she whispered. "And I'm not angry, Jo."

Mama was still wearing the getup from church. Her hair was flat and greasy looking and her face was plain, but up close Josephine could see it was still her beautiful mother. Josephine lifted her hand and brushed it against Mama's cheek. It was the only *I'm sorry* she could muster at the moment.

"You." Mama shook her head. "You just amaze me sometimes. I don't know how or where you learned such courage or why you have these instincts like you do." Mama was squeezing Josephine's hand too hard, but she didn't protest. "I was against this trip. All along I didn't want to drive down here.

I was worried about our car and didn't want to get tangled up in some family...thing. You know what pushed me to say yes?"

Josephine nodded.

"Can you talk, Jo?"

"I have a headache," Josephine whispered.

Mama frowned. "Is it bad? Should I call Dr. Pérez?"

"No," Josephine lied. "Can I have some water?"

"Of course," Mama said, and reached for the pitcher. She poured them both cups of water, and they drank, staring at each other.

Any second Mama was going to spring the awful truth on Josephine. "Where are my shoes?" Josephine said, suddenly panicked she might have lost them.

"The shoes are fine, Jo."

Josephine felt brave enough to hear the news. "You can tell me now," she said, and handed the cup to Mama.

"It was strange, you know," Mama continued. "The shoes left on our porch. Your obsession. It was starting to get under my skin. Those things in the mail. The real reason we're here is because I knew you'd never stop pestering me if we didn't come. And I wasn't sure how I could tell you to stand up for what's right if I wasn't willing to stand up for it myself."

Josephine's eyes were beginning to feel heavy. Maybe she'd fall asleep before Mama got to the bad part.

"I'm sorry. I'm going on and on like this, Jo, because I'm trying to protect you."

Josephine felt as hollow as any cave, and it didn't seem she'd ever be filled up again. Hadn't she known it would end like this all along? That her daydream of Molly joining her back at Happy World was a fantasy?

Mama sat on the end of the bed and looked into Josephine's eyes. "Dr. Pérez insisted I tell you this news as gently as possible. He doesn't want you excited, so try to stay calm, okay?"

Josephine's insides felt like they might explode.

"Molly's here, Jo. She's in the hospital just like you."

Inquisitive

Josephine was double-knotting her shoelace just as someone knocked on the door. "Come in," she called.

"Hey," a woman said. She was wearing a much-too-big gray sweater, and her black hair stood up in places.

Josephine stared at her.

"It's me, Helen-Dove," the woman said.

Josephine slid off the bed, but when her feet hit the floor, she went instantly dizzy. "I have a concussion," she said, and climbed onto the bed again. "And stitches." She peeled back her hair to reveal the bandage on her forehead.

"Mind if I come in and sit with you a minute?" Helen-Dove was unrecognizable with that terrible haircut.

"I don't mind," Josephine replied.

"The doctor said I shouldn't stay long."

Josephine scootched over and patted the place beside her. "I don't have to make my bed since I'm in the hospital," she said, explaining the messy covers.

Helen-Dove sat beside her. "I don't know how to say thank you. There is no thank-you, not for something like this. If I were a wealthy person, I'd write you a check for ten million dollars."

Josephine smiled at the thought of having so much money.

Helen-Dove sighed and put her hand to her throat. "I'm so sorry. I'm so sorry. I'm so, so sorry you got hurt. That you've suffered because of me." She shook her head. "And your poor mother..."

"It's not because of *you*," Josephine said. "It's because of those awful people."

Helen-Dove pressed her lips together and studied Josephine. "I would like to believe that, but I put you in harm's way. My desperation was no excuse." She sighed. "It's done, though. Like so many of my crimes. You'd think I'd learn, but..."

"I'm the one who ran out in front of a car," Josephine protested.

"You remember everything that happened?"

At the time she hadn't been frightened, but now, recalling it, she was.

"You don't have to talk about it. That's not why I came, Josephine."

"I saw them, through the windshield. They were looking at each other. Yelling. I could hear them. Then I don't remember much. I remember Joella being there. Her nose mostly."

"Her nose?"

"She was looking down at me when I was lying on the pavement. All I could see was her nose." Josephine didn't add anything about the size of her nostrils because that would be mean, and Joella had been so nice.

"Hog was nearby when it happened," Helen-Dove said.

"He was?"

Helen-Dove nodded. "Yes, thank God. His bike was hidden

251

in an alley. Joella was on the back of the bike. They were going to follow the car, but then..."

"She ran me over."

"And kept going, which is unthinkable. Joella stayed with you, and Hog drove off in search of Raylene."

"Then what?"

"Raylene drove into a ditch." Helen-Dove squeezed her thin hands together, and Josephine began to fill to the brim with dread.

"Tell me the rest," Josephine pressed.

Helen-Dove's eyes glistened slightly, but as quickly as the tears had come, they evaporated. "Molly's in a great deal of pain, but they—" She waved this off. "Everything will be fine, Josephine."

This was what adults did. They stopped shy of telling whole truths to keep kids from worrying, but it only made kids worry more. "Please," Josephine said.

"She has a broken leg. She'll be just fine." Helen-Dove smacked her thighs, an indication she was done with this topic. "Now, what I mostly came to say was thank you. You're a hero. A true hero. I mistook your interest for nosiness, and I'm sorry about that."

"But I was nosy," Josephine said, uneasy now. Molly had a broken leg, and what else?

"We'll call it inquisitive," Helen-Dove said. She grasped Josephine's forearms and held them tightly. "Doesn't matter. Okay?"

Josephine's head began to throb. Molly's window would still be dark. And the vision she'd had of best-friendship, of Molly sitting between them in the backseat of the car, it *was* a fantasy. "What about that awful Raylene?"

"She'll be out on bail soon."

"But she ran me over!"

"Claims she didn't see you. Claims it was an accident." There was anger in Helen-Dove's voice now. "She plays the innocent old lady very well, Josephine. It's maddening."

"But Molly's coming home? She's coming back to Happy World?"

"She's staying here for now. I'm staying, too. I won't let her out of my sight."

"But she *is* out of your sight," Josephine said.

"You don't miss a beat, do you?"

"Not really," Josephine replied.

"Your mother is with Molly. The hospital staff is on the lookout for Ray and Raylene."

Just then the door opened wider, and a nurse pushed a wheelchair into the room. "Time for this little hero to go home," she said. "And your girl is being prepped for surgery, Ms. Quiver. You can hold her hand right up until we take her back, but you better go on down there now."

Helen-Dove stood abruptly. "Penny Willoughby is with her, right?"

"Nobody gonna let your child out of their sight, ma'am. Not till we hear word straight from Judge Thomas' mouth."

"Who's Judge Thomas?" Josephine wanted to know.

"Nothing for you to worry about, little lady," the nurse said. "Now you come on over here and put your behind in this wheelchair. You're gonna be takin' it easy for a while."

Helen-Dove reached for Josephine's hand and kissed it. She gave a sad wave and was gone.

A Long Way Home

The trip home felt like a long week instead of a long day. And because of Josephine's condition, she had to stretch out in the backseat, no Barbies or coloring books or singing to the radio. She wore Mama's sunglasses so the glare didn't give her another headache.

Lisa Marie sat in front beside Mama and read *Blubber*. Every now and then she sniffled, so Josephine reckoned there were sad parts in that book. Sometimes Lisa Marie barked out a laugh, so Josephine guessed it was funny in places, too.

That dusky evening when they finally pulled into Happy World Trailer Park—*Dandiest Little Place on Earth!* Josephine looked around. It felt like she'd been away from home for weeks and weeks. And it did look dandy to her now. Lightning bugs were twinkling like stars fallen from the sky. The smell of charcoal hung in the air. Zeus strummed his guitar. An engine growled.

Hog and Joella were back, too, and like always, Hog was tinkering with his bike and covered in grease. Rufus and Jewell

Mooningham's trailer was dark and so was Helen-Dove's, of course.

The ole blue car bounced up the washed-out path, and Mama tapped her horn lightly to let their friends know they were back safe and sound. At number 17 she stopped. Granddaddy was stooped over pulling weeds, and he grinned from ear to ear when he saw them. It was his big gap-toothed grin, same as Lisa Marie's.

"Granddaddy!" Lisa Marie hollered, and scrambled out of the car. "I sure did miss you!" she said, and he swept her up into a hard-squeezing hug.

"I sure did miss you, too, shug."

"Can we get out and say hi?" Josephine asked.

"That's fine," Mama said. She switched off the ignition, and they both got out.

"Y'all had quite a time down there," Granddaddy said. He was shaking his head like he couldn't believe what'd happened. "You all right, shug?" Granddaddy was talking to Josephine now.

"I'm fine," Josephine said. "Jesus took real good care of me."

"Jesus takes care of us all, don't he?" Granddaddy replied.

Josephine wanted to explain she was not talking about *that* Jesus, but Mama shushed her, and started telling Granddaddy about Molly Quiver and the surgery and how Helen-Dove was staying down there and Raylene was probably out on bail by now, and Ray had skipped town or was hiding out, nobody knew which.

"We got some folks over at Cameron Mills trying to help with expenses," Granddaddy said. "Whatever sick time them people got, they done went and donated to Helen-Dove. They's a fund to pay her rent this month, too."

"That's a relief," Mama said.

"Dot Moncrief—she's the manager—was planning a talent show to benefit Buster Lee a while back, but that got canceled after he died. They planning to start that up again for Miss Helen and Little Bit." He glanced at Lisa Marie. "They might want you to sing, shug."

Lisa Marie shook her head. "I'm finished with performing. It's a hard line of work, and I ain't shaving my head again for nothin'."

Mama laughed. "She did put on quite a performance the night Molly was rescued."

"You're a mighty big hero, Josephine. Hog and Joella been tellin' me all about thangs." Granddaddy's eyes were shining, and he was looking at Josephine now, the lines in his face softening. "I knowed some brave folks in my life. Was in the service back in the day. This one here, her daddy, he was a mighty brave fella." Lisa Marie studied her feet, and Granddaddy patted her back. "We lost him in 'Nam."

"I'm sorry to hear that," Mama said.

"So was I." Granddaddy shook his head. "So was I," he said again. "Thank you for letting Lisa Marie come with y'all. I hope she wasn't no trouble."

"None at all."

"And thank you for my new dress!" Lisa Marie rushed toward Mama and gave her a big hug, and Josephine didn't feel jealous, not even a little. And then Lisa Marie did an unexpected thing and hugged Josephine, too.

⇒

That night Josephine took a bath instead of a shower. She didn't wash her hair in Gee, Your Hair Smells Terrific on account of she couldn't get the stitches wet. Twenty-seven stitches, and although Dr. Jesús Pérez promised she wouldn't have much of a scar, Josephine hoped she had a great big one so she could show it off to the kids at Brandywine Elementary when school started.

In her pajamas and smelling clean, Josephine climbed into bed, and Mama tucked her in. "When are you gonna put that fabric on my walls?" Josephine asked. "You promised you would do it weeks ago."

Mama sat on the edge of the bed. "Miss Connie has asked us to leave. You remember that, right?"

"But I don't want to leave now. I want to stay, and be with Lisa Marie. I haven't even held Baby Zephyr yet. Miss Connie can't make us go, can she? Not after everything we've been through. I'll show her my stitches. They're so disgusting she'll have to let us stay."

"She's looking forward to having her cousin here. I doubt stitches will change her mind."

"Rinky is a dumb name if you ask me."

"Jo, that's enough. She's an old lady. Now say your prayers and go to sleep." Mama kissed Josephine on the tip of her nose, then switched off the light. For a few seconds, she stood in the doorway. Finally she said, "Sweet dreams, beauty queen," and was gone.

⊃⟹

Soon Mama's sewing machine was *whirr*ing and *thump*ing along, and this lulled Josephine almost but not quite to sleep. She thought about the day she'd waved to Miss Connie and

Miss Connie waved back. She thought about the lonely way the old woman stood in front of the grimy picture window, cradling and rocking Bob Barker like he was her bundle of joy.

Josephine felt it then. The sad and the happy were swelling and swirling inside her like those foamy waves in the Gulf of Mexico.

Baby Dragon

J o, it's time to get up. I made cinnamon toast. We're meeting Miss Augustine at the store before it opens."

Josephine groaned. "I'm too tired," she said, and flopped
over.

"You feel okay? Your head isn't hurting you, is it?"

"Nope," Josephine mumbled into her pillow. "But my ears
are hurting because you won't stop talking to me."

"That's enough, Jo. You're sounding more and more like a
teenager every day. Lord help me. Now come eat your breakfast. I put your clothes out."

Josephine opened one eye. On her dresser were the
navy-blue shorts she liked and the matching top with capped
sleeves and red and white piping. She hadn't worn this outfit
in a while and she looked very cute in it. "Okay, fine," she
said, and climbed out of bed.

At breakfast Josephine slurped her grape juice and scraped
off the cinnamon with her knife. She hated too much cinnamon. "It sure is good to be at home in Happy World," she said.

"Josephine, you know we can't stay."

"I could talk to Miss Connie myself," Josephine offered.

"We have to make the best of the situation. Miss Augustine's rancher is nice. She has a big TV."

"It's nothing but reruns in the summertime," Josephine said, and slurped her juice again. "How 'bout you let me stay here with Lisa Marie today."

"Miss Augustine was planning on showing you some fabric and patterns for your junior bridesmaid's dress." Mama took a sip of her coffee. "They've set the date. October nineteenth. The big Presbyterian church downtown."

"I need to be with Lisa Marie," Josephine said. "What's she gonna do without me? That girl's been left by everybody. You heard what happened to her daddy, and Buster Lee died, and her mother must've left her, too, because she's not here. And now I'm gonna leave? It's not right," Josephine said, outraged by the injustice of everything.

Mama looked like she was thinking on this. "As long as you girls promise not to get into anything. But put on your play clothes, and no running around. Dr. Pérez says you need to take it easy. Remember you can't get your stitches wet, so no playing in the hose, either."

Josephine hurried from the table.

"What do you say, Jo?"

"Thank you for breakfast, except that toast had too much cinnamon," Josephine said.

<figure>⊏⟹</figure>

Granddaddy had gone to work, and Mama left for the fabric store. Happy World was mostly empty now, except for Rufus and Jewel Mooningham, but their trailer was quiet on account of the sleeping-all-day-and-cleaning-all-night business.

"What do you want to do?" Lisa Marie asked.

A lightbulb turned on in Josephine's head. "We could hold Baby Zephyr."

"I saw him be born. That was plenty for me," Lisa Marie replied.

"But I want to hold him, and I'm the one with the stitches who can't do anything."

Outside Zeus and Mercedes' trailer, they crouched down and listened to that baby squall. "He's sure got some lungs on him," Lisa Marie whispered.

"He might give me another headache," Josephine agreed.

They were about to slip off and find something else to do when Mercedes flung open the door and ran out to the porch. She leaned on the railing and rubbed her temples the way Mama did when the thread on her sewing machine birds-nested.

No way were they escaping now, so Josephine stood up and said, "You okay?"

"You sure do look a mess this mornin'," Lisa Marie said.

Josephine stomped on Lisa Marie's toe.

"Hi, girls." Mercedes' long, frizzy hair was flying every which way.

As if he'd just been cued, Zephyr sputtered, then cranked his squalling up a notch, and because Josephine couldn't think of anything else to say, she said, "I want to hold your baby. *Sometime.*" She added the *sometime* because she definitely did *not* want to hold him now.

"Oh, that would be a big help!" Mercedes said, her eyes hopeful behind the smudged glasses. "You girls come on inside."

"Now look what you done," Lisa Marie whispered.

Baby stuff was everywhere, and it smelled like dirty diapers. "You girls sit here," Mercedes told them, and then swept a pile of *Mother Earth News* magazines off the couch. "It's so hot I think I might melt. Zeus and I don't believe in air conditioning with HFCs polluting the planet. The smallest carbon footprint possible, that's our motto." She sighed. "So, instead we suffer. Or, I should say, *I* suffer. Zeus is at the music store all day. *With* air conditioning."

Josephine and Lisa Marie sat close together on the scratchy couch, and Mercedes plucked two diapers from an overflowing laundry basket. "Here you go," she said, and placed a diaper on each of their shoulders. "He has reflux."

"Do what now?" Lisa Marie asked.

"Reflux means he spits up. A lot," Mercedes said. "That's why he cries so much."

Josephine hadn't held a baby before. What if she dropped him? What if he cried louder?

Mercedes lifted Zephyr from his basket. "Who wants him first?" Josephine and Lisa Marie stared at her. "Here," Mercedes said, and plunked him on Josephine's lap. "Remember to support his head." She adjusted Josephine's arm. "There. Perfect!"

A baby dragon wouldn't be any harder to hold, Josephine decided. Zephyr was red-faced and wailing, kicking his legs and punching the air with his tiny fists.

"One of you gets tired, the other can take a turn," Mercedes said. "I haven't slept in two days, or showered in three. You girls are a pair of lifesavers! Afterwards, I want to hear about your adventures in Alabama. Oh, and Josephine, remind me to cut a piece of my aloe plant. It'll help you avoid a scar," she said, and disappeared down the hall.

Lisa Marie pinched her nose shut. "I hope you're happy. We'll be stuck in this dookiemobile all day."

Josephine stared into the baby's wide-open, toothless mouth. Zephyr took a breath, then geared up for another go-round and began crying nonstop. Josephine thought her arms might snap off, and she was certain Zephyr had busted her eardrums. "Please take a turn, Lisa Marie." But Lisa Marie shook her bald head and scooted away. "Pretty please with sugar," Josephine begged.

"Okay, fine. But you're the one who wanted to hold him in the first place," Lisa Marie said, and scootched closer.

Like she was handing over a ticking time bomb, Josephine placed the baby in Lisa Marie's arms. Zephyr settled against her, hiccupped once, then fell asleep.

After what seemed a hundred years, Mercedes came into the room again. She had on a flowy top and cutoff shorts and her long hair was wet. She sat cross-legged on the floor and began folding the clean laundry. Josephine had never seen so many diapers.

"Are all those just for him?" Josephine asked.

"Yes, he's a pooper machine," Mercedes laughed. "You girls rescued me this morning. I was coming undone. Breast-feeding is exhausting."

Lisa Marie gulped like she was choking down a bullfrog.

"Soon as I finish folding these things, I'll make us some lunch."

"Oh, we can't stay for lunch! My granddaddy already fixed us something."

Mercedes tilted her head, like she was trying to figure out if this was true or not. "Oh, well…another day then," she said, looking a bit hurt.

⊂⟶

The second they were out the door and standing in the hot summer sunshine again, Josephine scolded Lisa Marie. "You hurt her feelings!"

"You think holding that baby is bad, you should see what them hippies eat. I ain't fixin' to have *that* mess, not when we got Oscar Mayer wieners and a brand-new bag of Funyuns."

Josephine opened her mouth, all set to break into the *I wish I was an Oscar Mayer wiener* song. Instead, there was a terrible racket that made Josephine hold her breath. A crashing-smashing racket that went on and on. And *on*.

"What was that?" Lisa Marie whispered when it was over.

"I don't know," Josephine whispered back. "But it was coming from Miss Connie's office-house."

Catastrophe

Josephine and Lisa Marie clung to each other as they crossed the trailer park. They considered knocking on the Mooninghams' door, but the shades were pulled tight, and besides they wouldn't be able to hear them knocking.

"Let's go a little bit closer, but not too close," Josephine said.

"Maybe Miss Connie's roof caved in." Lisa Marie squeezed Josephine's hand.

"I already got a broken head. You trying to give me a broken hand, too?"

"Sorry." Lisa Marie loosened her grip.

They crept toward Miss Connie's office-house and stood bunched together by the flagpole out front. High above their heads, the Tennessee flag looked tired and tattered, like maybe Bob Barker had gotten hold of it with his claws. The grass needed cutting, and Miss Connie's picture window was even dirtier now since there'd been no rain in days.

"Aw, Josephine, I don't know about this. We ought to go back to my trailer and eat the Funyuns and watch *Hollywood Squares.*"

Josephine pointed to a sign taped to the picture window: "*One-bedroom furnished trailer for rent $200 per month. Available August first!*"

"That's the sign she had up before y'all came. It's your trailer she's advertising. Probably she's got it on the *Swap Shop* radio program today. Me and Buster Lee heard it advertised there last time. Buster Lee liked listening to *Swap Shop*, even though he never bought nothin'. I sure do miss him, Josephine. I sure am gonna miss you, too."

"Why is she advertising our trailer if that Rinky person is supposed to stay in it? And why can't he stay with Miss Connie if he's her cousin?"

"You seen what a mess her place is. Barely room for Bob Barker, much less anybody else."

"I'm gonna ask her myself," Josephine said.

Lisa Marie frowned. "Ask her what?"

"Why she's advertising my trailer. And why this Rinky person can't stay with her."

Lisa Marie groaned. "I don't know, Josephine. That woman scares me. Granddaddy says she's the hatefulest woman he ever met, and Granddaddy never says nothin' bad 'bout nobody."

Josephine put her hands on her hips. "Well, she can't be worse than a kidnapping granny who runs people over with her car. And do you want me moving away? Do you want to be running around getting into stuff all by your lonesome self?"

"No, but I ain't going near Miss Connie," Lisa Marie said firmly.

Josephine took a deep breath and let it out in a huff. "Well, then I guess I have to do everything myself."

Slowly Josephine inched toward Miss Connie's front door.

Now and then she turned to glare at Lisa Marie, hoping a mean look would make her change her mind. But Lisa Marie stayed planted by the flagpole.

Josephine was three steps from the door. Two steps. One step. Half a step. Her heart was beating hard. The backs of her knees were itchy. Just as she raised her fist to knock, a groggy wasp flew toward her. "Get away!" she cried, and dodged it. The creature hovered for a while near the door, then slowly zigzagged away.

Ever so gently, she knocked.

Nothing.

Silence.

Josephine knocked again, louder this time, but still nobody came. Josephine put her hand on the doorknob and looked back at Lisa Marie. "I'm going in," she said.

"Are you *crazy?*" Lisa Marie replied.

Josephine squeezed the knob and tugged. The door made a screeching-scraping sound. First with one Tiger Paw and then the other, Josephine stepped over the threshold. The cat smell was so strong it made her eyes water. "Oh, Baby Jesus," she said, and pinched her nose, "I sure have smelled a lot of yucky stuff today."

On the front counter, the office part of Miss Connie's office-house, was a giant ashtray with heaps of brown cigarette butts and stacks of papers and dirty coffee mugs and a jar of Tang and a dish with hard candy inside that was all stuck together. From another room a radio played, and Josephine could tell by the twangy sound it was the country station.

Feeling like the Pink Panther, she slipped into the house part of the office-house, to the living room. Except you couldn't really call it a *living* room. Nobody could live there. It looked like ole Fred Sanford, the funny junk man on TV, had unloaded his truck smack in the middle of the floor.

Broken-down lawn chairs. A toy wagon without any handle. Oodles of empty Pepsi bottles stacked in wooden crates and old *TV Guide*s and newspapers and magazines. There were cereal boxes and coat hangers and a toilet seat, even. Stuffed in a grocery cart, a *real* grocery cart, like maybe Miss Connie had swiped it from the IGA, were tangled Christmas lights and a plastic snowman. In a corner was one of those life-size dolls, her stiff plastic arms stuck straight out like she was sleepwalking.

"Miss Connie? You in here?" Josephine said tentatively. She took baby steps toward the kitchen. Donna Fargo was on the radio: "You Can't Be a Beacon if Your Light Don't Shine." "Hello? Anybody home?" Josephine's throat was dry with fear. Maybe she wasn't brave. Maybe her bravery was a one-time-only event.

In the kitchen, a closet door was off its hinges, and the shelves were broken and splintered on the floor. Bob Barker sat on the avocado-green stove, hissing and flicking his tail. Not in all her almost eleven years of living had she seen such a Guinness book record-setting mess of a kitchen: dirty plates on the counter and table, an overflowing sink with a missing spigot, broken flowerpots, cans of hair spray, an empty birdcage with a pair of panty hose draped over the top.

Most surprising, however, was the giant mountain of Lovin' Spoonfuls cat food. A cat food catastrophe is what it was. "Miss Connie?" Josephine whispered. "Miss Connie? You in here?"

"What do *you* want?" The woman's hateful voice cracked like a whip.

Josephine looked around but saw no one.

"Did I say you could trespass? *Huh?*" the voice said again.

"Ma'am? I don't see you," Josephine said.

"Down here! Are you blind?"

Josephine spotted a square of filmy pink fabric on the floor. Beneath the cat food cans was a very sprawled-out Miss Connie.

"If you're breaking and entering, might as well make yourself useful. Help me *up*, dummy! Don't just stand there!"

Josephine flinched at the word. Delia had called her a dummy plenty of times, and it was far worse than sticks and stones in Josephine's opinion. In a stern voice, she said, "Wait right there. I'll need Lisa Marie to help."

"Where you think I'm gonna go? *Huh?*" Miss Connie snorted.

"I would be more polite if I wanted somebody to help me." Josephine planted her feet on the sticky linoleum floor and raised her eyebrows.

Miss Connie blinked up at her. She nodded. A can of Lovin' Spoonfuls liver dish rolled across the floor.

⊏⟶

It took some doing, but Josephine and Lisa Marie managed to push all the heavy cans into a corner and get Miss Connie on her feet again.

"Are you alright?" Josephine asked.

"Oh, hush! Of course I'm alright. What do you think? I'm some frail old lady?"

Josephine shook her head. Scary old lady was more like it, but Josephine didn't dare say this.

Miss Connie plucked Bob Barker off the stove and held

him tight against her chest. She scowled at Josephine and Lisa Marie as if the doors busting off the hinges were somehow their fault.

Lisa Marie blinked. Josephine blinked. She wanted very badly to run, but her shoes were a little bit stuck to the floor.

Finally, Miss Connie knocked a bowling bag off the kitchen chair and flopped down. She heaved out a heavy sigh. And then Miss Connie broke out crying. It was the bawling sort of crying. Not hateful at all. Just regular old sad, miserable crying.

"What do we do now?" Lisa Marie whispered.

I don't know, Josephine mouthed back.

Miss Connie's shoulders shook and her back shook and it looked to Josephine like that woman had an earthquake happening inside her.

Josephine spotted a roll of toilet paper on the dish drying rack. She *squeetch*ed across the floor, grabbed the roll, and tapped Miss Connie on the shoulder.

"What is it!" Miss Connie's voice made a person want to shrink into a teeny-tiny ball and roll away.

"I thought you might need this," Josephine said. "For your tears."

"I *know* what *for!*" Miss Connie said, and snatched it from Josephine's hand. She dragged a long trail of paper off the roll and wiped her eyes and nose and mouth. She heaved and hiccupped and sighed.

When Miss Connie's noises died down, Josephine said, "Um...I was wondering..." She remembered Raylene's car as it barreled toward her. She pictured Dr. Jesús Pérez's perfectly shaped and sized nose holes. And then, in the calmest voice she could muster, Josephine said, "I was wondering if maybe that cousin of yours, that Rinky cousin—"

"Second cousin *twice* removed. And for the last time, his name is *Dinky*, not Rinky. Why do all y'all keep callin' him Rinky?" Miss Connie blew her nose again, loudly. "Hand me them cigarettes." She wagged a finger.

Among the piles and piles of stuff, Josephine saw a carton of cigarettes, but she didn't reach for them. Instead, she said, "Dinky's not coming, is he? We saw the ad. He's probably not coming because—" A peeping sound came out of Lisa Marie then, but Josephine continued. "It's because of your voice."

Miss Connie's mouth dropped open, and Lisa Marie gasped.

Josephine took a deep breath. She swallowed, then said exactly what was inside her stitched-up head: "You're hateful, Miss Connie. Your hateful talking makes people want to shrink into a tiny ball and roll away from here. That's why he doesn't want to visit you."

Except for the *Swap Shop* program, which was on the radio now, the room was still. The announcer's chipper radio voice said, "We got a furnished trailer for rent. Two hundred a month out in Happy World Trailer Park—Dandiest Little Place on Earth!"

It Ain't Right

It was mighty quiet for a while in Miss Connie's office-house. She sat at the kitchen table sniffling, first at Josephine and then at Lisa Marie. She cried some more, but not very much.

And then the most amazing thing happened. Miss Connie said, in a small voice, "It's just the way I am. It ain't right, I reckon, but I been talking like this my whole life. Veterinarians, grocery clerks, encyclopedia salesmen..." She shook her head and wiped her nose with the toilet paper again. "But Tadpole, he understood me. He took no offense to what I said, nor how I said it. Loved me for me. Nobody will ever love me that way again."

Ever so slowly it was coming to Josephine. Miss Connie was an actual, real person, with thoughts and worries and feelings, just like everybody else. "But you don't know that for sure," Josephine replied. "Somebody might come along and love you."

Miss Connie scowled. "Who are *you* to tell me what I know and don't know?"

Josephine flinched.

"I did it again, didn't I?" Miss Connie said.

Josephine nodded.

"Now see? I didn't mean nothin' by what I said. All I meant was nobody will love me like Tadpole did. I knew better than to think Dinky would come. Mother always said Dinky was a no-count good-for-nothin'." Miss Connie shrugged, and Bob Barker hopped off her lap. "I was just hoping for some company." She sniffed again. "I reckon you and your mama can stay. No reason why not."

Lisa Marie let out a squeal, then clamped her hands over her mouth.

Josephine wasn't sure she'd heard right. "What did you say?"

Miss Connie sighed and rolled her eyes. "I said you can stay! Good Lord, you want an engraved invitation? What do I care if y'all stay?" Miss Connie stood then and reached for the cigarettes. "Y'all pay rent," she went on. "Y'all don't make no mess. You two"—she wagged a finger at Josephine and Lisa Marie—"are right noisy sometimes with your carryin' on."

She put a cigarette between her lips. With one hand she flicked the Bic lighter and with the other she cupped the flame. When the cigarette was lit, she inhaled deeply and blew a long stream of smoke into the air. "But," she said, "to tell you the honest God's truth, y'all don't bother me much."

Another miracle, Josephine thought. First Molly Quiver's rescue and now this. "When you said that last part, I didn't want to shrink into a ball and roll away," Josephine said.

"I said not *much*! I didn't say not at all! So don't go yelling your fool heads off. Ain't everybody around here blessedly deaf like those Mooninghams. Lord, what I wouldn't give sometimes."

Josephine was feeling so good and generous she wanted to do something nice for Miss Connie. Sweep the floor, not that it would be easy with so much junk everywhere. Or wash a few of the dirty dishes, another difficult task considering there was only one spigot.

But Miss Connie snapped again. "Don't just stand there! Y'all go on and *git!*" she said.

"You ain't got to tell us twice!" With that Lisa Marie yanked Josephine by the arm and dragged her out into the Tennessee sunshine again.

August 9, 1974

Mama and Josephine and Granddaddy and Lisa Marie huddled around the television in number 17. Granddaddy and Mama kept shushing Lisa Marie and Josephine, who were playing Connect Four and making a racket.

"Thank you for letting us watch with you," Mama said. "I would hate to miss this. It's sad, don't you think? They all look so forlorn, even the Fords."

"Richard Nixon was a crook," Granddaddy said, and took a sip of tea.

Josephine and Lisa Marie stopped what they were doing to see the president of the United States give everyone a double peace sign and climb into a helicopter. In no time that guy was flying high over Washington, D.C.

"He's not the president now?" Josephine asked.

"No, he's officially a former president," Mama said.

Lisa Marie looked up from the stack of Connect Four chips. "Who *is* the president?"

"Gerald Ford. A veteran who served his country."

Granddaddy switched off the TV. "It's time to close that Watergate chapter for good. I'm sick of hearing about it."

"Me too!" Josephine chimed in, even though she hadn't heard much about it since they'd sold their television.

"And, Miss Penny, I sure am glad to know you and Josephine are sticking around Happy World. Lisa Marie would be mighty lonesome without Josephine. Two peas in a pod."

"They are that," Mama said. "Well, I've got a lot of sewing to do, and, Josephine, you need to get cleaned up before bed." Mama stood and smoothed out her skirt.

"But it's still light out! And we need a tie-breaker."

"That's enough for tonight. We've got to get you girls going to bed early again. School will be starting before long."

Josephine and Lisa Marie put their fingers in their ears and said "*Blah-blah-blah,*" which they did anytime somebody mentioned school.

Josephine took her fingers out just in time to hear Granddaddy say, "Is Josephine going to Hillwood Elementary?"

"I go to Brandywine Elementary," Josephine corrected him.

Mama gave Josephine a look. It was the kind of look she gave Josephine when she had something bad to tell her.

"What?" Josephine said.

"Did I say the wrong thing?" Granddaddy asked.

Mama took a deep breath and sighed it out. "Josephine has to hear this, and now is as good a time as any."

"Hear what? Miss Connie decided to kick us out anyway?"

"No," Mama replied.

"Woo-wee, changing that woman's mind was quite a feat, Miss Penny. She's a stubborn mule. Don't change her mind 'bout nothin'," Granddaddy said.

"Josephine gets credit for that," Mama replied. "My

daughter is a very persuasive person. I think Miss Connie met her match. Besides that, Rinky's not—"

"*Dinky!*" Josephine and Lisa Marie hollered at the same time.

"Oh, good grief. Who names a person Dinky, *or* Rinky, for that matter?" Mama said.

Granddaddy laughed. "I met him once. No great loss, him not coming. I rehung them closet doors of hers, too. Why, she must've had two hundred cans of cat food jammed in there. I told her she's gonna have to find someplace else to keep that stuff."

"I know what y'all are doing," Josephine said. "You're trying to keep me from thinking about whatever it is you don't want to tell me."

"This is how Granddaddy told me Buster Lee had cancer of the face," Lisa Marie said. "We were playing Connect Four, even."

"It's nothing like that," Mama said. "I didn't know how everything would play out this summer. Whether we would stay here at Happy World or move someplace else. But since we're staying..." Mama bit her lip.

"Tell me!" Josephine demanded.

"I'm afraid you'll have to go to a different school."

Josephine frowned. "You mean Brandywine won't be my school? I won't see Miss Lake? Not even pass her in the hallway?"

"I'm so sorry, Jo."

Josephine's mind hit Rewind. She thought about the playground seesaw, her favorite thing, and the school library, her other favorite thing. She remembered the squeak of the hardwood floors and the smell of hot buttered rolls in the cafeteria.

There was the crossing guard lady with her noisy whistle and the school store, which was really only a closet. It smelled so pleasantly of pencils. Josephine recalled the art room—finger paints and papier-mâché and those plaster figurines she'd molded and baked and painted.

"I'm sorry, Jo," Mama said again.

"Where will I go?" Josephine asked.

"Lordy, I sure shouldn't have brought this up," Granddaddy said.

"Your new school is a little country school not far from here. Instead of walking like you did at Brandywine, you'll take the bus."

"You'll be in school with me," Lisa Marie said in a shy voice.

Josephine's mouth dropped open. Her eyes bugged out. She looked at Lisa Marie and then at Mama. "I'll go to the same school as her?" She pointed to Lisa Marie.

"That's right," Mama said.

It was like the trailer was holding its breath, but then Josephine let out a whoop and a holler. The girls scrambled to their feet and hugged each other and jumped around.

Josephine paused and said, "What if we get in the same class?" And then they hollered some more.

Lisa Marie said, "And we can eat lunch together!" And they hollered again, until Mama said that was enough hollering. Granddaddy walked them outside and started filling a grocery sack with homegrown produce.

Josephine held Lisa Marie's sweaty hand and took a big sniff of trailer-park air. It sure did smell good here in Happy World—warm, dry grass and ripe tomatoes. Hog had spent the afternoon working on his motorcycle again, revving its noisy engine, so there was the faint smell of exhaust, too. Cicadas sang and lightning bugs flashed and flickered.

"We've had some wonderful vegetables this summer, thanks to you," Mama said.

Granddaddy handed her a full sack. "Ain't no way me and Lisa Marie could eat all this by ourselves. And y'all been mighty good to my little girl," he said.

Just then Josephine spotted headlights down by the Happy World entrance. Her stomach gave a funny lurch. She elbowed Lisa Marie and nodded toward the road. The car was stopped down by the mailboxes.

Lisa Marie squinted. "Wonder who that is."

Mama and Granddaddy stopped their chitchatting and watched the car bump its way toward the trailers.

"Officer Frye!" Josephine exclaimed.

"I hope nothing's wrong." Mama squeezed the bag of vegetables tighter.

They watched the car stop at number 7.

"Reckon Frye knows Miss Helen's still down in Alabama?" Granddaddy asked.

Lickety-split, Josephine took off running, and Lisa Marie went after her. They reached the car in time to see Officer Frye get out of the driver's side. "Evening, girls," he said, and smiled at them.

Josephine and Lisa Marie waved to him shyly.

"I got somebody I want y'all to see," he said, and just then Helen-Dove climbed out of the passenger's seat.

"It sure is good to be home," she said. "And it's good to see you girls."

Helen-Dove looked sturdier somehow. Besides that, she was wearing a new sundress, pale blue with daisies stitched across the bodice. Josephine was just about to tell her how nice she looked when she spotted somebody in the backseat.

Officer Frye went around to the trunk and pulled out a folded-up wheelchair.

"Molly can't walk no more?" Lisa Marie asked.

"She can walk, but it's painful," Helen-Dove replied. "A chair is easier for her right now."

Wide-eyed, the girls watched as Officer Frye and Helen-Dove helped Molly out of the backseat and lowered her into the chair. She was small and fragile. Josephine couldn't help but think how different she looked from the girl in the school picture. That girl seemed fearless. This girl looked scared. And she had a heavy cast on her leg.

Finally, Helen-Dove turned to them. "Girls, I'd like for you to say hello to my daughter. This is Molly. She has come home to live with me. . . ." She glanced at their faces. "With all of us in Happy World."

Josephine waved. Lisa Marie waved, too.

"So nice to meet you, Molly," Mama said.

"Welcome home, Little Bit." Granddaddy wiped his eyes.

Molly whispered something to her mother, and Helen-Dove smiled. "That's Josephine," she said. "And her mother, Miss Penny. You remember Lisa Marie. And Mr. Green?"

Molly nodded. For a few uncomfortable seconds, she studied Josephine. "You knew."

Josephine opened her mouth, but no words came.

"You knew I was trying to get myself home."

Molly Quiver in the flesh. Molly Quiver home in Happy World.

"I have markers." Molly tugged a small leather purse off her shoulder and reached inside it.

"You want to color? Right *now*?" Lisa Marie said.

Molly laughed. "I want you to sign my cast," she said, and laughed again.

Josephine hung on that laugh as if it were a trapeze swing.

Molly held up two markers. "Your favorite color is yellow," she said, and held out a marker with a yellow cap for Josephine. "And your favorite color is green." She handed the other marker to Lisa Marie.

Light

That night after Josephine had showered and washed her hair in Gee, Your Hair Smells Terrific, she crawled into bed and listened to the sound of Mama's sewing machine *purr*ing. Mama had been working her nice fingers to the bone on some curtains and pillows for Mrs. Morrison's next-door neighbor. Even though none of it was finished, Josephine could already tell it would be beautiful. And Mama promised—put her hand over her heart and everything—that when she was done, she would starch that fabric to Josephine's walls and even make a bedspread and curtains to match.

Josephine closed her eyes and thought about going to school with Lisa Marie, but there was some sad in her heart, too, on account of she would miss Brandywine Elementary. And she would definitely miss her favorite teacher of all time. No matter who else came next, Miss Lake would always be the favorite.

Josephine considered all the hunches and feelings she'd had these past few weeks. Hating it here, and then wanting to stay. She remembered Miss Connie calling her a dummy, and how it'd made her feel when Delia called her a dummy. She was done with that now. Josephine kept very still and tried to decide if this was really true.

Yes, it was true. She would not be friends with anybody, even if they had a canopy bed and a television in their room, if they called her a dummy. Or tried to make her feel like one.

It was strange to think you could make a decision like this and then have it be true. Josephine let this clarification settle over her for a minute. "Goodbye, Delia," she said tragically. "I've got a new best friend now. Two new best friends," she added quickly.

For her birthday Mama had promised one of those friendship necklaces. A lock and a key or a split-in-two heart. Now she would have to ask for both so there would be enough pieces for Molly Quiver.

Josephine stared at the ceiling, amazed by what she was feeling. Tomorrow she would write down Molly Quiver's story. The parts Molly didn't already know for herself, that is. Everything Helen-Dove and Officer Frye and Lisa Marie and Josephine had done to bring her home. The trip to Alabama and supper on the beach and the sharks coming out at night.

Josephine would pick up where Buster Lee left off, and maybe Molly would know, really truly know, deep down in her heart, how important she was to all of them.

Just then the bedroom door snapped open, and Mama stood in the crack of light.

"Hi, Mama," Josephine said.

Mama crossed the threshold and came to sit beside Josephine. She brushed Jo's hair back from her face, and kissed the place where the stitches had been. "You sure do make me proud."

"Except for when I act like an almost teenager," Josephine said.

Mama laughed. "How would you feel about getting your picture in the newspaper?"

Josephine blinked. "Huh?"

"Chub Depkins called while you were in the shower. He's a reporter over at the paper, and he wants to do a story about Molly. He'd like a picture of you girls together."

"I'm gonna be rich and famous?"

"Maybe slightly famous," Mama replied.

"When's he coming?"

"Tomorrow morning sometime, so you have to get your beauty sleep."

Josephine flopped down again, shut her eyes tight, and pretended to snore.

"Good night, silly," Mama said.

⊏⟶

After Mama's sewing machine was *whirr*ing and *thump*ing again, Josephine emerged from beneath her covers and looked out the window. A light was glowing across the way, a happy golden light shining from inside number 7. Molly June Quiver had come home, not just to Helen-Dove but to Happy World.

"Thank you," Josephine whispered, then pushed her prayer toward heaven.

She realized then, not fleetingly, not in such a way that

the thought might vanish in the night, but really knew, for sure knew, there was sweetness all around. Even when the inventory burned up. Even when you sold your stuff in a yard sale. And even in the middle of a trailer park.

The End (or just the beginning)

Author's Note

On February 4, 1974, members of a group known as the Symbionese Liberation Army kidnapped nineteen-year-old Patricia Campbell Hearst, a wealthy heiress and daughter of a newspaper magnate. Patricia Hearst later reported having suffered from something called Stockholm syndrome, which means the victim develops a psychological bond with their captors. Patricia Hearst suffered horrific abuse and her abduction went on for nineteen months. She wasn't found until September 18, 1975.

Patricia's story had a happy ending, though her journey was long and complicated. As of this writing, Patricia Hearst is alive and well and living in South Carolina.

I was ten years old when Hearst was kidnapped, and I recall watching footage on the evening news. While Molly's story is fiction, Patricia's is true.

There was another kidnapping around the same time, one not mentioned in my book. Nine-year-old Marcia Trimble lived about forty miles from where I grew up in Tennessee, and we were two years apart in age. On another winter's day, a little more than a year after Hearst's abduction, Marcia

Trimble was taken against her will. She was making a delivery of Girl Scout cookies to a neighbor on February 25, 1975, and never returned home.

For weeks and weeks, I worried about Marcia. *Where is she? Why can't anyone find her? She has to be somewhere! Kids don't just disappear!* Just as in Hearst's case, there were police officers and detectives and tracking dogs. It seemed everyone was looking for the missing nine-year-old.

Just when it was beginning to seem that Marcia really had vanished, her body was discovered, thirty-three days after her abduction, on March 30, 1975, Easter Sunday, only eighty yards from where she was last seen.

Marcia Trimble's story haunts me to this day. Her parents and relatives, her school friends, her neighbors, her church family, her Girl Scout troop members, and her dogs, Princess and Popcorn, must've all been feeling exactly as I was: helpless and frightened.

After Marcia's murder, the Girl Scouts organization forever banned its members from selling cookies door-to-door.

After thirty-three years of the Nashville community not knowing who was responsible for Marcia's death, her killer was apprehended, and on September 4, 2009, he was sentenced to forty-four years in prison for Marcia's murder. While Marcia was his youngest victim, sadly, she was not his only.

These are frightening stories, and as I write this, I think of my own three daughters and their safety. We live in a world that can sometimes be scary, but there are ways to protect yourself and others. Start with the National Center for Missing and Exploited Children, and learn about specific KidSmartz techniques to avoid becoming a victim at https://www.missingkids.org/education/kidsmartz.

If you are suffering abuse, sexual or otherwise, now or in the past, know it's not your fault. Tell a trusted adult, and seek additional help by calling this number: 1-800-THE-LOST (1-800-843-5678). You may also report sexual exploitation online at https://report.cybertip.org.

Acknowledgments

Sally Morgridge, what an exciting journey this has been! You're a dream editor—smart and knowledgeable and kind. Thank you for loving this novel and for understanding Josephine right from the start. You've made this process so enjoyable, and I'm forever grateful.

Thank you to my fearless agent, Ginger Knowlton. Your tenacity is the reason Josephine found her way into the world. Your gentle manner of ripping off Band-Aids is the reason I didn't quit. A million thank-yous and then some.

Without the expertise and insight of Joyce Sweeney, I would never have found my way to Ginger, so thank you, Joyce.

In the early stages of writing this novel, there were three readers who cheered me on. They also happen to be librarians and friends. Mona Martin Batchelor, Lawrence Horner, and Margaret Meacham, who is also an author, thank you for reading that very first draft and offering encouragement. I would also like to thank Sharon Sansosti, another amazing librarian, for her genuine enthusiasm for this novel.

In addition to my editor extraordinaire, Sally Morgridge, I also want to thank the Holiday House team who brought Josephine to readers: Mary Cash, Kerry Martin, Amy Toth, Lisa Lee, Judy Varon, Terry Borzumato-Greenberg, Michelle Montague, Sara DiSalvo, Miriam Miller, Derek Stordahl, Laura Kincaid, and Raina Putter. Many thanks to George Newman for his assiduous copyediting, to Regina Castillo for her sharp proofreading, and to David Curtis for his compelling cover art. Thanks also to Kirby Larson for so generously blurbing my book.

To Vicki and Steve Palmquist, I am deeply appreciative of your technical and artistic expertise, especially when it comes to website design. Your genuine love for children's books and their authors is demonstrated in so many ways.

To my family, Scott, Cassie, Flannery, Elsbeth, and John, you have loved me through all the celebrations and disappointments. Thank you for putting up with me and my imaginary people.

Finally, I want to thank Nannie, also known as Nancy Demastus Williams, my beautiful aunt. Thank you for all the late nights with Johnny Carson, the Sunday meals of fried chicken, the lemon mousses you made especially for me (okay, and Julie), the cheerful messages on my answering machine, the texts to make sure we've fared well in bad weather, and for being there when I needed you most. I'm so proud to dedicate this book to you. And to God, of course, because through Him all things really are possible.